Acclaim fo
UPSIDE DOWN

"UPSIDE DOWN is a refreshing and heartfelt New Adult contemporary romance."   —*USA Today*

"This story shows just how frightening it is to let yourself fall in love and be that vulnerable."   —HeroesandHeartbreakers.com

"Lia Riley turned my emotions UPSIDE DOWN with this book! Fast paced, electric, and sweetly emotional!"

—Tracy Wolff, *New York Times* and
USA Today bestselling author

"Where to even start with this book? Beautifully written, Australia, hot surfer Bran, unique heroine Talia. Yep, it's all just a whole lot of awesome. Loved it!"   —Cindi Madsen, *USA Today* bestselling author

"Fresh, sexy, and romantic, UPSIDE DOWN will leave you wanting more. I cannot wait for the next book. Lia Riley is an incredible new talent and not to be missed!"

—Kristen Callihan, award-winning author of the
Darkest London series and *The Hook Up*

"A rich setting and utterly romantic, UPSIDE DOWN will have you laughing and crying and begging for it to never end. I absolutely loved it!"   —Melissa West, author of *Pieces of Olivia*

"UPSIDE DOWN is a brilliantly written New Adult romance that transported me to another country. With vivid imagery and rich characterizations...I was completely smitten with the love story of Bran and Talia. I cannot wait for the rest of their story!"

—Megan Erickson, author of *Make It Count*

ALSO BY LIA RILEY

UPSIDE DOWN

DOWN

AN OFF THE MAP NOVEL
Book One

LIA RILEY

FOREVER

NEW YORK   BOSTON

Copyright © 2014 by Lia Riley
Excerpt from *Sideswiped* copyright © 2014 by Lia Riley
All rights reserved. In accordance with the U.S. Copyright Act of 1976, the scanning, uploading, and electronic sharing of any part of this book without the permission of the publisher constitute unlawful piracy and theft of the author's intellectual property. If you would like to use material from the book (other than for review purposes), prior written permission must be obtained by contacting the publisher at permissions@hbgusa.com. Thank you for your support of the author's rights.

"who are you,little i". Copyright © 1963, 1991 by the Trustees for the E. E. Cummings Trust, from COMPLETE POEMS: 1904–1962 by E. E. Cummings, edited by George J. Firmage. Used by permission of Liveright Publishing Corporation.

Forever
Hachette Book Group
1290 Avenue of the Americas
New York, NY 10104

www.HachetteBookGroup.com

Printed in the United States of America

RRD-C

Originally published as an ebook

First trade paperback edition: May 2015
10 9 8 7 6 5 4 3 2 1

Forever is an imprint of Grand Central Publishing.
The Forever name and logo are trademarks of Hachette Book Group, Inc.

The Hachette Speakers Bureau provides a wide range of authors for speaking events. To find out more, go to www.hachettespeakersbureau.com or call (866) 376-6591.

The publisher is not responsible for websites (or their content) that are not owned by the publisher.

Library of Congress Cataloging-in-Publication Data

Riley, Lia.
    Upside down / Lia Riley. — First trade paperback edition.
        pages cm.
    Originally published as an ebook.
    ISBN 978-1-4555-8572-4 (paperback) — ISBN 978-1-4789-0370-3 (audio download) — ISBN 978-1-4555-8571-7 (ebook) 1. Single women—Fiction. 2. College students—Fiction. I. Title.
    PS3618.I53279.U68 2015
    813'.6—dc23
                                                                        2014049855

To my matey—I still have a lot of time for you

ACKNOWLEDGMENTS

When it comes to sharing gratitude to everyone who made this book possible, my first inclination is to messy cry. First up, a simple fact. Talia and Bran would never exist without the vision and gentle encouragement of my agent, Emily Sylvan Kim. High fives to everyone at Team Forever, in particular, my editor ninja, Lauren Plude, for taking a mind-boggling leap of faith on this series and giving wise, thoughtful nudges to deepen shallow plot points. Elizabeth Turner, you designed beautiful covers that surpassed any poor imagining. Carrie Andrews, your copyedits made everything sparkle.

I'd like to dedicate a keytar solo to Christopher Peterson and Megan Taddonio for your advice during the initial stages. Infinite appreciation to the helpful elves who read rough words but shared love notes and/or a kick in the ass: Jennifer Ryan, Jules Barnard, Jennifer Blackwood, AJ Pine, Lexi Clemence, and Natalie Blitt. Also, hugs to my supportive lovies, Lex Martin and Megan Erickson. I'd interpretive dance my adoration, but none of you really want to see those moves.

Writing friends save lives, or at least sanity. A big toast o' Bigfoot juice (with a tequila chaser) to the '14 NAs. Shout-out to Roguers, woot woot, especially Marina Adair for letting me pester you with so many questions about fast-drafting and process. Hugs to RWA-Silicon Valley and RWA-Monterey Bay chapters.

To my parents, *grazie* for life, et cetera, still sorry about stealing the Bartles & Jaymes, but I turned out okay despite that whole "nighttime is the right time" phase. Hopefully, this is me putting that expensive college degree to good use. And to Helen and Dave, for your support and stepping up to watch the tinys so I could make word count. Kevin and Bridget, you're here to avoid the "no one ever says that about me."

To Passenger, your music kept me company during 5:00 a.m. writing sessions.

To J and B, who resorted to calling me by my first name to gain attention when I was in the zone, your frazzled mama adores you beyond the power of words. And Nick, who learned the hard way that when a girl says, "Hey, matey, I'm going to write a romance novel," that really means "Surprise! You now live with a frat boy who needs more showers." Thanks for learning to cook and digging American girls. We have so many of our own adventures left to write. I love you.

Author's Note

I'm the kind of girl who always says something, walks away, thinks of something else, and then wants to say more stuff. So...YAY Author's Note!

Okay, last year, I was working on another book (not UPSIDE DOWN) and while it was going fine, it wasn't fantastic. I started stressing, and suddenly, an old frenemy paid a visit. See, since I was eleven, I've struggled with obsessive-compulsive disorder, except I didn't call it by that name. It was rather "my thing." Yes, denial is more than a river in Egypt. Throughout my young adult and adult life, "my thing" waxed and waned. I'll spare you the gory details, but it wasn't until my younger sister (who happens to be a clinical social worker and therapist) matter-of-factly asked when I was going to deal with my OCD that it clicked. "Well, shit," I thought. And I sat with the idea for a week or so.

On one hand, the whole concept of having a "problem" filled me with unspeakable dread. On the other, it was a huge relief. I started therapy, got diagnosed, and began UPSIDE DOWN.

I didn't intend to write about OCD, but it was clearly "on the brain" (sorry, couldn't resist). When I realized how the story was taking shape, and featured this topic, I fretted a lot. Would I portray things right? Would people say WRONG! WRONG! WRONG!

THIS ISN'T HOW IT IS FOR ME! OR MY LOVED ONE! OR WHAT I SAW ON TELEVISION…whatever, you get the idea. Hyperbole is also a personal specialty. Talia isn't me any more than Bran or, gulp, her mom. But I have shared some of her experiences as honestly as was in my power. Your own experiences may be (and probably are) different.

But let's still be friends. And if you struggle with OCD, you aren't alone…

The National Institute of Mental Health estimates that more than 2 percent of the U.S. population (nearly one out of every forty people) will be diagnosed with OCD at some point in their lives. I'm no expert, but there are plenty of places to seek help. If you or someone you know has OCD, the National Alliance on Mental Illness (www.nami.org) or the International OCD Foundation (www .ocdfoundation.org) are great places to gain more information.

Moving along, I'd also like to say most places in the book actually exist. You can, and should, eat amazing Italian food on Melbourne's Lygon Street. If you ever venture to Tasmania, one of my favorite places on the planet, do drop in to the Museum of Old and New Art or wander Battery Point. Sadly, however, there is no "The Rock" surf spot on the Great Ocean Road. This is a very, very loose reconstruction of Winkie Pop, a famous break that many non-surfers reassured me didn't sound badass—even though it totally is.

UPSIDE DOWN

My brain is my heart's umbrella.

—Jeffrey Lewis, from "You Don't Have to
Be a Scientist to Do Experiments on
Your Own Heart"

I

TALIA

J breathe on my bedroom window and smear a spy hole in the condensation. Not much going on this morning. A lone crow dips over California bungalow roofs while in the distance Monterey Bay is shrouded in mist. I'm a Santa Cruz girl to the bone, love that fog like it's a childhood blanket.

The downstairs phone rings and Dad turns off NPR. He's a sucker for *Wait Wait...Don't Tell Me!* Once I get on the plane this afternoon, the only noise in the house will be that frigging radio. Guilt grabs me with two cold fists, right in the gut. I should be plopped beside him on the couch, trying to kid around, but I'm not even sure he wants my company.

My sister, Pippa, would know what to do. She was the expert in easy affection. She'd blow through the kitchen on a Friday night, swig a sip of Dad's beer, sling an arm around his neck, and torture him with wet cheek kisses. I've never been a hugger. My role was easy, the joke-cracking sidekick. But there's no work for a sidekick without a hero. These days, if I wander into a room, Dad's gaze automatically slides to the empty space beside me. Somehow, despite everything, I'm the ghost child. I don't want to haunt him, so I keep to my room.

My room.

Not ours. No one's slept in the other bed in a year and a half. My sister's one-eyed sock monkey, Seymour, reclines in the middle of her calico pillowcase, wearing an evil expression. *I know your secrets*, he seems to say. *What you keep hidden.* I give the monkey the finger and instantly feel worse.

Seymour and I go way back. To those days after Pippa died and my room was a safe place to shatter. He saw me research phantom medical symptoms until four in the morning, curl beneath my bed wrapped in the comforter so Dad never heard me weep, watched as I knelt in the dormer window seat and counted cars, closing my eyes if I ever spotted a red one because red was bad.

It meant blood.

Death.

Seymour the Sock Monkey knows me for who I am.

The leftover daughter.

"Sorry, Pippa," I mutter. Like my sister gives two shits about my relationship with her fucking stuffed animal. If she can see me from wherever she is, and that's highly suspect, I've given her far greater cause for displeasure.

Seymour's frayed mouth seems to sneer. We're in agreement on that point.

There's a knock on the bedroom door. "Hang on a sec!" I slip on my T-shirt and tighten the bath towel around my waist. My computer is open on the desk. WebMD calls my name, softly seductive, like Maleficent to Princess Aurora. In this case, I'm not offered a spinning wheel spindle but reassurance that I'm not going to die. Dr. Halloway urged me to block access to any health-related sites, but in the shower, the freckle on my right foot looked bigger. Bob Marley died from a melanoma on his toe, so I'm not 100 percent mentally unhinged—more like 85 percent on a bad day.

Despite my best efforts, I can't stop obsessing over what-ifs. What if I have early-stage skin cancer? What if this headache is a tumor? My mind is a bowl of water that I compulsively stir. I want my brain to be still and serene, but for the love of Sweet Baby Jesus, I can't quit agitating it.

There's another knock. More insistent.

"Seriously, I'm changing."

"Your mother's called to say good-bye," Dad says through the door. His voice is tense, pleading, like he holds something unpleasant, an old man's jockstrap, rather than the phone.

I turn the knob and stick my hand out to grab the receiver. "Thanks." I take my time putting it to my ear, humming the soundtrack to *Jaws* under my breath. "Hey, Mom."

"Alooooha." Wow, a perfect extension on the long *o* followed by a short, sharp *ha*. She's been practicing.

I mime a silent gag. "What's up?"

"Your cell went to voice mail." She doesn't like calling the landline. "You know I prefer not to talk to him."

I push up my glasses and roll my eyes. "Such an inconvenience." By *him* she means my dad, Scott Stolfi, the man she was married to for twenty-two years. She can't even say, "May I speak to Talia," without turning it into a thing. He was her high school sweetheart. They had one of those classic love stories, rich girl meets working-class boy. Now, a two-second conversation with the guy yanks her chain.

"You don't understand."

"And you say we never agree on anything." I bend and struggle with the zip to my overstuffed suitcase.

I bet two coconuts that Mom's sprawled by the infinity pool on the cliffside deck overlooking the Pacific. She's been holed up on my grandparents' estate on Kauai's north shore since she bailed last year. After they took Pippa off life support, Mom locked herself in the guest room for two days while Dad tackled an endless series of home repairs. When she finally emerged, he was mending the backyard fence. "You can't fix everything!" she'd screamed. Next thing we knew, she'd bought a one-way ticket to Hawaii. In lieu of a cheesy postcard, she sent Dad divorce papers from the law offices of William C. Kaleolani, Esq.

"Australia is just so far away. You've always talked about doing the Peace Corps one day, but to know you're all grown up…" Her gusty sigh is dramatic. This phone call is her pretending to care, a big show, part of the game she still plays called "Being a Mom." In all fairness, I shouldn't snark, because guess who's bankrolling my trip down under? As much as I hate to ask her for anything, I need this escape.

Mom comes from old Carmel money earned when my great-great-grandfather decimated two-thousand-year-old redwood groves. Environmental pillage made him filthy rich, but the money lost its stink over time, transformed into sustainable energy start-ups and progressive philanthropic causes.

I doubt the stumps rotting in the forest care.

"Has Logan's cookbook arrived?" Mom dials up the rainbow cheer. She's got to be grinding out that forced smile, the one that makes her teeth look like they're breaking. "His tour starts next week, LA and San Francisco. You could have joined us at the Esalen Institute."

The idea of soaking naked in a hippie retreat spa with Logan, Mom's hump buddy/Hawaiian spirit animal, is the stuff of nightmares. To date, I've successfully avoided an encounter with the Wunderchimp. In her photographs, he sports a mean chest 'fro. He's a personal macrobiotic chef to the stars and wannabe guru.

His book, *Eating from Within*, recently released and she mailed me a personal signed copy like I give a one-eyed donkey.

I jam the phone between my ear and shoulder to shimmy into my skinny jeans. "What about the breatharian section? Like, was he serious about gulping air for sustenance?"

"The detoxifying effects are incredible."

Whatever. I'll wager my own enlightenment that she's dying for one of Dad's famous cheeseburgers.

"I've lost five pounds since we got involved." There is a faint noise on the other end of the line, suspiciously like a wine bottle uncorking.

Hawaii is three hours behind.

Please don't let her be drinking before noon.

"Hey, um, are you—"

"Sunny put a new photo of you on Facebook." Mom's a ninja at deflection as well as a social media junkie. She posts daily emo statuses about self-discovery alongside whimsical shots of waterfalls, out-of-focus sunsets, and dolphins. "Are those new shorts? I swear your thighs come straight from your father's side." She makes it sound like my genes sport cankles and triple chins, but she's got a point. I did sprout from Dad's southern Italian roots: Mediterranean curves, brown eyes, and olive skin.

I slip on my shoes, turn sideways in the mirror, and pooch my stomach. "Had a physical last week with Dr. Halloway. Still well within normal range."

"Aren't they stretching those numbers to make big girls feel better?"

Mom is a size 2. To her, everyone is a big girl.

Pippa was Mom's doppelganger. They shared hummingbird-boned bodies and perpetually surprised blue eyes. I shove away the quick-fire anguish, slam my lids shut, and count to ten. The number nine feels wrong, so I do it once more for good measure.

"Talia? I need a little advice." Mom hushes to a "just us girls" level.

"What?" She's going to bash me and then get all buddy-buddy? Who replaced my real mother with this selfish hag?

"Male advice."

"Um, wait, you're joking, right?" This is above my pay grade.

"I just read online how pineapple juice improves semen flavor. Any tips for how to raise the subject with Logan?"

I open my mouth in a silent scream.

"He claims he doesn't enjoy the fruit. But what about me? My needs? He tastes like—"

"Enough." I flop beside my bed, grab a skullcap, shove it on, and yank the brim tight over my eyes in a futile attempt to hide. "You have got to be—"

"I come from a land down under, where women glow and men plunder." Sunny bursts into my room in a whirlwind of sandalwood essential oil and peasant skirts. Beth follows behind wearing the same hand-painted silk sheath gracing the cover of the latest Anthropologie catalogue.

"Hey, I gotta jam. Beth and Sunny arrived to say good-bye." *My mom*, I mouth, pretending to stab the receiver.

They roll their eyes.

"*A hui hou*, Ladybug. Australia waits. Discover your bliss." When Mom gets philosophical, her voice takes on a theatrically British accent for no reason.

"Bye, Mom." I toss the phone on my dresser and fake a seizure.

"Sounds like Mrs. S was in fine form." Sunny tugs off my cap.

Beth's jaw slackens. "OMG, Talia, what did you do to your hair?" She runs her fingers through her own dark flat-ironed locks as if trying to reassure herself of their continued flawlessness.

I skim my hand over the top of my head. "Box dye. Sunflower blond. You hate it, don't you?"

"You'll be easy to find in the dark." Sunny waggles her eyebrows in pervy innuendo. Nothing fazes this girl. I could tattoo a third eye on my forehead and she'd chat about opening root chakras. That's why I love her.

Beth halfway sits before realizing my bed's buried beneath an avalanche of travel guides, bikinis, underwear, power adaptors, and multicolored Australian currency. She never touches Pippa's bed. They were best friends. Beth had been riding shotgun in her Prius when the tweaker ran a stop sign and plowed through the driver's side door. She never talks about that day. Neither of us do. We've been too deeply hurt.

For a long time after the accident we remained optimistic. Pippa's brain showed limited signs of activity, but eventually, hope devoured the heart of my family until nothing remained but ashes and bone. Dad finds solace in warm beer and cold pizza and my mom in baby men. Me? I'm still digging out of the wreckage.

"Earth to Talia." Sunny presses a matcha green tea latte into my hand with a wink. "We picked up your favorite swamp water."

"Hey, thanks." I fake a sip, not having the heart to reveal I cut off caffeine and the accompanying hamster-wheel jitters. It's part of the Talia reboot. Talia 1.0 is outdated and it's time for a new model. Talia 2.0 isn't an anxious freak and is more than Pippa's tragic sister. She didn't lose her virginity to Tanner, her dead sister's long-term boyfriend after the BBQ held to commemorate the one-year anniversary of her passing, and she doesn't count precisely ninety-nine Cheerios into her bowl at breakfast to feel "right." And she certainly isn't going to focus on the fact that she's not graduating in six months—a secret that no one, not her parents or even her best friends, knows.

Old Talia may have royally screwed her GPA. New Talia is focused strictly on the future. A shiny tomorrow. A new-car-smelling do-over.

These girls are everything to me, but they don't have a clue how far I've fallen down the rabbit hole. I'm already one big sad story. Do I really want to be like *Hey, how about my freaky compulsions?*

Pretending to be a normal, functioning member of society is exhausting stuff.

"You're wearing that on the plane?" Beth inventories my jeans, purple Chuck Taylors, and Pippa's favorite tee.

"What?" I glance at the red-stenciled words crossing my chest—HOLDEN CAULFIELD IS MY HOMEBOY.

"There's no way you're getting upgraded," Beth says.

"It's a full flight. Besides, I needed to…" A shrug is my best explanation. The night before Pippa was removed from life support, I pinky-swore my beautiful, brain-dead sister that I'd live enough life for two. This shirt helps remind me of my promise.

Fortunately, Sunny is the resident expert in deciphering vague Talia gestures. "You want to be close to Pippa. I get it." She toys with her feather hair extension and shoots Beth a "let it go" death stare.

"There's an X Games competition in the city next weekend, so Tanner's back in town." Beth's tone is controlled, far too even to be natural. "Did he stop by?" She gazes at me like an implacable jury forewoman, about to pronounce a verdict of guilt.

"Nope."

The ensuing silence makes me want to curl into a catatonic ball and stare as dust motes filter through the air.

I don't mention watching Tanner land heel kicks and pop shu-vits while walking past Derby Skate Park last night. Or how he stared right through me. He'd been in love with Pippa since she was twelve. She and I had been walking home from Mission Hill

Middle School when a classmate cornered the two of us on Bay Street with rape threats. Tanner spotted the encounter from the front stoop of his trailer, marched over, and clocked the kid over the head with his skateboard. When Pippa told Mom what happened, she took Tanner out to Marianne's Ice Cream parlor for sundaes. By ninth grade, he and Pippa were going steady and that was that, until the year anniversary of my sister's death.

Tanner will never forgive either of us for the night we got trashed, and then naked, under the Santa Cruz Wharf. I'm sure he guilty-conscience confessed the whole sordid story to Beth, but she never called me on it, a form of punishment in itself.

"What's up, girls?" Dad appears in the hall dressed in well-worn board shorts and a ratty surf competition T-shirt. He looks more like a beach bum than a coastal geologist.

Beth gives him a little wave. "Hey, Mr. S."

His head grazes the top of the door frame. He's huge, my dad, but quiet, more a gentle giant. Mom used to run the show around these parts, a high-strung Chihuahua to his laid-back golden retriever. Now he wanders around like he forgot where he hid his bone. He's not in the right headspace to deal with my crap. All I need to do is fake happy and stay alive.

"You finished yet?" He shifts his weight, eyeing the mess spread over my bed. "We've got to hit the road soon to beat the traffic. Don't want you missing your flight."

Sunny leaps up with a squeal and wraps me in a fierce bear hug. "Safe travels, honeybunch."

She's the only person who occasionally calls me by Pippa's old nickname. I miss hearing it but don't have to look at Dad to know he flinches.

"Remember your promise." Sunny presses her forehead to

mine. "You can't call either Beth or me while you're gone. We'll be fine. This time's just for you. Relax. Get a tan. Ride a platypus. Throw a shrimp on the barbie and whatnot."

"Got it." I nod as she gives me a final squeeze. Sunny's firm in her belief that we can't communicate until I return home. She wants me to escape from my family train wreck, and you can't get much farther than Australia. I'll have five months to screw my head back on straight.

Beth steps forward with a steely look in her gray eyes, but maybe I'm imagining things because in another second it's gone. She rumples my hair. "Don't forget to have fun, Tals."

"Never do," I crack. When's the last time I let go, lived without an invisible boulder crushing my chest? Can't even remember.

"Good times." Dad grabs the suitcase with an easy swing while I cram the rest of my stuff in the bulging duffel. "There's going to be a lot to celebrate when you get home. You three, almost ready to graduate." He casts a hesitant smile in my general direction. He was the first kid in his family to go to college. I know it means the world to him that he can provide me with an opportunity for higher education.

My lungs go on strike. A full breath is impossible.

He'd be so proud to learn his only surviving daughter is a liar and a failure.

I'm letting him down.

Like mother, like daughter.

My core grows cold. The letter from the history undergraduate committee is torn into a hundred pieces in the trash. They denied my petition to extend my senior thesis and the resulting F is a nuclear detonation in my transcript. My GPA is blown and because I didn't pass a mandatory class, I'll have to repeat the semester. Dr. Halloway offered to write a letter requesting medical exemption, but that would mean owning a crazy-ass diagnosis like obsessive-compulsive disorder.

Even before Pippa's accident, there were warning signs. Indicators like being hyperconscious about unplugging electrical devices or rechecking that I locked the front door in a certain way that felt "right." Over the last few years my compulsions intensified. I had to eat my food in pairs, not one M&M, not three M&M's, but two every time. Don't get me started on setting my alarm clock, changing a car radio, or trying to fall asleep. Over the course of last semester, I became convinced I contracted leukemia, thyroid disease, and MS. My nights were spent symptom Googling my way to academic probation.

After breaking down in my childhood doctor's office a few weeks ago, Dr. Halloway wrote me a prescription for a low-dosage antidepressant. He says the medication will increase my serotonin levels and in turn decrease the severity of my symptoms. It's got to work. I can't continue being a closet freak. Dr. Halloway also strongly advised cognitive behavioral therapy, stressing it would be helpful—vital, in fact—in controlling OCD impulses.

Right now, escape is preferable to weekly psychologist meetings. Once Santa Cruz and its ghosts are behind me, I'll feel better.

"Peanut?" Dad's frowning, so are Sunny and Beth. I've zoned out again, lost in my navel-gazing bullshit.

"It's all good." I flick on a megawatt smile because that's what I do best, fake it until I make it. "Australia's going to be great. Just think, tonight I'll be passing the International Date Line. I'm going to Tomorrowland."

Leaving is the only way to move forward.

If I never get lost, I'll never be found.

2

TALIA

*T*he door to my cramped studio flings open and Marti, the Quebecois girl from next door, peeks in. "Bonjour, hi," she chirps in her customary greeting.

She arrived from Montreal the day before me, and we live on the fourth floor of Melbourne University's foreign student residence. Our friendship began during orientation a few weeks ago and her direct, take-no-prisoners style cut straight through the tentative getting-to-know-you stage. During the bewildering first few weeks, we helped each other decipher campus maps and dodge cars driving on the left-hand side of the road. Soon we traded giggles over the odd language hiccups like how *uni* means "university," *capsicum* is a pepper, or that an *icy pole* is, in fact, a popsicle.

"How was the excursion?" Marti sashays into my room. Her hair is swept into an intentional messy bun with blunt cut bangs. Heavy eye makeup and a silver nose ring accentuate her bold features.

A history geek to the core, I've signed up for every single International Student Club sponsored outing: the Melbourne Museum, the Immigration Museum, and the National Gallery of Victoria. Today's big adventure? The Werribee Open Range Zoo.

"A keeper let me help feed the kangaroos." I remove my black-frame glasses and stand in front of the cracked mirror to pop in contacts. "A cute idea in theory until one head-butted my crotch in front of a bunch of Japanese tourists. Keep an eye on YouTube for that little chestnut."

Marti smirks before cocking a penciled eyebrow toward the various outfits laid out on my narrow bed. "Going somewhere? Big date?"

"Not a date." I knead vanilla-scented body cream into my calves. "More like a hangout."

"With Idiot Boy? Jazza?" She grabs the lotion and helps herself. "Pfffft, such a stupid name."

Jasper really, but he was all "Call me Jazza." He's a part-time surf instructor and full-time President of the Handsome Club. He's a few sandwiches short of a picnic, but an easy, surface-level relationship holds a certain appeal. This is the perfect opportunity to kick-start my Talia 2.0 reboot, one where I'm the kind of girl who lets loose and has good times.

People tend to regard me as cheerful, almost relentlessly happy. Yeah, sure, a little high-strung, but fun loving. I've worked my ass off to cultivate that persona, ground my nails to bloody nubs to make this impression take root. People want to be with the sunflowers, those who rise and face the sky. Who prefers fungus, moss, things that grow in the world's dank and shadowed places?

No one.

Marti and I met Jazza at the Espy, a grungy pub near St. Kilda beach last weekend. He'd hit on Marti first until she'd informed him in no uncertain terms that she was a card-carrying Lesbertarian and he down-geared in my direction.

After shots, my tequila-hazed mind dimly registered his shaggy blond mop and broad shoulders. Our stunted conversation didn't deepen beyond quick fact trading. Jazza lives at his parents' beach house and he ventures into the city for weekend parties. His eyes glazed while I gushed about my Victorian Sexuality class and he veered the subject to Mavericks, a big-wave surf spot up the coast from Santa Cruz that hosts an invitation-only competition.

I cracked a few jokes that flew over his head. My interest flagged until he stretched, revealing a ladder of perfect abdominal muscles. My tongue flopped out like an accordion and next thing I knew we were dirty dancing. Despite my buzz and his looks, when he kissed me, nothing happened. No fireworks, not even a sparkler. I didn't feel a single sensation except sloppy wetness. Maybe it's the medication—my brain does seem calmer—but that's a sucky trade-off if the price for sanity is zero sex drive.

On the bus home from the zoo today, I unearthed his number crumpled at the bottom of my bag, scrawled on an art postcard I'd bought at some museum gift shop. It's a painting of a guy on a tired horse riding through the outback. He's dressed in strange armor and instead of a face under the helmet, there's only sky. I don't know why, but the image struck me—a certain defiance despite the loneliness.

The time has come to break out of my comfort bubble. I hadn't traveled down under to scuffle with captive kangaroos. Would Pippa have filled her days with long, homesick rambles along the Yarra, the wide brown river flowing through Melbourne's heart? Or spent weekend nights curled in the study lounge reading Australian classics like *The Thorn Birds*, *Cloudstreet*, and *Picnic at Hanging Rock*?

No way.

It's time to fulfill my promise to her, put myself out there in the big, bad world and make a few stories of my own.

Marti rifles through my clothes and wrinkles her nose at a short-sleeve plaid button-up before lifting the drop-waist dress. "Ooh la la, cuteness."

"Think I can pull it off?" The white lace dress is a Sunny cast-off and cut lower than anything else I own. Higher too.

"You want to get lucky? Wear it." She gives a sage nod. "The boy is a boob hound."

"Takes one to know one." I wink. She's been going hot and heavy with a voluptuous British chick who works at the coffee shop around the corner. I drop my towel, slide into the tiny dress, and unearth red lipstick from my dusty makeup bag. So what if Jazza isn't Prince Charming? He is Prince Hot Enough for a Friday Night.

———

It's a little after seven and the temperatures have yet to drop. Lygon Street is packed with commuters, students, and townies trying to beat the February heat. I don't hurry, geeking on the eclectic late-Victorian architecture with the fancy cast-iron lace work. The concrete is damp from a fleeting late-summer downpour and the scent of rain lingers beneath the other smells: exhaust, espresso roasts, and the Italian cuisine being served in any one of a dozen trendy cafés. I pause as a cute couple at a cozy sidewalk table takes turns feeding each other bites of pasta. I wish I'd made the melon gelato I inhaled last longer.

The Southern Hemisphere's reverse weather doesn't throw me. Summer is generally one gloomy, fog-locked season back home while winter is all blue skies and shorts weather. Still, in this humidity, even my sweat has sweat. Moisture trickles down the tight valley between my breasts and puddles in my bra. I miss the cool Northern California coastal breezes and still can't quite believe I'm here, at the bottom of the world, ten thousand miles from home. So far the second-guessing doomsayer that hijacks my thoughts has retreated to the background. Even my body is calmer, no pulse racing to 160 over a surprise quiz. I haven't had a panic attack since arriving. Maybe Santa Cruz really was the problem and all I needed was new surroundings.

"It's wankers like you who fuck over everything. Take, take, take. When will it ever be enough?" An oddly muffled male voice booms from up ahead.

"Bloody environmental Taliban, that's what you are." A man in a well-tailored suit runs backward, straight in my direction. A koala wearing a T-shirt emblazoned with the words TREE HUGGER gives chase, elbows people out of the way. A grinning gray-furred mask belies his menacing posture.

For once my reflexes are lightning quick. I dive to safety, back pressed against a lamppost.

"You hippies are the real polluters, mucking up the gene pool. You're a poster child for abortion, mate." The suit's paunchy gut bounces in time to his words.

The koala responds with a crazy jujitsu move to the guy's nose. "I'm not your fucking mate."

I let out an inadvertent squeal, immediately woozy from the red drops splattered on the concrete. I can't handle blood—at all.

The koala wheels in my direction. The businessman takes advantage of the temporary distraction to flail forward. He wrenches the lid off an alleyway trash can, pivots, and drives the metal disk hard into the side of the koala's mask, making it impossible to see out. Blinded, the koala can't defend against the wing-tipped shoe when it connects square in his stomach.

Whoever's inside goes down hard. The suit's eyes gleam as he lands another vicious kick to the ribs.

"Hey!" My anger rises at the pot shot. I kind of want to run away, but blatant injustice raises my hackles. "Pretty tough kicking a guy who's down."

"Want a piece of this?" The businessman's fists are raised and his expression is pure bloodlust.

Great, there goes me and my big mouth, biting off more than I can chew. My knees loosen. What the hell am I going to do now? Before I can even begin to form an answer, the koala stirs. "Muss a hair on her head and they'll mop you off the streets."

Whoever is inside sounds dead serious. I don't know who he is, but I'm glad he's got my back.

The suit glances at his fight stance and recalibrates in an instant. "Jesus." He shakes his head, as if surprised to find himself returned to an ordinary businessman rather than a heavyweight boxer. He scuttles off, swallowed by the crowds.

"Hey there." I kneel next to the koala and place my hand on his mangy, threadbare fur shoulder. "You all right? Thanks for standing up for me."

Stony silence ensues.

"Um…" I look around, helpless. No one pays us any attention. "Is there someone I should call—"

"I'm fine, just taking a nap." The koala's freakish frozen smile is a sharp contrast to the deep and surly Australian accent.

"Well, I can't leave you here." I reach to take his arm, help him to his feet.

He jerks back. "I'm sure you mean well, but time to piss off. Show's over."

"Wow. Nice, real nice. Jesus, sorry I bothered." I stand and wipe my palms on my scalloped-edged skirt, shouldering my bag, irritated at my hurt feelings. "Guess no good deed goes unpunished."

"Sorry to let you down, sweetheart." He brushes off his arms. "I'm no knight in shining armor."

"Duly noted." I take a step backward. When he threatened the suit on my behalf, he meant every word. In some way, I knew, deep down, that he'd keep me safe. So why rush to my defense and then push me away?

And why overanalyze?

This is a dude in a koala suit. He clearly lacks vital screws.

The dive Jazza selected for our not-a-date squats across the street. I give the koala a frosty parting glare and stalk away. Maybe it's my imagination, but I swear he watches me go.

Whatever, cuckoo koala.

Tonight's plan was to seek adventure, and an altercation with an escapee from the *Island of Dr. Moreau* must count to that end. Time to grab a beer and chalk the encounter up to a good story for once I'm back home.

The pub's cavernous wood-paneled interior is dim. The White Stripes blast and the whole place reeks of vomit and male sexual frustration. Charming.

Jazza's easy to spot, beyond the pool tables, towering over a cute girl with a choppy bob. Okay, crap—what if he's found a better opportunity? I back away and make myself smaller, going from fight to flight mode. This whole not-a-date is a bad idea. Jazza's gorgeous, but in a bland, beefcake way. Maybe I'm not cut out to be a good-time girl. I mean, in five minutes, I could be back in my room finishing *The Thorn Birds*.

What would Pippa say? *Come on, honeybunch, live a little.*

The growing crowd propels me to the bar. "Victorian Bitter." I order the cheapest beer on tap. Mom—and her family money—might foot the bill for this Australian adventure, but no need to be greedy. I take a sip and focus on the cricket match broadcasting on three different flat screens. Sports don't interest me as a rule but the sight of fit men in pristine white uniforms running back and forth between a couple of sticks proves an incongruous distraction.

"California!" Jazza appears beside me. I turn at the exact moment he leans in for a cheek peck and give him a mouthful of nose. That's how I roll. Not at all uncomfortable.

"A table's free in the back." He recovers nicely and nods to a shadowy corner. I resist stiffening when his gaze rakes my too-short dress. This is what I want, right?

We've just taken our seats when a familiar shaggy body saunters through the throng. I clutch the edge of the table. Intense heat flares in the pit of my stomach even as my shoulder blades slam together. What's he doing here?

It's the jujitsu koala.

3

TALIA

*T*he koala has his mask tucked under one arm; dark hair half cloaks a clenched jaw. My thoughts scatter like fresh-shot marbles. Never expected a grown man in an animal suit would be quite so easy on the eyes.

"No bloody way." Jazza tips back his chair and throws up an arm. His barrel-like biceps flex. "Bran, over here, ya dirty dog."

"Wait, this guy's a friend of yours?" I hiss as the koala saunters in our direction, radiating arrogance despite his ridiculous suit.

"Yeah." Jazza's sideways glance is curious. "We go way back."

"Hey, pisshead." The koala stops before us, giving Jazza a curt nod. The guy's cat-eyed gaze arcs from my date's cheerful face to me.

An invisible blow strikes me bone deep. The ache radiates from between my pressed kneecaps, through my femurs, settling inside my pelvis with an intense throb. It's like I've been clipped by a city bus, but in a good way. He's not as generically handsome as Jazza, but his unflinching features are more interesting. My optic nerves register the slashing brows, bold nose, and a paradoxical mouth that wavers between ironic and vulnerable, but that's not what has my breath quickening like I'm at the end of a mile-long sprint. Who'd have imagined such soulful eyes lurked beneath the disturbing koala leer? He frowns and his next blink seems to last a fraction longer than necessary.

"Grab a seat, bro. Check that getup. You're sweating like a pregnant nun in confession." Jazza drags his chair close to mine and drapes an arm casually behind my shoulders. "Talia, meet Bran Lockhart. Bran, this is…uh, Talia. She's from California. Cool, hey?"

I want to shake Jazza off, deny the Cro-Magnon possessive gesture, but that would create a scene. I hate scenes.

"You're an American." Bran's tone implies this fact amuses him for some reason. Despite his flushed features, he doesn't appear to have sustained serious injury. He lounges back, one leg bent casually at the knee. While the two guys exchange quick banter, I count in my head, fast as I can, until my breathing slows.

He keeps staring at me, giving nothing away. The ambiguity is unsettling.

"How was your nap?" I'm flustered, so the words come out snarkier than intended. Still, we didn't exactly part on excellent terms.

"Plagued by dreams about Good Samaritans." Bran's lips crook in the corners.

I narrow my eyes, and his cocky smile intensifies in response.

"Hold up, so you two know each other?" Jazza's befuddled gaze bounces between us like a Ping-Pong ball.

"Not exactly." I trace a star in my pint glass's condensation. "We—"

"Met each other once, briefly." Bran props the koala head beside the table and wipes his brow. I swear he purposely angles the face toward me so that I'm right in its creepy sights.

Discussing the universe's most ridiculous fight is off-limits?

O-kay. I arch one of my brows at him, a talent of which I'm exceedingly proud.

And am totally ignored.

"Yo, bro," Jazza breaks the long silence. "Still going hard for the greenies?"

"What's a greenie?" I'm out with a guy who says "Yo, bro." The idea hurts my heart.

Jazza clasps my bared thigh, higher than appropriate for a not-a-date. "My man Bran here works for the Wilderness League. Gonna save the world, hey?"

"Just doing my bit." Bran's gaze drops to Jazza's handsy move with a heavy-lidded watchfulness that makes my stomach leap. "Today we're holding a city-wide collection drive, raising money for a new campaign."

I cross and recross my legs, casually deflecting Jazza's sweaty palm. "So, the koala suit's like a uniform?"

"Like, yeah." Bran's Valley girl accent is everything mocking.

I take a deep breath and force a sweet smile. He seems the type to kill with kindness. "And here I thought you were a furry."

He chokes on his drink and this time my grin's 100 percent natural. *All the points to me.*

"Hold up." Jazza is confuzzled. "A furry? What's that?"

Bran and I exchange glances. "So," I say, "you want to enlighten him?"

"No, no, be my guest." He makes an exaggerated courteous hand gesture.

"A furry is a person who dresses in an animal suit, like mascots or whatever, and you know, gets off in them."

"Wait…" The dawning look of realization on Jazza's face is priceless. "People root each other in animal suits?"

"Technically more like dry humping," I deadpan. "It's called yiffing; think it refers to the sound foxes make when mating."

Bran's laughter is deep, rowdy, and surprisingly infectious.

Whoa—hello. Dimples? That's my weakness. My mouth dries, makes it hard to swallow. For a second he looks like a naughty boy, and my fingers twitch with the urge to muss his hair.

"How do you know about these freaks?" Jazza eyeballs me like I'm a sexual deviant, and he can't decide if that's a good thing.

"Google." I smother a grin. This evening has turned out nothing like I expected, and yet, somehow so much better. Hanging out, tossing around sass is fun. I can almost recognize my old self.

"That's some strange shit." Jazza stands and cracks his neck. "I'm gonna grab another round."

Bran regards me for a long moment. His irises are dark green, devoid of any mottling browns or hazel, like a jungle's underbrush, intriguing, but likely dangerous. At last, he speaks. "You enjoy scandalizing innocent minds?"

"I seriously doubt your friend's a pure little snowflake."

His infuriating grunt could be interpreted a hundred different ways. "He's a bit slow on the uptake." He bangs out a staccato rhythm on the scratched table. "So, you two? How long's that been going on?"

I shake my head harder than needed. "There's no me and Jazza."

A small groove appears between his brows. "He clearly digs you."

"He's a total hornball. It's not me, specifically, but me, in a general sense. I mean, look, when we first met, he hit on my friend Marti. She's way cuter, but bats for my team, if you get my meaning."

Stop babbling.

"I doubt that."

I tilt my head, confused by the pushback. "Trust me. I've endured salacious tales about her and this one coffee shop girl, so—"

"No. I mean…I doubt she's cuter than you." His voice lowers in pitch and when he briefly worries his lower lip, the flash of his teeth, his tongue, gives me an odd jolt of intimacy.

"I…wait, are you getting flirty?" The unfiltered words zoom from my mouth before I can slam the brakes.

"No! Jesus, of course not." He stares at me like I'm a total idiot. Which I am. "But I'm not blind either." He takes a slow sip of beer. "Jazza's a good guy." That tone isn't going to win any enthusiasm awards.

"Yeah, he's great," I mutter.

Bran's hands fiddle with a coaster and are oddly fascinating. Must be some primal instincts at work here. Just a couple of minutes ago, he face-punched a man on the street. My DNA is logically programmed to be attracted to a guy who could defend me from saber-toothed tigers. That's all that's happening here. "Why didn't you want me to mention the fight outside?"

"Don't need to alert my mates to the fact that I got my ass kicked by a fat forty-plus titan of industry."

"You hung in there," I answered. "The guy fought dirty."

"Suits always fight dirty," he states, too quickly. "I was collecting donations outside his office, an international mining company. They're lobbying to put an open cut iron-ore mine square in the middle of pristine cool-temperate rain forest. The dude told me to shove off. We exchanged words. End of story."

"You swapped a lot more than words."

Jazza reappears, balancing a tray with three fresh beers and a steaming bowl of thick wedge-cut fries. "Who's keen for chips?"

We all dig in and munch for a minute.

Bran's gaze locks on me, his expression speculative.

I tense, press my knees together. "Can I help you?"

"What's with the twos?"

I freeze. "The huh?"

"Twos." He points at the bowl. "You pick up two each time."

"That's crazy." My molars set on edge. Is he for real? He can't have seen that. It's impossible. No one has ever noticed. It's like I'm suddenly naked.

Jazza chuckles to himself, engrossed in a marathon texting session.

"Go on, then." Bran slowly pops a fry in his mouth and chews, fingers steepled like a comic book villain. "Prove me wrong. Take one."

"I refuse to humor you." My voice struggles to stay light. I can't take one, or three. Only two. Otherwise something bad might happen. Yes, it's irrational. No, I can't stop. I've tried so hard to hide these compulsions, but maybe it's obvious to everyone. The thought makes my mouth taste sour.

"Consider it a dare."

I suck in my cheeks. "What are you, like five years old?"

"Twenty-three." He shoots me a lazy smile that would be totally hot if I didn't want to strangle him for shining a spotlight on my rituals.

"Knock it off," I whisper.

"Huh?" Jazza looks up.

Bran pushes the bowl in my direction. "Nothing."

"Not hungry." I smooth my eyebrow, a gesture that helps calm me down. "Hey, who wants to get their ass kicked at pool?" My mom's not the only conversational ninja in our family.

I teach the guys Cutthroat, where we are each assigned a set of numbered balls. "So," I conclude the brief tutorial, "the mission is to be the last player with at least one ball remaining on the table."

Bran leans back, one foot propped against the wall. "A player's turn continues so long as he can knock a ball in with each shot?"

"Yep."

"I can knock a ball in." Jazza guffaws.

"Ladies first," I say, neatly sending one straight into the pocket. I can't walk and chew gum, but I can play pool. Go figure.

"Ripper," Jazza says with an admiring wink.

Five minutes later they're frowning as I own the table.

"Nice superpowers, Captain America." Bran bends to adjust his belt. He shed his koala suit right after the game heated up. He wears a pair of well-worn jeans and a tight-fitting T-shirt with a picture of a unicorn and the words I BELIEVE. I'd have teased his hipster garb but the lean cords of muscle running up his forearms distract me.

Bran isn't crazy muscular like Jazza, but his wiry body holds its own appeal. Too bad he's determined to be a self-righteous ass.

There are only two pool sticks. When I finally scratch during the second game and pass mine to Bran, our fingers slide against each other. He smells like nothing special and yet everything amazing, a combination of plain soap and an indistinct but manly musk, unforced and natural. Our sudden proximity sends blood racing around my heart in a confused eddy. This guy has me on high alert, and that's dangerous for someone with OCD. Not good to be amped up. Makes the crazy flair.

My not-a-date is a far safer choice, although it's hard to pretend Jazza's charming while he ogles my boobs. Caught out, he flashes what is obviously intended to be a winning grin. "So, you're liking Australia?"

I know the guy's trying hard, but enduring his conversation is the equivalent to receiving a paper cut to the eyeball. I suffer from smalltalkaphobia.

"Yeah, Melbourne's great. I needed to get away for a while. So far so good. Can't stop playing with the light switches. They work opposite to the ones back home. Pretty neat."

Neat? Jazza's going to know I'm humoring him.

"Yeah, neat." He reveals a mouthful of perfect teeth.

Or not.

"What did you want to get away from?" Bran asks.

I must be getting drunk because his focused attention is enthralling. I fiddle with my hair and freeze when I realize he's doing the same. Oh God, am I unconsciously mimicking his actions?

My smile wavers. "It's a sad story."

"Captain America has a sad story?" Two lines bracket his mouth as he snorts. "What's the tragedy, your parents never took you to Disneyland?"

Who's he to pass judgment? My fists involuntarily clench. Bran is obnoxious. I should let it go. Feign calm. Not give him the satisfaction of knowing how much his well-timed jackassery jars me.

"Aw, poor California." Jazza's all up in my personal space and heavy on the beer breath. "I'll be your shoulder to lean on. Who wants another round?"

"Me," Bran and I say at the same time.

"I'm on it." Jazza pushes back his chair and struts to the bar.

In the quiet second that follows, Bran and I lock eyes. There are five thousand acceptable comments to make, a wry aside about the music or a jokey comment acknowledging the bartender's spectacular mullet. Instead, his gaze disorients me and I blurt, "I'm not graduating when I get home."

Damn, it's like he compelled me. It's not the truth, the whole truth, and nothing but the truth, so help me God. Still, it's a whole lot more than I'm used to sharing.

Bran frowns. His eyes hood, and even though his posture grows deceptively lazy, I sense it's an act. A trick to make me drop my guard. "That's it. Nothing else?"

I grab my beer and drink deep. Best way to shut myself up before I start sharing how my sister never woke up from a coma or that I slept with her grief-stricken boyfriend. Don't forget Mom leaving. Or when I started to believe I was dying, like all the time.

Bran's not interested in my jugular; he goes straight for the soul. Tonight was shaping up to be fun, carefree, and easy. But I forgot. Nothing is ever easy for me.

"My transcript's screwed," I say at last. "That's a big deal. Huge. My dad will commit late-term infanticide when he finds out and I can kiss any decent grad school, or shot at the Peace Corps, good-bye."

Bran's expression turns strangely tight. "Yeah, well, shit happens, Captain." He lifts his glass in salute. "To the grisly past."

"Are you making fun of me?" I can't believe this guy. He's got all the delicacy of a thorn to a blister.

Bran raises his brows in exaggerated innocence. "Of course not."

"You are. You're doing it now."

"You doubt my sincerity?" He rests a mocking hand against his chest.

"With all my heart."

He shrugs and mutters something under his breath.

"Excuse me?"

"Nothing." His lips compress. "Don't worry about it."

"Go on." I lean into my words.

"Drama."

I wrinkle my nose. "Drama?"

"Dra-ma." Bran draws the two syllables out. "Girls say they hate it, but really they can't get enough."

"Hardly," I mutter under my breath. Bran's like an itchy rash—contact dermatitis. My chin trembles as I stand. I don't want to be here anymore. This guy sees too much, sniffs out my weaknesses like a bloodhound, and I can't take it another second. Thoughts of Pippa, my mom, that fucked-up night under the wharf crowd my mind. So much for Australia being an escape. What a joke. There's no escaping the truth or my defective brain.

Jazza returns with another round. "Going to the ladies?"

My smile is tight, the carefree, relaxed feeling from earlier nothing but a distant memory. "Sorry, I just got super tired. I'm going to head out."

Jazza glances at another girl walking past. "Need me to take you back to uni?"

"That's okay." I hug my chest. He's ready to move on, and so am I. This night is a bust. "The streets are busy. I'll be fine."

"All right, girl, catch you later." His phone rings and he answers, laughing loudly.

I ignore Bran and plow through the drunk-ass crowd. When I get outside, I take a deep breath and reach for a positive affirmation.

Everything is absolutely okay.

Fuck, it's so not. Instead of playing cool, I totally lost my shit. I've alternated between sleepwalking and counterfeit smiles for so long that lying is my new normal. Nothing prepared me for my reaction to Bran. Why does it take a rude jackass to flick an honesty switch inside me?

Because he noticed more about me in an hour than my closest friends have in two years.

Stupid, needy, traitor brain.

Someone grabs my elbow and I whirl around. "What the—"

"I was a dick, okay?"

Air whooshes from the atmosphere. Bran's penetrating eyes have me on lockdown. I'm five foot six and he's got maybe another three inches on me—barely. Normally I like my guys taller, but no one's ever knocked me out with such weird magnetic voodoo. For a split second I swear he sees through all my lies and cuts straight to my demolished heart.

"It's fine." My accompanying sniffle tells a different story. "Really."

Bran's fingers burn my already warm skin and even after he lets go my arm tingles from the memory of his touch.

"Right." His wide mouth jerks into a bitter smile. "You're fine. I'm fine. We're both fan-bloody-tastic." He forks a hand through his hair. "'Night, Captain. Maybe I'll see you around."

"Wait a second." I break free of my own head and peer into his face. Intensity and desperation etch his features. He shifts his gaze to a crumbled candy bar wrapper on the concrete.

Yeah, guy, it's hard when someone peeks at your soul, isn't it?

Before I can ask a single question, he jaywalks across the street. The traffic lights illuminate his lean body, and then he's safe on the other side, swallowed by darkness.

4

BRAN

*T*al-i-a." I tangle my tongue on those three sexy syllables while kicking a half-crushed can along the footpath. Jazza is a tosser, too distracted by her tits to see the truth—his hot American isn't the type to get down for a casual root.

That girl's a watcher—those expressive eyes didn't miss a trick. One look at their depths and I sank. Basic survival instinct kicked in. Probably took her less than .5 seconds to classify me as a dickhead.

And she's not wrong.

I do think with my dick. Makes things easier. Tonight's the first night in a year that I chatted to a girl in a pub without trying to get in her pants.

Big fucking deal. Doesn't exactly qualify me for a Medal of Honor.

She fronts a cute-as-hell smile but is wound tighter than a clock. Sadness hangs over her like an invisible cloud. That's the reason I chased her outside. I poked too hard. No fair hurting someone who's down.

She said so herself.

Even now, the memory of her quivering bottom lip lingers. If I still had a heart, Talia's the type of girl who'd shoot an arrow straight through its core.

Lucky for me, I'm a Tin Man. Can't slay what's not there.

I look up—almost home. The Bean Counter's shuttered for the night. I angle around a parked car toward my place. A light shines out the back window. My housemate, Bella, waits up. Her barista shift's done. She's like me, after only one thing. Physical distraction quiets my churning thoughts.

The evening got overcomplicated. Better to keep things simple. My actions boil to one rule: Don't get involved. Bella's an easy choice. She doesn't push my buttons; I don't ask her questions. Rule #1 protects my ass, but just in case, here's Rule #2: Never, ever get curious about girls—especially cute American ones with sad eyes.

5

TALIA

I can't believe you're ditching out on the weekend." I throw my hair into a loose ponytail and secure it with an elastic band from my wrist. "Are you positive I can't bribe you with a handful of vitamin C?"

Marti sniffles in response. "My sinuses are getting stabbed by an ice pick." Her nose matches her oversized magenta bathrobe.

Jazza called out of the blue and invited me to bring any and all friends to his "oldies" beach house down the Great Ocean Road for a party. I accepted because my Talia 2.0 reboot has stalled. But I only have one real friend in Melbourne, and she's busy making love to a bottle of cold and flu medicine. I don't have Team Sunny and Beth to fall back on, or Pippa with her free and easy people skills.

If I want to get out in the world, I'm going to have to do this solo style.

Given I'm without a car and his house lies well beyond the reach of the city bus line, Jazza promised me a ride. My phone buzzes; that must be him. I check the text and my heart crams a few extra beats into the next second. Looks like he left the city early to surf and Bran offered to give me a ride instead. He'll be here anytime. This sudden change in circumstances calls for a few deep breaths. Looks like I'm enduring a two-hour car trip with the human equivalent of a splinter—a sexy splinter.

I will have to face down Bran, and those perceptive green eyes, sans backup.

"You really too sick to come?" I flash Marti my best pout.

"Sadly." She gives a seismic sneeze. "No orgasms today."

I snicker like a twelve-year-old boy. "That's not what I meant, horndog."

"I know, but it's still true. A tragedy."

"Get some rest, recharge your mojo. Tell that girlfriend of yours to do a soup home delivery." I plant a kiss on Marti's forehead, grateful her theatrics lowered my anxiety about the upcoming drive, and grab my duffel.

"No worries, mate," she mutters sardonically, waving me off with her bunched-up tissue.

I slow in the lobby and check my phone. Should I assume Bran has my number? Will he call? What's the game plan? The questions don't last long because there he is, right out front, lounging against the lone tree sprouting on the sidewalk. The white Wilderness League T-shirt provides a distracting contrast to his tan biceps. He's built like a rock climber, lean and muscular. He's reading but senses my stare and glances up.

His tight smile reveals that distracting dimple. His fierce features are all outlaw, dangerously charming. He's the kind of guy who in a sword fight would manage to coax a kiss off a nearby girl without missing a thrust.

"Hey." I eye the book he shoves into a beat-up backpack. *Walden.* "Oh, good choice. '*The mass of men lead lives of quiet desperation.*'"

"Yeah. I guess." A muscle tics in his jaw as he checks his watch. So much for an impromptu book club.

"Traffic's going to be a nightmare," he mutters.

"Not my fault."

"Never said it was." He thrusts his arms through the straps and starts to walk.

I trot to keep up. "Your tone." I raise my voice over the tram rattling past. "It says differently."

"Bloody hell." He casts me a side eye. "Are you always this defensive?"

"No." *Only with you.* Bran's burrowed under my skin in a big way. "Why are you hanging around campus?"

"You think I shouldn't be here?" *Tap-tap-tap.* He beats out a rhythm against his leg.

"That's not what I meant...just, why, it seems like..." My tongue snarls in serious knots. "Never mind."

"I tutor a few classes, natural resource management and GIS over there." He jerks his head toward the Environmental Studies building across the street. "I'm not always dressed like a koala, Captain," he says curtly. "The day we met, I was filling in for a kid with a family emergency. Mostly, I do freelance campaign work at the head office and work on campus."

"Oh." I process Bran the rogue hippie becoming Bran the academic. Both ideas hold a certain appeal.

"Shouldn't be so judgmental about how someone earns their way."

"You misunderstood me."

"Maybe. Maybe not."

I might be forced to shove him into oncoming traffic if this conversation continues in the same vein. I slow my pace to trudge two steps behind him all the way to the parking garage. He beelines

straight to a vintage cherry-red car with a short board strapped to
the roof.

I do a double take. "You drive this?" Red cars are a trigger. My
defective brain considers them unlucky, a dangerous threat. But this
one isn't setting off any irrational murder vehicle warnings.

"It's my car, if that's what you're asking." Bran unlocks the passenger side door before heading around to the back. "Here, pop
your stuff in the boot."

"What boot?"

I'm practically Rip Van Winkle by the end of his lengthy sigh.

"The trunk, Captain. The boot is the trunk."

"Oh, right." I pat the glossy panel.

Will you keep me safe?

I take my internal temperature. No signs of panic. Amazing.
I drop my shoulders from my ears; for once I can be a regular girl,
one who doesn't make a giant deal over everything. "This car, it's
so…" *Cool* is the word I want to use, but no need to further inflate
Bran's ego. "What year is it?"

"She's a sixty-nine Holden Kingswood. Restored her myself.
Hate seeing old beauties go to the junko. Such a waste."

I dump my bag on top of his and turn around, bumping into
his body. My hands splay against his chest, my fingertips tingling at
every point of contact. He's hard in all the right places. My cheeks
must match the paint. He's close, so close I can spy the spot where
he missed shaving this morning. A deep-rooted instinct urges me
to rub my lower lip over that scruff. Jesus Henry Christ, I'm almost
tempted. What is wrong with me?

"I…" He makes the single word sound dragged through gravel.
The Sphinx is a million times more expressive.

"You never mentioned you surfed." I turn away and tap the board's fins to hide my shaky inhalation.

"Well, here's me saying it."

"Your parents get a refund on your charm school lessons?" Zing. I'm throwing out sass like it's my job. Easier to provoke than concentrate on the fact that he unsettles me. My reactions to him are magnified, and that's dangerous. Sure I want adventure, but getting lost in my mind's jungle isn't fun times.

"You ever surf in Santa Cruz?" His gaze drops to my waist.

Shit. My tank top's ridden up. I yank the fabric, covering my exposed belly.

The way he listens, it's like I could tell him anything. But he's not exactly Mr. Warm and Fuzzy. Better to proceed with caution. "My dad once had big hopes for me and surfing, but after a stint in the Junior Guards, I kind of lost interest."

Add another item to my running tab of disappointing everyone.

"If you get bored during the weekend, I could take you to a few breaks," Bran says casually, yet I get the sense he's not being polite, that he'd like to take me in the water.

"Sure, maybe." I shrug like "no big" even as my stomach flip-flops. For all he knows, attractive men offer me private surf lessons every day of the week.

"Cool." He slams the trunk—boot—whatever. "Ready to hit the frog and toad?"

I jerk my head to the side. "Are you hating on amphibians?

He bursts out laughing and there they are again, my new best buds, the sexy dimples. "I asked if you wanted to get on the road."

"I need a How to Speak Australian dictionary."

"It's easy, I'll give you a quick lesson. Fuck."

I lean back. "Huh?"

"Just add fuck to everything. Fucking hell. Fucking wanker."

"Wow. I thought you were going to say something like *arvo* means 'afternoon.'"

"But you've got that one all figured out." He steps toward me.

"Yes." I take a step back. He has this pull to him, a pull that I'm not sure is a good idea.

"Telling you something you already know is about as useful as a one-legged man in an ass-kicking contest." He keeps coming and I keep retreating until we reach the passenger-side door.

"Well, when you get all poetical about it…"

He stretches an arm out and for a half second it appears he's reaching for me. Before my brain cells die off in panicked delight, he opens the door. "In you get, Captain."

We're soon on the highway, trying to exit the city, like a million other people parked alongside us on the Westgate Bridge.

"Do you have an atlas?" I ask, opening the glove compartment.

"There's a Melways under your seat, but no worries—we don't need it. I've been to Jazza's place a hundred times."

"I like to keep track of where we're going."

"Controlling much?" Bran shoves his elbow out the open driver's side window and rocks his head against the seat.

"Here we go again." I curl my toes, flex, and release. The traffic isn't even at a crawl. The drive has barely begun, and it may never end.

"Hey. I never said thank you for last week. When you stopped to help me on Lygon Street. That was cool."

"Well, I'm a cool kind of girl." Really? Those actual words came out of my actual mouth? His unexpected friendliness clearly gave me whiplash. I tug down my shades and make a fleeting wish to shame-melt into the vinyl seat.

Bran motions to flick on the radio and before I can think, my hand flies out, catching his wrist. "No, wait. Don't."

"What?" He stares at my fingers, locked on his skin.

I release my grip and massage my eyebrow. "Doesn't the passenger always get to pick the station?"

"Go ahead, if it means so much."

I exhale and casually tap all five buttons before turning on the dial. This is one of my things. A ritual. It's what I do.

"What the hell was that?" Bran's look is incredulous in the extreme.

My mouth dries. "Where I'm from, the passenger chooses the music. Common courtesy, try it sometime."

"Where I come from, girls don't finger every radio button."

"Enough with the conspiracy theories, all right? It's nothing." Sweat beads in the small of my back. "Can we turn on some air, please?"

"The Kingswood predates fancy amenities."

I pull a water bottle from my bag and take a deep swallow. "Want some?" I hold the stainless steel canister out like I'm offering a peace pipe.

"Sure." His gaze is impenetrable and I have no clue what he's thinking. Probably wondering why he's stuck in Friday night traffic with a twitchy freak. He drinks deep and hands back the bottle. I fight the stupid urge to put my mouth right where his lips touched.

The silence grows excruciating. Anything I think to ask or say seems beyond lame.

He breaks first. "Know how to play Never Have I Ever?"

I shake my head.

"It's simple. Here's the rules: One of us says 'Never Have I Ever' and finishes the sentence. If you've done whatever the thing is, you drink. Yeah?"

"Capisce." I salute and he laughs. The unfamiliar sound makes my chest untighten.

"Ladies first. That's your style, right?" He drums his fingers along to the Led Zeppelin song wailing on the radio.

"Chivalry's never out of style. My dad drilled that into me." I stare out the window for inspiration. In the distance, skyscrapers from the central business district stretch toward the deep blue sky. A police car's stalled beside us. "Never have I ever worn handcuffs."

He cocks his head. "In bed or out?"

"Har. Har. Har."

"I'm serious," he says after a beat.

"Oh." Wait, we're chatting handcuffs and bedroom play? Jesus, I really am in Oz. "Um, let's see . . . bed."

Oh God, what you are doing, Talia?

Bran reaches over, yanks the lid off the bottle, and takes a sip.

"Really?" My stomach gives a sick lurch at the idea of another girl within five feet of him.

"Once. Wasn't for me. I prefer more control in the bedroom, know what I mean?"

Nope—not really. My sex life is shorter than a haiku.

I bite my inner cheek, pretending not to notice his curious gaze slant toward me. "All right, Kink Boy, your turn."

He considers. "Never have I ever done something I regret."

He looks dead serious. Not sure how to handle that statement, so I do my usual—fumble for a stupid joke that will make everything okay. "Wow, that must make you alone in the universe." I dust off my best wry grin and drink.

"Your smile, it lights up your whole face, but your eyes always stay sad."

Is he being serious or is this yet another bait? "Never have I ever sleepwalked," I say, darting to a safer subject.

Bran drinks. "When I was eight, my neighbors woke up and I was in their bedroom. Don't remember a thing. Lucky they didn't call the coppers."

"That's nuts. Do you still do it?"

"Sometimes. Lock your door tonight. Let's see…never have I ever shot a gun."

I don't drink.

He makes a sound of disbelief. "Isn't that anti-American?"

"I'm a pacifist. Never have I ever had a big romantic kiss in the rain."

"That fact is the single most depressing thing I've ever heard."

"Hence my sad eyes." Traffic starts moving. I hang my hand out the window and let the wind blow through my fingers. He's spinning me every which way, but I think I like it, even though I'm dizzy. "Bran?"

"Natalia?"

I stiffen, immediately on edge. "No one ever calls me that except for my mom. How'd you know my full name?"

"Read the luggage tag on your bag—Natalia Stolfi."

"Oh, right." I shake my head and regroup. "Is it true you have no regrets, not even one?" Hopefully he has no idea how dead serious I am in his response.

"There's no point." His fingers tighten infinitesimally on the wheel. "The past is the past. That's it."

"Like whatever doesn't kill you makes you stronger?"

"No, that's a dumb-ass cliché. I mean there's no meaning to life, despite what people pretend. Once I figured that out, everything got easier."

"Has anyone ever said you are intense?"

"Since the day I was born." He checks the rearview mirror. "So I've got to ask you something. Maybe I'm presuming but—"

"If that's your lead-in, then you're probably correct."

"You don't fool me."

He's right. No matter how hard I try to hide and pretend away my crazy, Bran sees too much.

"But you try to fool everyone, don't you?" He turns and catches me staring. "With the act. You, all breezy, cute as hell, always smiling like we're at some big-deal party. You know what I think—"

"No, actually." *Wait, I'm cute? He thinks I'm cute?*

"Not sure what your issue is, but—"

"I'm fine," I mutter tightly. Reality wanders back, as unwelcome as a drunk uncle at a family picnic. Let's face it, no one wants to be around a girl with issues. "Really, I'm all good." Right, I sound like a five-year-old watching worms die in puddles.

"Whatever you say, Miss OCD." He glances from the open atlas on my lap to my pursed mouth with a thoughtful look.

"I…I…" Anxiety locks me in an invisible chokehold while my abdomen spasms. But Bran's gaze isn't mocking. There's an unexpected sweetness there that's coaxing me from my familiar fortification. "I guess maybe it's something like that." My whispered words rise above my head like a toxic balloon.

"Must kinda suck."

People don't kid if they think you're crazy, right?

"Sucks donkey balls."

He grins. "An unpleasant flavor."

Suddenly I can breathe again. "And you'd know how?"

A second crawls past. He keeps his veiled eyes trained on the road.

"Bran?" Finally, I can't take it. I need to say something. "You acting nice is unfamiliar, and, frankly, uncomfortable, territory."

"Is being interested a crime?" He kneads the back of his neck. The deep, massaging rhythm is mesmerizing. His thumb is a little wide. He keeps his nails neatly cut.

"You're interested?" I'm off-kilter, like I've taken back-to-back rides on the Tilt-A-Whirl at the boardwalk.

"In your quirks. Let's hear another one."

"One more. That's it. Then we're done for the day." I kick off my flip-flops and cross my ankles. "I can't fall asleep without reciting this long poem, *Paul Revere's Ride*."

How is this even possible? We're talking about my most shameful secrets like it's just another thing. Why isn't he pointing a judgmental finger at me, crying, *Shun her, shun the freak*?

"And you call me kinky? What do your boyfriends say when they sleep over?"

"I repeat the words in my head, not out loud. And I've never had a boyfriend."

"Wait, how is that even possible?"

"What? The no-boyfriend situation?" The words make me sound like a bigger loser when spoken aloud. There's a very good reason. Too busy obsessing over my sister's big love. But I don't say that. Even in this sharing mood, some words strangle. Still, I've hinted at my blackest secret and wasn't smote down, laughed at, or ridiculed.

A new song starts that's all angsty and instrumental—dramatic violins, slow guitar riffs, and measured drumbeats. I don't want to go dark, not right now, when everything almost glows.

I spy Bran's iPod up on the dash and reach forward. "We need different music—"

"But we haven't finished talking about—Wait! Hold up." His hand darts but I'm quicker.

"What?" I dangle the iPod out of reach. "Cool guy like you have something to hide? Maybe a secret Beyoncé playlist or..." I flick on the screen. "Oh to the Em Gee."

"Go on." He heaves an exaggerated sigh. "Don't hold back."

"Justin Bieber?"

"I watched my nieces yesterday. They have a dance recital to the song next week. I helped them practice their routine."

"You? That's so normal." *And sweet.*

"Yep. I broke it down to the Biebs."

"Please, tell me there's a video."

"I'm secure in my manhood, Captain."

"Clearly." I can't hold back a snicker and within seconds we're both doubled over. My heart swells until I feel like I might burst with pale, pink light.

The feeling lingers until we turn off at a faded, salt-worn sign that reads POINT ROADKNIGHT. After a few sharp turns, we pull in front of a sleekly modern beach house, all steel lines and wide windows facing the Bass Strait coastline. Dozens of cars line the sandy street. Heavy bass throbs from inside.

Jazza bounds through the crowded balcony, leans over the rail, and raises a rum bottle in greeting. "What's up, bro? California! Lookin' gorgeous, baby."

I give a little wave before glancing back. Bran's bent deep in the trunk.

"Are you coming up?"

"Nah, not yet." His voice is muffled. "Tell Jazza I'll be around in a bit." He emerges with a wet suit flung over his shoulder and deftly unstraps the board from the roof rack, avoiding my eyes.

"What we talked about—"

"Don't forget your thongs, Captain."

My brain blanks, rational thought grinding to a halt. "Excuse me?"

He opens the passenger side door and grabs my flip-flops. "Your thongs," he repeats slowly, holding them out.

Holy God, talk about being lost in translation.

"Wait, you thought…bloody hell." He smirks as my blush extends to the tips of my bare toes.

I'd be perfectly content if the ground beneath me happened to be quicksand.

"Sorry. Guess I'm never going to get this Aussie lingo down," I mutter, sliding my feet into my thongs, flip-flops, things-with-a-sole-and-toe-strap.

"No worries, Captain. Don't get your knickers in a knot." He moves to turn away.

"Hey, wait, one last thing…"

He freezes and I bite my top lip. There isn't anything profound to say, yet something should be offered to recognize the connection we shared in the car. Bran's practically a stranger, but now he knows some of my most classified information. I carry all this weight inside me, each secret, a tarnished stone. This afternoon it's like I've split my belly, pulled one out, and washed it clean.

"Thanks for listening." I take a deep breath and say the next words super fast, afraid they won't come out if I overthink. "You're a good guy, underneath the general saltiness."

His gaze darkens as his jaw sets.

I cross my arms. "Maybe we can, you know, be friends?" My words hang like a half-flown peace flag. A single foot separates us, and the narrow space hums with a hidden current that spreads goose bumps up my neck. My shorts ride up my thighs and I tug the legs down. The fidgety gesture draws his attention toward my exposed skin. I shift and my cotton underwear rubs between my legs. This sudden oversensitivity isn't doing wonders for my inner calm.

"I'm off to check the waves." His voice is carefully bored. Too careful. He's not going to accept my offering. "You should head inside, have fun with Jazza and the crew."

We'd shared a brightness, something flitting and elusive, like a late-summer firefly hovering just out of reach, but the moment's gone, lost in shadow.

He doesn't hold my questioning gaze. Instead, he shrugs, face expressionless, and strides away down a narrow footpath through the heath-covered dunes.

My swallowed response sticks in my throat. The one where I almost said, "But I'd have more fun with you."

6

TALIA

J hunch alone against a stark-white wall in Jazza's living room. The airy home is lifted straight from the pages of *Dwell* magazine and brims with beautiful tanorexics and ripped surfers trading inside jokes and easy banter. I'm as vital to the scene as the angular modern sculpture to my left. A few steps ahead, three dudes in identical neon Ray-Bans slaver over a ridiculously fit girl named Bunny. Either that's an unfortunate nickname or her parents were porn stars.

Jazza, the only person I recognize after Bran ditched me in the driveway, perches on a stainless steel barstool, holding court before shaggy-haired guys who hang on his every word. I catch enough stock phrases—*sick ground swell, hell munched*, and *caught inside*—to know he's getting off on some chest-beating big-wave story.

He catches me staring and before I can divert my attention to the massive abstract painting above the fireplace, the one that vaguely resembles two tangoing penises, he shouts, "Yo, California, get your bad self over here."

Add being the center of attention to things that churn my

stomach. Wingman is so much more my speed. Time slows as I shuffle across the state-of-the-art kitchen, openly scrutinized by unfamiliar faces. What if I say the wrong thing? Accidently insult someone or make a complete and utter fool out of myself?

Deep down I know I probably won't, but the what-ifs send my heart slapping between my spine and ribs.

Because what if this time's different? What if this is the time when I blow it?

Jazza casually hooks his big, wide hand around my waist, drawing me close while his crew scatters. "Having a good time?"

"Yes. Great. Amazing. This place is incredible." Three lies and a truth. The house gleams with natural light and sleek architecturally designed lines.

"Bangin'." Jazza's fingers travel up my shorts and I shift toward the bar. He's drunk and flirty, and I'm neither.

"What should I have?" When in doubt, trust in alcohol. Maybe a drink will take away the sting of watching Bran walk away.

If Jazza notices my subtle rebuff, his cheerful face doesn't let on. The bronze skin around his turquoise eyes crinkles and his hair is sun-bleached nearly white. He's unquestionably gorgeous. So why is my inclination not to tear off his tight Rip Curl shirt, but rather pat him on the head like an oversized man-boy?

"You dig shots, California?" He leaps up and fists a saltshaker.

Maybe if I pretend his cheesy nickname for me doesn't make me want to tie my eardrums in knots, it will be so. Funny how when Bran calls me Captain, it has the opposite effect. "Well, let me see. I have kind of a love-hate relationship with tequila."

"Tonight is all about the love." He pushes me a glass and flashes an orthodontic-swooning smile.

Three shots and a beer later, the sixty-odd faces take on a

dreamy appearance. The floor-to-ceiling windows capture the steely blue waves under a sky exploding in a fiery sunset. A few surfers bob near the point.

Which one is Bran?

Jazza offers to give me a tour and staggers up the crowded staircase, pausing occasionally to clap a guy on the back or chat with some girl in a string bikini and microskirt. As soon as he opens a door and tugs me inside, it becomes clear there's only one stop on this itinerary.

His bedroom.

My fight-or-flight response kicks in hard. There's a framed poster on the opposite wall. A surfer crouches inside a massive barrel, enclosed by a whitewater tube that looks poised to crush down, consume him whole. Neither the Talia 1.0 nor 2.0 version thinks being here alone with a heavily inebriated Jazza is wise. "Hey, you know what? I forgot to go and—"

"You drive me mental, know that?" He digs both hands into my back pockets and hauls me close, grinding his pelvis into my upper stomach. No way he's wearing boxers beneath his board shorts. "What colors are you wearing underneath?" His cologne makes me woozy and not in a good way. "I'll bet black, tell me black silk."

"Wait, Jazz—" But he's already in for the kiss. His tongue flicks over my tight-closed mouth while he makes these creepy, guttural grunts.

I struggle free. "Seriously, this isn't—"

"We're not leaving the room until one of us comes." From the frantic way he's mouth breathing, it won't be long before he whips out little Jazza for a playdate. His hands reach for my breasts like overeager octopuses. Or is it octopi? Who cares—I'm not getting off tonight. I've never been close, and I don't feel even the slightest whiff of attraction toward him.

"Easy, Tiger." I clamp Jazza's wrists.

"What?" He pants hard but freezes.

"You are super sweet, Jazz, but I can't do this."

He stiffens. "Why not?"

I stroke his ridiculously chiseled jaw. "I want to be friends, not get complicated."

"Fuck buddies." Jazza's face lights like he just solved a riddle. "That's cool."

"Wait, what?"

"I get it. You don't want anything serious. Me neither." He swoops in for another kiss.

Yeah, he so doesn't get it.

"Yes to the buddies." I plant my hand firmly in his sternum. "No to the fuck."

"No?"

I shake my head gently.

"Really?" The feverish expression fades from his eyes, leaving behind vague puzzlement.

"Truly." Something tells me getting denied is new territory for the Jazzster.

He runs his tongue over his bottom teeth. "Bloody oath, I feel like an ass."

"This is going to sound so cheesy, but it's all me, not you." And I mostly tell the truth. He's a bit of a slow bear, but still a nice enough guy. From the way other girls check him out, I doubt he'll lack company for long.

A muscle twitches near his ear. "Bran was bloody keen to drive you here."

My heart forgets to take the next beat. "He was?"

"He asked a lot of questions about you, after that night in the pub."
Really?

His lower lip juts out. "Am I pissing in his pool?"

"First, sorry, I'm not a pool. Second, no way are Bran and I a thing." I scrub my hands through my hair to erase the tiny voice whispering, *Maybe.* "Absolutely not."

"I don't check out dudes or anything, but chicks don't find him repulsive."

"He's so…" Cocky, brash, nosy. An all around pain in the ass who's a magnet for everything I want to remain deeply buried.

"He's Bran." Jazza completes my sentence with a sage nod, or at least a knitted brow.

"Yeah." I reach out an open hand. "So are we cool?"

He meets me with a halfhearted fist bump. "Sure, California."

I wake from restless sleep to someone puking down the hall. Sweat prickles my chest and my mouth fills with saliva. Bodily fluids aren't my strong suit. Vomit ranks just behind blood on my personal gross-o-meter. I kick free from tangled sheets, rearrange my camisole, and survey the empty guest room. After our failed make-out session, Jazza proceeded to get blindly obliterated. As did pretty much everyone else at the party with the exception of me. Bran never put in an appearance. What gives? He wouldn't go back to the city without me, right?

I go to the door and turn the knob and step into the corridor. An open condom wrapper lies on the polished hardwood floor. Thank Christ I took preventive measures and locked the door before crashing. The house is a black vault of silence. The time is probably well past midnight, nowhere close to dawn, but the coast is clear as I pad toward the kitchen, holding my breath while tiptoeing past Jazza's room.

The kitchen is empty, at least of sentient beings. Drained beers, crushed chip packets, shot glasses, and demolished limes litter the marble countertops. I hunt through cupboards, unearth a champagne flute, and run it under the tap. Tangy salt air blows in from the open window, caressing my face. Three empty tequila bottles guarantee the pukefest is sure to continue upstairs. Crashing out on the peaceful balcony is a vast improvement over a return to the vomit lairs.

I slide open the glass door, step out, and tilt my head toward the star-filled sky. The ocean's rhythmic roar washes over me. I could almost be home, except the Southern Cross constellation replaces the Big Dipper.

"Nice night." A deep and already familiar voice cuts the silence.

My breath catches. "I didn't know anyone was out here."

"What're you doing up?" Bran sprawls on a rattan lounge, his face cloaked in shadow.

"I'm good," I respond automatically, realizing a second too late that wasn't the question. And that I took off my bra to sleep, leaving on my tight-fitting white camisole.

His gaze drops, takes in my unbound girls, and he clears his throat. "Uh...okay."

I fold my arms across my chest, hunting for anything to reduce the tension. "I didn't think anyone remained standing."

"Me neither."

"Yeah, yes. Good. All right." I need to shut up or get to a point sometime this century. Bran has no idea Jazza grilled me about him. Does he? Or is that why he can't sleep? I chew the inside of my cheek. Unlikely. Guys never talk. "So..."

"So what?"

"Where were you tonight?"

"Haven't been to the beach in ages." He swings his legs to the ground and shoves to the far side of the couch to make room. "Surfed until after dark and then went for a walk."

"Loner much?" I take a seat.

His broody expression lightens. "A regular Scott."

Thrown, I cock my head. "Excuse me?"

"Scott No Mates. It's a childhood burn on the play yard."

"Like calling someone a loser." I set my water on the armrest and try to ignore the fact that the dimple in his left cheek kills me. Can he tell my heart gears into fifth from his proximity?

"Yeah. As in, 's got no mates."

His posture relaxes when genuine laughter erupts from my chest.

Even from here, I smell his clean soapy scent and a lingering hint of sunscreen. Tingles spark behind my knees. A shiver skims my spine. Here he goes again, casting that magnetic voodoo that wakes up my whole body.

His green eyes glow in the porch light. He has smooth, olive skin. Despite his dark hair's rumpled, scruffy appearance, the texture is thick and glossy—definite Latin ancestry. "Do you have a little Spanish in you?" I blurt.

One of his brows arch, a talent we apparently share. "Is that your version of a pickup, Senora Random?"

"Egotistical much?"

Surprisingly, he looks more amused than annoyed. "Indirectly Spanish—Mum's from Argentina."

Jesus, this guy's genes don't play fair.

"Your mom?"

"I didn't hatch from an egg, Captain."

"What? No, of course not."

Silence marches on until I'm almost reduced to humming the *Jeopardy!* theme song.

"Party looked all right." Bran inclines his head toward the house. The dim security light reveals his calves are cut. A runner?

"Just your average wasted gropefest."

"Great." His hands clench and release. "How'd you do? Any conquests? Where's Jazza?"

I choke on a sip of water. "Otherwise occupied." Last I saw him, he had the lovely Bunny set in his crosshairs. She seemed to welcome the target.

Bran faces me dead-on and his pupils are huge. "Can I have a drink?"

My hand shakes a little as I pass the champagne flute. "The kitchen's a mess. Couldn't find a normal glass."

"I'm sure we can find a reason to celebrate."

Anxiety swims around my stomach like a trapped snake. Did he sidle closer? No. Must be my imagination. Don't forget to breathe. Oxygen. Get some.

"Do I make you nervous?"

My intended world-weary chuckle comes out more terrified field mouse. Warmth floods my breasts despite the cool ocean breeze. "I have a confession," I murmur.

He pivots his hips in my direction. Wait, I swear his foot is nearer to mine. My fingers close on my knees. His eyes are prettier than any guy has a right to own. "Go on."

"You're not that scary." I reach behind me and toss a throw pillow at his chest. My choice is clear. It's joke or explode from the mounting pressure.

"Hey, watch it, Captain. I can be scary. Very, very scary." He walks his fingers along the back cushions—just out for a casual Saturday night stroll.

"Whatever."

He's less than a hand width away. Comes closer. Closer. My head pounds. My pulse rivals a hummingbird.

"You should be careful," he murmurs. Our legs brush and I'm full, aching. The underwear against my skin is too much friction. I'm going to burst into 4th of July grand finale fireworks if he kisses me.

"Maybe I like to live dangerously," I whisper.

"Maybe I do too." He stares at my mouth. His lips part.

Holy shit. Holy shit.

Below the deck comes a scuffle. Something's knocked over. Glass breaks. A muffled laugh. Bran and I fly apart as footsteps trip up the stairs. Jazza and Bunny appear, smirking and disheveled.

"Yo, mate. We passed out on the beach. The tide came up and…" Jazza halts, notices me, and gives Bran a flinty look.

"I'm beat." Bran jumps to his feet. He saunters for the stairs. "Gonna go crash in my car." He's gone without looking back.

"Let's shower." Bunny traces one of Jazza's bare pecs. "I'm all sandy."

He gives me a tight nod as they slip inside.

I crush a pillow against my chest. I wanted to be alone anyway.

And I tell myself I mean it.

7
TALIA

*I*nvulnerable to hangover blues, Jazza rallies everyone for a predawn surf mission at the Rock—a world-class point break up the coast. I failed to scrounge contact solution before leaving his house. My dry, slept-in lenses threaten to pop from my skull. The freezing cliff-top parking lot numbs my bare feet while below, set after set of clean head-high waves roll in. The surf is big and I haven't been in the water in a good long time. I could make an excuse, say my eyes are bothering me, but that seems like a cop-out.

Dr. Halloway said in our last appointment that the key to mastering the mind is observation. I need to learn to ride thoughts like a wave rather than get pummeled onto shore. My lungs expand in a deep, intentional breath, but my mind jigs like a demented circus monkey.

I edge farther from the group. Better to have a little privacy to gather my nerves and gyrate into my borrowed wet suit. Someone unearthed one for me that must belong to an eight-year-old boy. My boobs pancake to my chest—the twins clearly unhappy to be bound—while I grapple over my back for the Velcro close.

I realize I'm about to paddle into waves bigger than any I've ever attempted—and for the world's most stupid reason.

"Need help?" Bran steps behind me. He tugs my wet suit closed and pulls the zipper. My skin ignites when his knuckles graze the hypersensitive skin between my shoulder blades.

Yep. I'm trying to impress the Southern Hemisphere's most unimpressible guy.

I turn around, wishing the skintight neoprene was a smidge less revealing. Each and every curve is highlighted in bright neon.

"Sure you're up for this, Captain?" His lips are pressed tight. "The Rock's a fast wave."

"Yeah, totally." This is the third time he's asked. The first two times were in Jazza's driveway before leaving. Why does he pretend to care? I don't get it. He blew me off hard last night and now stares with bedroom eyes. I take a skittish step backward, a rabbit before a curious panther.

Finally, I manage to break his gaze. A big mistake, as his wet suit is only half on. The top flops over his narrow waist and hard-cut abs. His body isn't framed with bulky "sexy and I know it" musculature. Instead, he's got this lean, agile thing happening, like he gets his muscles from use rather than gym worship.

"Ready to head?" I fumble for the dinged short board Jazza's given me on loan.

"Lead the way. Don't want you perving behind my back." Suppressed laughter lurks in his voice.

I hook the board against me and plow down the steps toward the water's edge. "Right, because guys hate getting checked out."

"Is that what you were doing?"

His playful side totally charms me. "Want the truth?"

He leans in, eyes lively. "Always."

"I'm trying to remember what part of jumping into a frigid ocean before sunup is a good idea."

"Dirty little liar." He nudges the back of my knee with his toe. That smile is so, um, so...swashbuckling. "Hmm." *Translation: Let me plunder you three ways to Tuesday.*

When we reach the cliff bottoms, he nods toward the crowded lineup. "We need to walk over the reef and paddle through the oncoming waves."

"Don't worry, I'll be fine." I bite my lip and hope my face looks stoic rather than panicked. The locals out there are exceptional. Jazza's white-blond hair is starkly visible as he carves a giant face. In the distance, thunderheads cling to indigo water. Sweet. We have violent limb-tearing surf conditions bolstered by an impending typhoon. At least I poured over the fine print in my traveler's insurance. The repatriation of remains is fully covered. Dad won't have to fork out for my coffin's 747 ride home. I lean down and casually knock a piece of driftwood twice for extra luck.

Craggy orange-streaked sandstone rises at our back. The cliff face is gouged from centuries of the wild weather for which the Bass Strait is famed. I'm caught in a twisted version of that childhood rhyme "Going on a Bear Hunt." Can't go over it. Can't go under it. "I'll have to go through it," I mutter, stepping onto the knobby reef.

"All good?" Bran moves beside me.

"Where should I go if I hypothetically wanted to steer clear of everyone's way?"

He gives his chin a musing rub. "Uppers and Middles are the preferred spots—that's where everyone's headed. We could paddle this direction." He points closer inside. "Lowers. No one's there yet. The waves are smaller, but it can get shallow fast."

All I register is "we" and "smaller." I like the small part but refuse to rope him into babysitting duty.

"Thanks, I'll hang there. I haven't surfed in a while and don't want to cramp your style. Go on, have fun."

"Who says I'm not having fun?" He doesn't budge.

"Um..." I restrain myself from giving the parking lot a last desperate look. "Okay, sure. Let's go do this." Foamy whitewash runs over my feet and my lungs constrict. The water temperature hovers at a cool 60 degrees.

Bran paddles up on my left. The tips of his hair are wet and in his black wet suit he looks sleek, hot, and utterly confident. "Follow me. You're gonna do great." His brilliant smile snatches what little air remains in my chest.

When he's like this—nice, open—it's dangerously appealing.

Everyone else congregates near the bigger waves. We float alone, straddling our boards. A slow swell rises.

Bran points. "This one is all you."

I hesitate.

"Go on, take it. Unless you want to sit around waiting to be shark bait."

Sharks? Great. Add that to the list of things that will kill me before breakfast.

He ignores my scowl, all business. "Here it comes, quickly now."

I point my nose toward shore and paddle.

"Harder," he orders. "Like you want it."

I dig deep, my fingers numb. The wave gives lift. "Come on, girl," I mutter, shoulders screaming. Spray peppers my face. Bran whoops my name. There's a surreal moment of weightlessness and then—I'm on. Holy shit, I fucking did it. I caught the wave.

I leap to my feet and drop into a low crouch, smiling so hard my cheeks hurt. For the next few seconds time slows even as I gain speed. Every thought flies from my head as joy floods my limbs. I've never had an orgasm, but no other sensation seems even remotely as blissful or fleeting. Already the wave dwindles and I sink back into the ocean.

I flick my head to face Bran and he pumps a fist. I can't wipe the grin off my face. No point pretending to be cool when I'm this stoked.

He gives me a friendly splash when I paddle back. "Well, how was it?"

"Freaking amazing. Fantastic." For those few seconds I existed in the present. Why haven't I been going out back home? This is exactly the activity that could sort out my head.

"Did good, Captain."

"You doubted my mad skills." I don't add that I questioned them even more.

"Who, me?" He holds up his arms, cat eyes bright with mischief. Another wave approaches. "All right, Captain, this one's calling my name." A few easy paddles and he pops up, the perfect mixture of power and grace.

We don't talk much, only the odd back-and-forth trade. I catch almost every ride and while I'm waiting, the sight of Bran's easy grace keeps me warm.

A gull swoops close enough to reveal shiny black eyes and a red-tipped beak. The bird looks as if it drank blood. I paddle for a new wave when Bran shouts. Not understanding him above the ocean's roar, I stand—what the hell? Bunny slides over the crest on a hot-pink board and blocks my ride. We make quick eye contact, enough to register her mouth, *Mine.*

My jaw slackens. The twat! She dropped in on me. That's breaking a fundamental surf law. Rather than risk a crash, I pull back, but the board shoots from under my feet. I wipe out, hitting the water without time to cover my head as the wave's foamy maw devours me. The ocean seizes me like a child with a new toy. Salt water fills my mouth and ears, bends my body as I kick hard. My foot scrapes gnarled coral.

Shit. Shit. Shit.

If we were at a sandy-bottomed beach, I could push off the sea-floor, shoot myself to the surface. But this is a reef. I don't want to risk getting my foot caught.

My lungs burn, desperate for oxygen. I open my eyes for orientation and my contacts are gone in an instant. Stupid. So stupid. Panicking makes things worse. Stay calm. Impossible. I'm going to die, right here, right now, in five feet of water. My diaphragm jerks against my rib cage. I was an asshat for making light earlier. If anything happens to me, Dad won't survive the loss.

The moment the thought enters my head, my face breaks the water. I kneel, hands cutting on the reef, and draw a sobbing breath.

"Talia!"

I turn toward Bran's alarmed voice. Another wave barrels forward with my board poised directly at my head. My reflexes are slow and before I can protect myself, the fiberglass collides with my left temple in a sick crunch. The fin slices across my cheek as if in afterthought. I sink into the wash, ears ringing. The world retreats into a murky shroud.

Strong hands yank me to my feet. Why so rough? Can't stand. Gagging. Mouth tastes like bitter metal. Can metal taste bitter? The question blooms through my brain, crowding every other thought. Arms brace my shoulder and under my knees. I'm lifted like a baby.

"Hold on, Captain."

That voice. Warm as sunshine even as the darkness settles.

"Talia, Talia, Talia."

What? What? What? Jesus, shut up.

"Come on, let's see those pretty eyes."

Pretty? Must be someone else. Someone who didn't have an ox tap-dance across their temple.

"Talia."

"Too loud." My voice is thick and scratchy. I force my lids apart. Bran is at my nose. His eyes widen and he sits, goes all blurry.

"I can't see."

He hisses about twelve different curses. "Okay, calm down. You're going to be fine."

"I'm not losing it. Lost my contacts in the wipeout." Even half blind I can tell we're in the parking lot. "You carried me up the stairs?"

"She good?" Jazza's smeary outline appears overhead.

"I'm fine." Did everyone witness my little accident?

Jazza makes a grunt of approval.

"Bunny dropped in on her," Bran says tightly. "I think she has a concussion."

"That sucks." Jazza sounds distracted. "Can you hang with her for a bit? The swell's epic."

I brace my head and wish away the mounting nausea.

Wish denied.

"I'm taking her to the hospital. She lost consciousness."

"I'm sure it's nothing serious." All of Jazza's attention appears trained on the water. "She said she's fine. You're cool, right, California?"

Bran gives his head a half shake. "I'll leave her board and wet suit by your van."

"No worries, bro." Jazza gives my shoulder a brief squeeze and is gone.

"No hospital." I mean it. The idea of getting anywhere near an emergency room ratchets my queasiness to gut-shredding levels. But maybe my brains are scrambled. What if I'm bleeding internally, a ticking time bomb—a small jolt away from total brain hemorrhage?

"Talia?" No *Captain*. He's using a serious voice, tight and über-purposeful. He kneels beside me and my hands disappear into his. How can his skin be so warm after the freezing ocean? The universe's origin seems easier to decipher. "Natalia."

Natalia now? A sure sign of impending catastrophe. I'm screwed; something must be really wrong. Please, God, don't let me bleed out my ears like an Ebola monkey in front of him.

He's vanished. Where? I float, alone, the sensation not entirely unpleasant.

"Hey." Bran's hands gently grip my jaw and tilt my head. "I backed my car into the space behind you. You don't have to walk far. Or I can carry you."

"No, that's all right." I accept his hand and haul onto unsteady feet.

"Here." He hands me a faded striped beach towel. "For your face."

My fingers fly up to my burning jaw. I jerk my hand free and stare at the blood. "Oh no."

"A little scratch, from the fin—"

I vomit salt water across his bare feet.

8

TALIA

I huddle in the emergency room's sticky plastic seat while Bran asks the two dour nurses at the triage station if I'm next, even though we've only been here ten minutes. I shove my heavy black glasses up my nose, the ugly Buddy Holly pair I keep in my purse in case of contact failure. No point trying to make an impression. I already puked on him.

The antiseptic hospital smell clogs my nostrils, intensifies my already sizeable headache. Bran flashes a charming smile and I swear one of the women almost fans herself. I don't blame her. His smile lights fires when he chooses. I wonder if he knows? Probably—he's not exactly modest. He turns and saunters back across the green linoleum. Holy God, his skin is golden even under the glary fluorescent light. He really is sexy as hell.

And I'm a rag doll who's been run through the wash.

"The nurses say we can go wait in back. A bed opened. You can lie down."

I want to nod, but it hurts. "Sounds great."

He helps me from the seat and keeps a firm grip on my arm

while I shuffle through the hospital's warrenlike halls. I lean into him and he lets me, his arm protective on my waist. We reach the assigned hospital bed and he tugs the privacy screen closed. It's weird, and nicely intimate, letting someone take care of you.

I climb onto the mattress and ease myself against the thin pillow, staring at a cracked ceiling tile. Pippa lingered in this kind of place for too long, over a year. Then came the day Dad, Mom, and I huddled together, watching a nurse turn off her ventilator. The doctor chewed gum while he removed the breathing tubes. His snapping jaw was all I heard once the life support went silent.

My calves tighten while a cold sweat breaks out over my belly.

A chair scrapes against the floor. Bran sits and takes my hand.

I jump when he interlaces his fingers in mine, startled by the unexpected physical contact. "When you do that, I feel like I'm dying."

He massages my knuckles. "You're cold. It bothers me."

"How are you so warm?"

"I'm a human furnace."

"Hot." My attempt at a smile is marginal, so I let my lids flutter shut. The headache is less intense lying down.

"This your first time in hospital?"

I slowly inhale and exhale. Shit. I'm gripping his hand really hard.

"The nurses say I need to keep you talking until the doctor comes."

"No."

"Can't let you fall asleep, Captain."

"Sorry. No, it's not my first time in a hospital."

"Me neither." He keeps his voice easy, conversational. "Shoved a lolly up my nose when I was five."

"Oh God." His admission shocks me back into the present. "What?"

"I remember the examination table and the crinkly paper. My sister brought me. Must have been almost Christmas because some drunk in a Santa hat tried to punch out a doctor."

"Where were your parents?"

"Dunno. Maybe Frankfurt...Hong Kong? Dad works in finance. Mum goes where he does."

I let that sink in. "They left you and your sister alone for the holidays?"

"Gaby's much older." He surveys my face, no doubt noting my pallor, the way I keep chewing the inside of my cheek. "Let's see, what else is there to say? Mum was almost forty-three when I came along. She never recovered from the shock. When I was ten, they packed me off to boarding school across the bay at Geelong Grammar. That's where I met our mutual friend—Jasper Bartholomew Kingston, the third."

"Jasp—wait a second...Jazza?"

"The one and only. Our fathers play golf together."

"Do you see your folks much?" I follow his words like breadcrumbs, hoping they lead me from the encroaching panic.

"Nah. The family homestead is in Portsea—on the Mornington Peninsula—but they're in Singapore at present."

"Sounds lonely."

"I'm used to it."

"And your sister—"

"Enough about my boring family. How about you? Overprotective sisters? Crap parents?"

"My dad's great. Mom sucks."

"Only child?"

"I had a sister." I tug a loose string on the sheet's edge. "Pippa. Almost exactly one year older." I lick my dry lips. "She died a while back." Sounds like I'm discussing what I ate for breakfast. A few scrambled eggs, half a cup of coffee, dead sister. Can someone pass the cream?

I'm no better than that fucking gum-chewing doctor.

"I'm sorry."

Everyone is sorry. I nearly drowned in other people's sympathy. Yet when Bran offers his condolence, it's like a life raft I can cling to for a moment, keep my head above water.

"Me too." My chin gives an involuntary quiver.

His hand doesn't leave mine. I like the contact. Makes me feel human, less a husk.

The air conditioner rattles through a vent overhead.

"What's your favorite movie?" Bran asks.

"Serious?" That's not what I'm expecting him to say.

"I won't ask you to discuss your dead sister. Unless, of course, you want to."

"I don't." I relax a fraction. "At least—not right now. Not here."

"*Empire Strikes Back*. That's mine."

"Old school."

"Don't watch much new stuff."

"An excellent choice, except when Yoda gets all creepy about the dark side. That part used to give me nightmares."

Bran's lips part. I glimpse his tongue and a slightly crooked incisor. These little details, I can't stop gathering them like a kid seeking fistfuls of dandelions. My heart starts racing and the bewildering warmth sends goose bumps up my arms. My body is as confused as my mind how to react to this guy.

"The world's divided into two kinds of people." I pause to clear my throat. "Those who love *Star Wars* and idiots."

"Where have you been all my life?" He leans close and I can see the exact spot where his scruff ends beneath his jaw.

I duck my head, aware my thighs are clenched. "Sorry, Tiger. Han Solo and I have this thing going on behind Princess Leia's back. It's my destiny."

The screen yanks open. A doctor stands there with a beard that would make Chewbacca jealous. He gives me a once-over, rechecks my chart, and turns to address Bran. "How's your wife? Surf accident?"

Wife? Is he for real? I dissolve into full-blown hysterics. Tears course down my cheeks from my head's stabbing pain even as I choke back hiccups. Lack of sleep and a hospital phobia are leaving me borderline mentally incapacitated.

"Yes, my wife, Natalia," Bran deadpans. He goes on to effortlessly describe the accident and my symptoms.

The doctor performs a quick examination, checks my short-term memory, and cleans the wound on my temple. "Probably spot-on about the concussion," he concludes. "I don't think we need to keep her here. Why don't you go home and keep an eye on her over the next twenty-four hours?"

Home.

Bran.

Twenty-four hours.

My mind short-circuits, unable to compute. Is the doc positive I don't need a CAT scan?

"What do you say, sweetheart?" Bran's mouth curls into a trace smile. His soft accent is utterly seductive. "Shall I take you home?"

———

I enter my cramped student room, Bran at my heels. On the drive from the hospital, I tried to release him from any obligation. He ignored me, making it clear that he meant to stick around. If I wasn't so drained, I'd be psyched to keep hanging out.

"I like what you've done with the place." Bran glances around my bare beige walls while depositing my duffel, which he'd retrieved from Jazza's house, next to the twin bed. Besides a cheap set of drawers, it's the only furniture in the room.

"I try not to be in here too often."

He takes in a deep breath. "Smells like you."

Wait. I freeze, swallowing hard. "Is that good or bad?"

"Sweet."

"Oh, right, that's just my body spray…" My tongue falters on the word *body*. The room, already a veritable shoebox, seems to shrink while Bran's presence fills the space, like when Alice in Wonderland ate the "grow bigger" cake.

"Why don't you climb into bed?"

I tug the bikini strap underneath my tank top, mouth dry. "I've got to get out of these clothes."

Bran's Adam's apple bobs and he coughs into his fist.

It's a fight not to bury my face in my pillow. Why can't I be assigned an emergency button to hit when I need to stop talking?

From the way my face burns, I must sport full-blown fire engine cheeks. Not a flattering look on anyone. I turn, fumble open my dresser drawer, and grab the first thing my hands graze—yoga pants and a Santa Cruz hoodie. I sling the bulky clothing over one shoulder, wishing I could be effortlessly sexy. My underwear doesn't even sport lace.

Bran pulls back the blinds and stares at the street traffic through my grimy window. "I live around the corner, across from the Bean Counter."

"Oh, I know that place. It looks cool." With this new information filed away, it's pretty much inevitable that I'll resume consuming my body weight in coffee.

"Yeah, they make good..." His eyes drop to my chest. The Foreign Student Hall is serious about air-conditioning. It's like we're training to forge the Arctic tundra. My nipples have responded accordingly.

Yoohoo! The twins seem to wave. Here we are—boobs!

I cave my shoulders. "I'm going to run to the bathroom and change."

"No."

I freeze midstride. He wants me to undress here? In front of him? Invisible sirens sound. Heat speeds from my cheeks, down my neck as a fire lights in my belly.

"I'll go." He grabs his backpack and digs out his water bottle. "And fill this. Hydration will help the lingering headache. You've got an hour before I can give you another Panadol." The over-the-counter pain reliever the doctor told him to dole out.

I'm snuggled under the duvet when he returns. He wordlessly hands me the water, staring at my mouth while I drink deep.

I dab my lips self-consciously. "Want to watch a movie or something?"

"Mmmm...something."

"What?" My voice squeaks on the *t*.

He hooks his thumbs in his pockets and flashes a fleeting grin. "A movie's fine, Captain."

Bran wasn't kidding about not knowing recent movies. He let me make all the selections off my iPad. We have our own mini film festival: *Juno, Garden State*, and *(500) Days of Summer*. Good thing I've seen these flicks about a thousand times because the fact that Bran sits three inches away is more than a little distracting. I'm hyper-cued into his every fidget.

Eventually, my vigilance wears me out, my eyes droop, and I let out a big yawn.

"Those are some cute tonsils." He knocks his foot into mine.

"Shut it." I knock my foot back. "I'm exhausted."

He tucks the sheet around my shoulders. The tender gesture catches me off guard. Again there's that lovely, off-kilter feeling of being looked after. Protected. I mean, I can take care of myself, more or less, but it's nice that he wants to. Really nice. What if it could be like this all the time?

He must feel me tense. "Go to sleep, okay? Everything's fine. I'll keep watch and read." He grabs the book beside my bed. *"Discipline and Punish?"*

"I'm taking a class on Foucault," I mumble into my pillow. The mattress creaks as he eases beside me. I force nonchalance, as if cute guys commonly frequent my bedroom. The twin mattress is narrow, so I roll onto my side and face the wall to make room—and to hide the fact that my heart's threatening to leap from my mouth. His chest brushes my back. This feels good, normal even.

Despite Bran's proximity, the day's been long. Sleep shoots out tentacles, drags me into the blackness. I'm dreaming, such a nice dream. One where he settles a hand on my hip, buries his face into the back of my hair.

I wake to him gently shaking my shoulder. "Hey there."

"Mmmmmrf," I garble, tongue thick and eyes gritty. Surely it's been what? Five minutes?

"You've slept almost two hours. Time to eat something."

I burrow back into my pillow. "Not hungry. Sleepy."

He pokes the base of my ribs.

"You value that hand?" I snarl, still not quite conscious.

"You're a little bear, Captain."

"Grrrrrr." I flip over and land half across him. Whoa, didn't realize he was so close. My hips press against his, and his jeans are rough through the thin cotton of my yoga pants. His eyes widen and I gasp at my impulsive gesture. His face doesn't lose its frozen expression, even as he hardens against me. His mouth is perfect. His hands dip over my waist, slide to my hips.

Here we go.

He gently rolls me off, swings his feet to the floor. "There's a milk bar across the street." His voice is husky.

"Milk bar?" What the hell is going on?

Or rather, not going.

"A corner shop. Carries small groceries, newspapers—"

"Milk. I get it." *Why didn't you kiss me?*

"Want some juice? What kind do you like?"

"Apple." *Am I repulsive?*

"Nuts? Chocolate?"

"A granola bar would be awesome." *Clearly far more awesome than me.*

"Okay, back in a tic."

I maintain until the door slams. Then I throw the blankets over my head and let out the world's largest groan like the world's biggest idiot.

A low-pitched buzzing sounds and I emerge from my cocoon to grab my phone. Wait, this isn't mine. A text flashes across the screen.

Bella: I miss our good night kisses. You awake?

Bella?

I'm sitting on the end of my bed when Bran returns.

"You can go home," I say in a low voice.

His brows pull together. "But the doc said twenty-four hours—"

"I checked in with my friend, Marti, next door. She'll look after me." I hand him the phone without comment.

His face blanks when he checks the screen's text. "Right." He tosses an apple juice bottle and granola bar beside me, pockets the phone, and slings on his backpack. "Talia."

"You don't owe me any explanations." At that moment, all I want is for Bran to get out, give me space. His presence is too close, too much, too confusing, pressing against my secretly raw places. I don't want to take this anywhere if he's involved with another girl.

"Look—I'm not seeing anyone, not anymore."

"Sure, whatever. Not my business. I'm really tired, okay?" No way I'd hook up with a guy who's been recently involved either. My few drunken hours with Tanner were enough torture for the rest of my life. I'm not a masochist; being the rebound girl isn't my idea of fun.

For a split second he looks like he wants to explain more. But then he battens down the hatches. His face a cool mask. "Right." His voice is flat.

"Right," I repeat, squashing the little voice inside me that whispers, *Wrong, this is so wrong.*

9

TALIA

My fingers absently travel to the mouse and I click open Facebook. Bran doesn't have a profile page, so I troll Jazza's looking for information scraps, party pics, anything.

Zilch.

I Google Bran's name and the same well-trolled information appears. Not that I'm a stalker, just someone very aware of the scholarships he's won. And of his posted high school swim meet results. And that one paragraph mentioning him in a research project at the University of Tasmania's Institute for Marine and Antarctic Studies.

Okay fine, I am a total stalker.

But my spy skills only extend so far. Google's last hit remains a stubborn mystery. The link is in Danish except for his name, Brandon Lockhart. Other than that, all I can decipher is that the site is a wind-turbine manufacturing company headquartered in Copenhagen. Weird.

Not as weird as Bella.

I press a finger to my jugular vein and brace my elbows on

the library table. Crap, my heart rate is over 100. In the hospital, every time I sat with Pippa, her monitor *beep, beep, beeped* in the background. I'd never paid any meaningful attention to heartbeats before. Why would you? The body beats, breathes, whatever. It's like turning on a light, or getting water from a tap, little ordinary miracles in our day-to-day lives. But during those empty hours, listening to Pippa's heart, things turned complicated. Breathing's difficult if you overthink the action, like staring at the word *the* for too long. Grows unnatural, bizarrely wrong.

My inbox pings—message from Bran.

Oh God. Okay. Shit. He can't tell I just Googled him, can he?

The e-mail has an ellipsis in the title bar. No hint to the message's content. Bran may be closer to a stranger than a friend, but I know him enough to sense this behavior is typical.

I hold my breath and open the message.

To: Natalia Stolfi <natalia.stolfi@ucsc.com>
From: Brandon Lockhart <blockhart@melbourne.edu.au>
Subject: …

Can I see you?

"Bonjour, hi." Marti drapes over my study cubicle. A hot-pink stripe slices through her inky hair.

I try to refocus, act like I'm not freaking out.

"No more study today, *mon petit chou*." Marti flicks one of my highlighters to the floor. "Give the brain a rest."

I pick the marker up and tap the tip against the desk. "But I need to finish—"

"Pfffft, it is Friday night. You need to go out. Besides, you do not work. You are e-mailing…oh la—what is this?" She peers at my laptop screen. "Who is it that wants to see you?"

I slam my computer shut. "Nobody."

She gives me a knowing look. "Did you write this nobody back? Say yes to the boy. You must get some sexy time before you die of boredom and your own hand."

"Marti," I hiss, glancing around at the nearby students.

"Don't be such a prude. You are young. Beautiful. Be alive and make love to real live people. Not the vibrator."

I wrinkle my nose. "Like I have one of those."

"No…vibrators?" Her tone is aghast.

"No. Or vibrator, for that matter."

"So you only…" She mimics a frantic fiddling gesture by her crotch.

"Jesus, God. No!" I jump to my feet, gathering my notebooks. I have to drag her out of here before she gets us arrested for sexual misconduct.

"But how do you—"

"I don't, okay?" I flee toward the stairway.

She keeps pace. "You've had no Big O?"

"Never."

"*Tabarnak*," Marti mutters her favorite swear word, crossing herself. Apparently in French Canada, swearing consists of vague Catholic references like tabernacle and chalice. But right now I'm not charmed like usual. I'm totally shamed.

We walk in silence and she doesn't speak until we exit the library.

"You're a virgin?"

"No."

"But—"

"I've slept with one guy, but I've made out and stuff with others. It's"—I give my head a half shake—"kind of overrated. Nothing ever felt amazing."

She scrapes one index finger over her other in a gesture of admonishment. "This changes, right now."

"I'm flattered, but you're not really my—"

"Oh, please." She rolls her eyes. "Hand over the computer."

"You can't write him back."

"Him? Yes! I knew it was an e-mail from a he. Wait, it's not the Idiot Boy, Jazza?"

"No."

Not that Idiot Boy.

"Computer, now. I need it." She tugs my purse, ruthless as a German shepherd with a chew toy.

"Fine." We stop at a university bench beneath a wide eucalyptus. "Knock yourself out. Campus is fully Wi-Fi equipped."

Marti goes all Mozart on the keyboard and within thirty seconds, an alarming grin slides across her face. "This is where we go."

The page she displays burns my retinas, all gaudy pinks, lurid reds. The flashing words *Pleasure Den* plaster across the header.

I flap my hands like an agitated duck. "Are you insane?"

"*Non.* But you will be—tonight. And afterward you shall write this mystery man. It's time for Talia to get lucky."

"Luck and I aren't really on speaking terms."

"How old are you, twenty?"

"Twenty-one."

"*Tabarnak.* Twenty-one and not even one teeny-tiny O?"

"Can you tone it down?" My voice rises and two passing students slow down.

"Orgasms are not brought by fairies." Marti speaks a fraction quieter. Great, now only people within a quarter-mile radius can eavesdrop.

"Yeah, I get it. But I don't know, maybe my va-jay-jay's not wired in that way."

"You've not properly tried. The woman must take responsibility for her own pleasure."

———

Marti ushers me through my first sex shop experience with the air of a seasoned pro. I trail her high hot-pink ponytail past butt plugs, flavored lubricants, and nipple clamps to a wall bursting in a veritable rainbow of silicon cocks.

"No way." I cover my mouth.

Marti rolls her eyes. "Get over yourself."

"I'm sure each of these big boys deserves a good home but come on, I just…can't." I point out an engorged, veiny, twelve-inch monster. "How could I sleep near that beast? It looks like it will come alive after midnight. Chase me around the bedroom."

"Pfffft. Such drama. No one expects you to jump in the deep end."

"If that's the deep end, I don't ever want to leave the kiddie pool."

"What about this?" Marti points to a more realistically endowed creation.

"Neon green doesn't scream sexy time. And seriously, what gives with the color? Looks like it has contracted an infection."

"You're picky." Marti makes a judgy noise in the back of her throat.

I answer with a noise of my own. And a finger.

"Fine." She takes my elbow, steers me toward a glass display case. "You're choosy. Maybe this is good."

"It is?" I spend five minutes trying to decide what socks to wear in the morning.

"Better to be, how do you say? Discriminating."

In the end, Marti cajoles me with a classy pocket-sized vibrator called a Leora. Sounds rather cute, like a perky friend you'd meet for a gab over coffee. She's white and vaguely obelisk, and pricier than the endowed competition. I fork money to the uninterested cashier and try not to overthink the fact that my grandpa's inheritance is funding my first sex toy.

———

I sit cross-legged and stare at the white box on the center of my bed. Leora nestles inside. I give my dorm room a helpless scan. This is ridiculous. I'm twenty-one and haven't the first clue about how to proceed. Marti might be pushy but she's got a point. Time to quit whining and take responsibility—get all "sisters doing it for themselves."

What about music? There we go. Brilliant idea. I shuffle to my iPad and select a moody dub album before catching my reflection in the mirror—skinny jeans and a vintage Ramones tee. Not so good. I'm overdressed for a date with myself. I wiggle from the tight denim. Leave it puddled on the floor. All I need now is a little inspiration.

I climb onto the bed and type the name Brandon Lockhart into the search engine. There's a single picture of him online. He stands beside a podium to receive a scholarship. For once he's clean-shaven. His jawline is strong if awkwardly clenched. His forced smile looks painful but still reveals those adorable dimples. My stomach fizzes like I gobbled a packet of Pop Rocks.

I ease Leora from the velvet-lined box. "Okay." I roll onto my back, concentrating on Bran's picture. "Let's do this."

Cool plastic touches my heat. Bran stares back with that

uncomfortable, trapped expression. My gaze flicks to the ceiling stain, the one that resembles spilled tea. Hmmmm. Maybe I should close my eyes after all. Yes. Better. I hit the button and jump at the loud buzzing. Oh no. Will everyone hear? Know and judge my masturbation? Hard to stress because holy shit. My vagina startles awake with a "what the?" I jerk. My lower back arches from the bed. My thighs quiver. Holy fucking shit. Pulsing warmth builds between my legs. I grip Leora harder. If my clit had a voice, she'd hit operatic high notes.

Three mind-blowing orgasms later, I am reduced to a loosey-goosey-limbed mess, humming the theme song to *Aladdin*. Leora is stored under my bed before I literally kill myself from self-pleasure. Is that possible? Probably. There's always too much of a good thing, right? Every action creates an opposing reaction and whatnot.

So that's what I've been missing. Jeeeesus. I'm ready to pen an Ode to a Vibrator. Turns out my girl parts are indeed wired correctly. They just haven't had the right sort of treatment.

Could a guy ever give me the same addictive rush?

Maybe one guy could.

After trying and failing to sleep for an hour, I jump on my e-mail. Nothing more from Bran. I reread his last one.

Can I see you?

What if he's waiting for me to make a move?

I'm no longer Talia Sans Orgasm. I'm Talia Sex Goddess. Bold, confident, saucy. I can do this.

I one-finger-type my response.

Sure.

10

TALIA

I haunt the Bean Counter because Bran mentioned he lived near the coffee shop. It's a violation of the New Talia caffeine ban to drink myself into a severe jitter attack with several long blacks, the Australian version of an Americano. But what the hell, I'm not sure any of my best-laid plans are working out so well.

I recheck my e-mail and take short, fast breaths—two new messages. My neck prickles while I open my inbox.

Ack.

Only updates from Mom and Dad.

Bran's killing me here. I reread his cryptic message for the billionth time.

Can I see you?

And my reply.

Sure.

A terrible thought occurs to me. If the coffee shop wasn't filled to capacity, I'd bang my head on the table until I forgot my own name. What if he hadn't meant to write this message to me? Or what if he changed his mind?

Gah. What-ifs are the worst.

Why did I ever freak out on him in the first place? I mean, there I was with a hot guy, in my room, being cool—wanting to take care of me. And I order him to leave.

But the look on Tanner's face the moment he pushed inside of me is imprinted on my brain. The last twelve months haven't erased the memory of the way he looked—pretending I was someone else. When I woke alone on the beach, hungover and cold, I swore that I'd never hook up with another guy who was in any way on the rebound.

But Bran isn't Tanner. When Bran looks at me, it's like he sees me—all of me. Even the irrational, bad parts I don't like to notice.

I need to distract myself, so I read Dad's short note. He chats mostly about the weather. A little boring because Santa Cruz comes in two flavors: sunny or foggy. He'd returned from a geological conference in Santa Barbara. On the way home he drove through Big Sur, stopped at Pfeiffer Beach. What's left unsaid between his brief words gnaws my stomach lining. We scattered Pippa's ashes on that windswept beach during a dreary, wet morning.

I try to swallow the painful lump gathering in the back of my throat. What if I'm no better than Mom? I left too. My heart ratchets into overdrive.

No. The word bursts from my brain, gives me an involuntary start. I'm going to return home in the end.

I'm nothing like my mother.

Take her e-mail as a case in point.

To: Natalia Stolfi <natalia.stolfi@ucsc.com>
From: Bee on the Island <beelight@gmail.com>
Subject: Love & Light

Aloha Natalia!

Just returned from my first Bikram yoga class and another step toward divine balance. I'm also five days into the new master cleanse that Logan's trialing. Today's elixir is Tahitian noni juice, fresh squeezed lemon, agave, and cayenne pepper. Let me know if you want him to send you the menu.

Remember, honey, feel light—live light!

Bliss,

Mom

I mean—where do I even start? This coming from a woman who used to open cans of soup and call that dinner.

My e-mail pings again and I can't contain an epic eye roll. Jesus, Mom—there is no part of me that wants to go on Logan's crappy cleanse. Noni fruit smells nauseating, like Parmesan cheese left to rot in a public toilet stall.

Hold up. I do a double take at my computer screen. New message—Bran Lockhart.

My stomach flops like a breaching whale.

I close one eye and hit open. *Oh, please, please, please.* I'm not even 100 percent sure what I'm praying for. Mostly an avoidance of total self-humiliation.

You're a woman of few words.

Relief drizzles through my veins like honey on a hot day.

Sometimes. I suck in my breath and hit send.

His response is immediate. You have a cute smile.

I trace my finger over my lower lip and take another sip of coffee.

Another ping. Is it true that American girls prefer nonfat-mocha-frappa-what-the-fuck lattes?

My head shoots up.

Wait, what? Is he here? Like here, here? I scan the crowded coffee shop but don't recognize him at any of the tables.

I peck back my response. You're not going all creepy stalker serial killer on me...are you?

"I told you, Captain." A deep whisper heats my ear. "I'm dangerous."

I whip my head around. Bran's sitting right behind me, striped stocking cap shoved over his unruly hair, sporting aviator sunglasses. If getting punched is ever good, that's how I feel. "Are you kidding me? How long have you been here?"

"Since before you arrived." He tipped onto two chair legs. "You've ignored me for at least an hour."

"What's with the incognito look?" Am I relaxed enough, cool and nonchalant? "You pretending to be a celebrity in hideout?"

He tugs off his shades and his green cat eyes glow. "I've got a reputation to uphold."

I snort. "Being a creeper?"

His lazy smile and accompanying dimples activate a previously unknown nerve that begins behind my eyes and ends between my legs. The Leora rewired my circuits during the last twenty-four hours and my body is ready for a little electricity. The sensations Bran elicits in me—yeah, I've got names for them now. Want. Desire. Need. I grind my thighs. At last I get what all the fuss is about. And I want more fuss. With Bran. Right now. His expression alters, almost imperceptibly, but enough to suspect he can tell that I masturbated the shit out of myself to him last night. And once this morning.

I peer into the murky brown liquid and my face reflects in miniature. I'm too wide-eyed, clearly overexcited. Need to settle, pretend like I'm halfway cool, collected.

He tugs off his hat and rumples his hair. His eyes flick to the healing cut beneath my left temple. "How's the wound?"

"The perfect souvenir." I trace the thin jagged line the surfboard sliced on my face. "Can't wait to brag back home about how I wiped out and almost drowned in five inches of surf."

"It was at least six inches." He wraps his arms around the back of his seat. "You left your thongs in my car."

I start. "My—oh, right. My flip-flops. I always think of the other kind of thongs. It messes with me."

His answering smile is more than a little wolfish. "No, if you left those in my car, I wouldn't give them back."

"Pervert." I wipe my hands on my jean skirt.

"Proudly." There's that dimple again. I kind of want to lick it.

"Do you have a girlfriend?" I need to clear this up before we can tread another inch farther.

"No."

"Have you recently gotten out of a relationship?"

"No." When he watches me, it's like I'm the only girl in the room, the only girl he's ever seen. His awareness is magnetic, addictive, a total rush.

"Who's Bella?"

"A friend."

"I didn't mean to check out the text, but she came across as more than a friend."

"Maybe she's the kind that came with occasional benefits. But that's over. So, you want your shoes?"

I fight off the sharp stab of jealousy. He can't be expected to live a monastic life. "Yeah, I should rescue them. Don't want you sitting around sniffing my thongs."

He laughs out loud, an infectious sound that rises over the coffee shop and is followed by the sound of shattering glass. I turn to see a vibrantly red-haired barista glaring behind the counter before she dips to collect whatever she dropped.

I tear a piece of my napkin and roll it into a little ball. "Apparently humor is frowned upon in these parts."

"Isn't that the MO of Hipsterland?"

I set my mouth. "You'd know."

He kicks at my chair's leg. A lock of his hair cuts across his cheekbone.

I want to tuck it back so bad.

"So...shall we beat it to my place?"

"When you put it that way, how can I resist?"

Breathe—just breathe. I am cool. I am collected. I am losing my shit.

He rises and mumbles to the floor tiles, "You know...I missed you, Captain."

My stomach gives a delicious lurch at his unexpected sweetness.

The flame-haired barista shoots me a death stare while I shut down my laptop. Like I committed a capital offense by daring to joke and smile. I arch my eyebrow and she returns to wiping down the pastry case. Tough crowd.

"After you." Bran grabs my bag from my hands.

"Seriously?"

He stares down at himself. "I must have at least one chivalrous bone in my body."

"Don't worry, I'll keep it a secret."

"Thanks, don't want to ruin my rep."

"Guys who wear sunglasses indoors have to be careful about such things." I give his chest a playful push, feeling the hard pectoral beneath.

I am calm. I am collected.

"How else can I covertly spy on you?" He grabs my hand and doesn't let go.

I am calm, I am—fuck this. I want to touch him so bad that the need verges on painful.

"Next time bring a newspaper. It'll be more subtle."

"You didn't notice me." His smile's a little smug.

"Sometimes I'm blind."

His gaze intensifies. "Me too."

He opens the door for me and we step into the sunlight.

11

TALIA

I never noticed Bran's dingy terrace, veiled behind a thick bottlebrush hedge, during my previous neighborhood-recon jogs. The mildewed bricks appear ready to sprout mushrooms, and a basil sprig browns in a cracked pot at the entryway. He fiddles with the lock and the door swings open to reveal a dim corridor crammed with mountain bikes, mismatched shoes, and a cracked computer monitor.

A guy in plaid boxer shorts snores from the couch in the lounge room to my left. Chinese takeout props on his hairy gut and a cat perches on his chest, buried to the ears in the white noodle box. Acrobatic porn flashes on the flat screen while a bong tilts precariously between his pasty, splayed thighs.

"That's hot. He a friend of yours?" I turn and discover Bran's lips only inches from my own. He watches me in a lazy, hooded-eye way that makes it difficult to draw a full breath.

"Not exactly." He snorts. "This place is just a dodgy share house. We all crash together for the cheap rent and killer location. Miles, over there"—he juts his chin at the snorer—"he's a bouncer at one of the downtown nightclubs."

"Wow, he looks charming."

"Wait until he speaks." Bran sidesteps a dirty sock and continues down the bleak hall, which smells of mold and old pizza.

I follow close at his heels. "Are you waiting for your trust fund to kick in, or what?"

He pivots until our hips graze. My belly performs a quick series of impressive gymnastics.

"Whoever said anything about trust funds, Captain?"

"I assumed...stop looking at me like that, will you? It's just that you spoke about the private schools, fancy houses, rich parents, and this place is all—"

"You interested in my bank account balance?"

"No...seriously, God, no. My mom has crap-tons of money and she's the unhappiest person I know so—"

"I haven't touched my dad's cash since I was eighteen." His voice is so quiet, a borderline whisper.

"Why?" I rest my hand against his cheek. A muscle in his jaw tics, but then his body stills, all that lean energy harnessed like the hushed moment before a storm. This is intense. How can I feel such a powerful connection to an almost stranger? A surly guy who during a few, fleeting moments looked past my shields, my battle-worn armor, and saw...me? He leans closer and my body responds, the pull as natural as the tide to the moon.

A warning ripples in my belly. Anxiety stirs, uncoiling, sensing an opportunity to strike.

Wanting is scary, the kind of thing that might open Pandora's box. If I allow one feeling to escape, what's to stop the others from pushing their way free, the darker, uncontrollable kinds?

The idea of him—us—is so good, why spoil it with reality?

Bran's move is sudden, faster than the speed of fear. He grabs my wrist and plants a kiss on my palm. His lips heat my skin and the sweet torment drives back doubts. I could shut down and protect myself, or maybe there are times, little life moments, too big for thought.

"You always smell so good." His voice drops an octave, slightly husky, but the tone is almost accusatory. The pulse in his neck quickens, and the hungry look on his face—I can't even. I'm two seconds from jumping out of my skin. Currents fire through my body's length. The storm comes closer, a glimpse of lightning.

"Fuck it." His hands span my waist as he propels me into what must be his bedroom. His forehead presses to mine as he back kicks the door closed and spins me against the wall. Our next inhalation shares the same ragged note. When our bodies press flush, the fit's perfect. I could stop, protect myself, or throw the chips to the gathering wind and see where they scatter.

"Fuck it," he repeats, closing his eyes. His fingers flirt with the hem of my shirt, dip under to graze my bare stomach. "I told myself, I *ordered* myself, that I wasn't going to do this—but here's the funny thing, Talia." His lips brush my eyelids, my cheek, hesitating a fraction of a second over my mouth. "I can't stay away."

His lips cover mine and we hold still, so still, breathe each other's breath like the last two people left on Earth. The unshaven hair on his jaw prickles my skin, but I like it. I offer something between a gasp and moan before our kiss grows hot and desperate, a tangle of lips and teeth and tongue. I taste coffee and a hint of spearmint toothpaste. His hand covers my breast and my thighs shiver in response. He rumbles a few urgent words, but I can't decipher anything other than my name.

"Please, don't stop." Any restraint on his part would shatter me into a million irreparable pieces.

"I've no intention." He lifts me off my feet and I hook my legs around his hips, unwilling to sever even a fraction of contact. My hands sink into his hair; the texture's impossibly soft, better than anything I'd imagined. I'm vaguely aware he's walking us backward and then I'm eased onto a futon. I don't have time to study his room. My vision's filled with the sight of Bran staring at me as if he's adrift and I'm some sort of anchor. Time slows down to a dreamlike trance.

He sits back on his knees. His hands slide up my legs, under my skirt, and—bang—there goes my underwear, just like that. Wait. *Crap.* I forgot to shave my legs this morning, didn't—

"Fuck." A muscle tics deep in his jaw. His cat eyes fix on *me*, my exposed sex.

Okay, okay, be cool. How would a normal, more experienced girl react to this situation? My brain peeks through invisible fingers and shrugs. It's got nothing.

"Oh, Talia." His voice gentles, almost prayerful. He leans in and kisses me—there—and within three toe-curling seconds all my worry dissolves in a warm pool of holy-shit-goodness.

I once read in a magazine that a guy should go down on a girl like they're writing the alphabet with their tongue. Bran composes a sonnet. I'm consumed. My secret places alight as a fierce ache gathers in my belly, quakes through my limbs. I pull him closer, shameless in my need. He pins my hips and anchors my body to the mattress. His thrumming moan vibrates to my core. His mouth demands everything, so I give it. It doesn't take long. My thighs clench, unclench in cadence to the spasms rocking me from the inside out.

Afterward, he holds me close, gently rubs circles across my lower back as I return to myself.

"Um…" My voice is hoarse, like I've been screaming. Oh God, did I scream?

"Yeah." He kisses the center of my forehead.

"That was—"

"Incredible."

"Implausible."

"You're perfect." His heart beats a hard rhythm against my cheek.

"Sadly, no."

"Perfect for me, then," he whispers in my ear. "You're only perfect for me."

There's no way he can miss my tremble. I've always felt out of place, the odd duck waddling behind Pippa the Swan. I close my eyes and increase my grip on his shoulders. I've been shut tight for so long, but every lock has a key, right?

Maybe Bran fits me.

Maybe I fit him.

I trace his lips. That mouth earned a gold star. "You feeling lucky?" My whisper is husky with all the words I'm unable to say.

"Fuck, yes."

I grin at his fervency. "Let me amend the question. You want to get lucky? I can't be selfish, right?"

He rearranges us so that I straddle his hips. His brown hair is mussed, boyish, in sharp contrast to the fierce, hypnotic heat in his green eyes.

His hardness drives into my thigh. A full, pulsing ache spreads between my legs. Wait, I just came so hard. I can't be ready to go again this quick, right?

"You're nervous." He frowns, noticing my shiver. "Talia. Are you a virgin?"

Wow, I'm putting out all the sexpot signals.

"No." I bite my lip and still. "That's okay, right?"

"This ain't the sixteenth century, Captain." He pokes my navel. "I'm not negotiating with your father, twelve goats for a hymen."

"Sick. Don't ever use the words *father* and *hymen* in the same sentence again." I tweak one of his nipples through his shirt and he clamps me harder on his lap. I'm not wearing any underwear and he's rigid beneath his jeans. My laughter fades, amusement replaced by growing urgency. "This is crazy."

"What?" He sounds hoarse.

"Don't you think? You? Me? Like this?"

"Crazy good." He pulls off my shirt, explores my stomach's geography. I can't believe he's done so much to me and I'm still wearing my bra. Well, not for long. He opens the clasp with one hand and I gasp—loudly—when air brushes my bare skin, like I'm being strangled. I'm not sure it's attractive, but I don't really have a choice. My entire body is almost unbearably sensitive.

"Got to say"—he circles my nipple, watches it harden into a tight button—"I'm digging those little noises."

"You are?" I try to hold on, not pass out.

"They're cute as hell." He moves on to my other breast. "Like you, actually. Too fucking adorable for your own good."

"Are we going to..."

He arches a brow.

I arch mine back and wiggle it a little, hoping humor can mask my nervousness. "You know what I mean."

"Do I?"

"Come on, don't make me be an idiot." I fold my arms, blocking my breasts from his veiled gaze.

"Will we have sex?" He chews the side of his lip. "Not sure. I kinda don't want to mess this up."

"Sex will mess us up?" I don't ask my other question—*Is there an us?*

"I don't know." He presses my lower back, gathering me closer, until we lie hip to hip.

"So what to do, right?"

His lazy smile makes me light-headed. "Do you make those cute sounds whenever you get off?"

My cheeks must turn five shades of red. "Negative."

"Don't believe you." He drags a finger down the valley between my breasts and grins at the way my stomach hitches.

"I don't make noises. For anyone. Ever. Only...you." I rub my knee against his. "You're the first guy who's ever made me come."

A deep rumble sounds in his throat. His eyes flash in a primal way I don't quite understand. "You fucking slay me, you know that, sweetheart?"

I'm flipped onto my back and his clever tongue traces my breasts, my belly, and lower until I'm a goner.

———

I wake to discover Bran facing me. We somehow drifted off, nose to nose, in a midday siesta. A dark lock of hair tumbles over his closed eyes and in sleep he appears younger, sweetly innocent. I sort of want to trace my thumb over his spiky eyelashes before kissing the corner of his mouth where the dimple hides.

"It's creepy to stare at someone sleeping," he mutters, his lids tightening.

I stare cross-eyed, tongue poking out until he dares a peek.

"You goon," he chuckles, burying his face in the pillow.

I throw my leg over his, realizing he's still dressed and I'm totally naked. "And what is that exactly? Like a brat?" I trail my hand over his chest. He's gone down on me twice and I've hardly touched him. That situation needs to be rectified.

"You're getting warmer."

"Am I?"

He kisses the tip of my nose before cradling my head into his hard chest muscles. Bran's a cuddler, who knew? We stop talking and hold each other—it's pretty much the best way I've ever spent five minutes. On the wall above the futon is an art poster; the image is familiar, a lonely man in strange armor, on a tired horse in the bleak outback. It's the same picture I bought as a postcard at the museum gift shop. Maybe he can tell me what—

"You asked me before, why I live here, with people like Miles," he mutters. "About my dad. His money."

The art history chat will have to wait. "I shouldn't have said anything. None of it's my business. You don't owe me a single explanation."

"But I want to tell you."

"Really?" This moment feels more intimate than anything else we've done so far. Bran's actually going to talk—about himself. Any second the sky will probably start falling.

"His wealth is tainted."

"Embezzled?" I whisper the word.

The creases in his forehead lighten. "No, nothing like that. His blood money comes from perfectly legal means. He invests in primary industries, mostly mining, destroying Aboriginal land in western Australia, desecrating pristine beaches, and occasionally dabbling in the African diamond trade—which produces child soldiers and bloody civil wars as a by-product. At nineteen, I joined an activist conservation group, engaged in direct action against one of his best mate's timber companies by padlocking myself to a bulldozer."

"Jesus."

"A national newspaper was on the scene and snapped a dramatic photo that received front page treatment—Brandon Lockhart, only son of Bryce Lockhart, president of Lockhart Industries. Dad went ballistic and I couldn't take his dirty money anymore. Not if I wanted a prayer of looking at myself in the mirror. So I took out school loans, lived cheap, taught surf lessons near Jazza's house during the uni holidays. Got a scholarship for an honors year after finishing my bachelor's, a way to fast-track into a PhD."

"Doctor Lockhart...it has a certain ring."

He traces my mouth. "I want to investigate climate change—the single biggest environmental threat our planet faces. My family's made a killing plundering the earth. One of us needs to play for the good guys. Reset the karmic balance."

"But you're not in a PhD program, right? Don't you work for the Wilderness League, tutor at the uni?"

"I fucked up." His expression darkens and his gaze locks on the ceiling. "I'm still trying to find my way back."

I wait a few beats but nothing more is offered. Of course, I'm wildly curious but don't want to pry into unwelcome territory. God knows I have my own secrets.

"Come on, Captain." He slides from the sheets and hands me one of the T-shirts crumpled on the end of his bed. "Let's go shower, see if we can get any dirtier."

12

TALIA

*B*ran's small bathroom is cluttered by a motley assortment of well-used towels, soap, toothpaste tubes, and shampoo bottles.

"How many people live here?" I ask, inventorying the lavender body gel and pink razor on the tub side.

"Three, give or take, depending on the week." He peels his old T-shirt up and over my head, licks my clavicle. "Seriously, sweetheart, how'd you get so bloody cute?"

He traces the undersides of my breasts and my next breath is forgotten. Forget any witty comebacks. I forget to suck in my stomach to look hotter. I forget my own name.

His grin is wicked. "You like that." It's not a question; he sees that I do.

I nod, hesitant.

"I want to know everything about you."

"Yeah, those are famous last words." My smile can't quite hide the discomfort undercutting my tone.

"Doubt it." He keeps up his lazy explorations.

I hear his words again, from before. *"You're perfect. You're only perfect for me."*

What if this is the start of something bigger, like a song that opens one way, but gradually veers in an unpredictable direction, building to a crescendo? This could be just such a moment.

A moment where everything changes.

"Tell me," he murmurs. "What else do you like?"

"Um…" I lick my lips, no idea what to ask for. In my limited prior hookups, I haven't enjoyed much. "Why don't you surprise me?"

My eyes close as he skims the sides of my breasts.

"You're sensitive here?"

"I…I guess so, yeah. I like it." I arch deeper into his touch. I don't know why Bran's different, but every time his fingers pose a question, my body answers in the affirmative. Yes. Oh, yes. Uh-huh. Yep. Okay, okay, wow, yeah, yes.

He drops his head to my nipple, gives a quick nip, and then slides his tongue across the skin to intensify the ache. I clap my hand over my mouth to keep from crying out.

He inches his fingers between my legs and we both groan.

"Jee-sus." His voice is gruff and we both look down between us. His fingers are lost inside me. "You're so wet, it's unreal." He circles my clit. My ache is impossibly sweet. I dig my fingers into his shoulders.

"Fuck, Talia." He steps back and fists his shirt over his back. He sports a tattoo, right on his heart. At first I think it's a circle but realize the ink forms a serpent, eating its own tail. He fumbles with his belt. I'm unable to tear my eyes away from his dick when he jerks his boxers down.

Tanner was a decent size, more than decent. But this…

"What?" He hesitates as something approaching uncertainty crosses his face.

I wave my hands helplessly. "I had no idea you had all of that going on."

His eyes darken. "You. In the shower."

The warm spray hits my back as I reach to take him in hand. His silky hardness jerks against my palm. He makes a desperate sound that I need to hear again. I don't know—and don't really want to discover—how many girls Bran has been with. His moves are solid; I'm willing to bet the number is high. How can I compete? Eclipse their memory. Make *my* name choke from his lips, brand on his brain. Inspiration strikes and I grab a bottle of his housemate's body gel, flip the cap, and squeeze the contents over my shoulder. Cool, creamy gel slides down my lower back.

"What are you—"

I stop him with a finger to his beautiful mouth and shake my head once before turning around to nestle the small of my back against his abs. My ass is positioned right in his hardness. He's not a ton taller, so our fit works. I slide my arms backward, taking a second to explore the cut muscles bookending his abdomen, enjoying when he flexes from the attention. I lock him to me and rub the cleft of my ass against him. The slippery shower gel eases the friction. His dick jolts. His hands reach to anchor on my breasts. Up and down I grind until his breathing is erratic and his lips fasten on the crook of my neck. I increase my speed and pressure until he bites my skin.

"Talia." He groans my name in a way that's almost violent as fire shoots over my skin, the liquid hotter than the shower water.

I turn to loop my arms around his shoulders.

"Hey."

His lips part. The way his hair flops on his forehead makes him look surprisingly vulnerable. "Hey."

"So…um…was that oka—"

His fierce kiss is an eloquent reply.

———

Bran bends to tie his shoes, providing me a nice view of his surf-hardened lats. He grabs a blue toothbrush from the medicine cabinet, squeezes paste on, and shoves it in his mouth. "I want to call in sick."

Watching Bran be normal is fascinating. Especially when he's shirtless.

He catches me checking him out from my perch up on the sink counter, spits, rinses his mouth, and steps between my legs.

I hike my legs around his waist and press my palm against his forehead. "You look awful."

"I do, do I?" He kisses the tip of my nose.

"Coming down with a bad cold, no wait, pneumonia. You'll be bedridden for a week."

"That would be a tolerable prescription if you were to play nurse." His mouth runs a trail from my clavicle to the base of my throat, right at the sensitive place he'd discovered earlier.

I arch against him. "Did you ever think this would happen?"

"What?"

"I don't know, this, us, hooking up or whatever."

"Not going to lie, I thought about it heaps."

"You did?"

"You drive me mad."

"In a good way?

"Look at you fishing. Yes, Captain." His lips cover mine and he punctuates each word with a kiss. "In the best kind of way." His tongue finds mine and minutes pass before he finally pulls free. "Fuck. I need to go, have to tutor and then take part in a phone meeting. I'm trying to regain my honors placement down in Hobart, at the University of Tasmania."

"Tasmania?" Hobart is the capital of Tasmania, the island state below Melbourne, across the Bass Strait. I've seen the ferry, *Spirit of Tasmania*, docked at the port. And there's the Tasmanian devil. And that pretty much sums up my breadth of knowledge regarding the place.

"Yeah, there's a project going with a climate change study, modeling ice sheet trends in the Antarctic. My old supervisor is willing to give me another shot—which is cool seeing as I bailed before at the last minute."

"Why?"

"Because I'm a dickhead sometimes. If the call goes well, I'm going to head down and talk things over in person. My uncle lives there; I can crash with him. He might share my dad's DNA but he's cool."

This information is helpful in point of fact. Bran and I have a fleeting amount of time, can't afford to get overly involved. I'm leaving; he's leaving. That's the situation.

Hear that, brain? Don't get attached.

My heart runs in circles, saying, *Nananananana, I can't hear you.*

Yeah, that's so not helping.

"You share your dad's DNA too." I push his hair back from his face, troubled by his shadowed expression. "And I think you're kind of an all right person."

"Kind of?" He kisses the corner of my chin.

"In a roundabout way." I inhale sharply as his lips return to the hollow in my neck.

"Oh shit." He freezes.

"What?"

"I'm sorry."

My heart pounds harder. "Seriously, what?"

He tilts my head to face the mirror. Beneath my ear is a quarter-sized hickey. "Oh shit." I echo him and prod the purple mark.

"I didn't mean to."

I laugh despite myself. "Guess who's wearing scarves the rest of the week?"

"You're mad?"

I should be irritated. But I'm a little turned on. The hickey will be a temporary reminder when I'm back alone in my room that this afternoon actually happened.

"Not your fault." I smooth away the worry lines creasing his brow. "I bruise easily. Anyway, that's great. About the interview, Hobart and all." I plaster on what I hope passes for an imitation smile. Apparently our time is shorter than I originally envisioned.

"You think so?" He catches my chin, eyes searching.

I forgot Bran's uncanny abilities to get a read on me. I lean to distract him with a kiss that turns out to sidetrack me as well. "I should leave, let you get going," I murmur at last into his mouth.

"Don't want to." His grasp tightens around my neck.

"Think of your future."

He releases his hands only to slide his palms down my body's outline. "All I can think of is making you give one of those little moans."

I grab his wrist and point to his watch. Don't get me wrong; I'd like to moan again too. But he's got places he needs to be and that fact's distracting me.

He peers at the timepiece. "I'm so late."

"Go on, run. I can get dressed fast and let myself out."

He hesitates. "What are your plans for later?"

"Today? Nothing much." *Replaying the last few hours in blow-by-blow, dirty detail.*

His smile is mischievous. "Why don't you hang out in my bedroom? I'll be done in a couple hours."

"Oh, really?"

"I'm thinking we can pick up where we left off."

"You're clearly a genius." He leans in for another kiss and I clap a hand over his mouth. "Okay, get to school. Embrace your potential."

"Yeah." The intensity in his heavy-lidded gaze makes me shiver.

After he leaves, I splash my face with cool water. My cheeks are pink and my eyes shine. I look different—happy—deliriously so.

I whistle under my breath as I yank open the bathroom door and narrowly avoid a collision with a red-haired girl waiting outside. A housemate, no doubt. Oh man, I hope she didn't hear Bran and I going at it in the shower.

"Sorry." I drop my gaze, wanting to avoid direct eye contact, and pretend to massage my neck to cover the hickey.

"Enjoy yourself?" No mistaking the catty tone.

Whelp, guess she heard us.

"Excuse me, please."

She blocks my attempted sidestep. "American?"

Startled, I raise my gaze. The girl's red hair is styled in funky vintage victory curls. She's perfectly voluptuous and striking. Her A-line emerald dress with a white Peter Pan collar and black kitten heels completes the glamorous '50s pinup girl look.

"American?" she repeats, tapping her foot like I'm taking up both time and valuable hallway real estate.

"What?"

"You. Are. An. American?" She speaks with condescending slowness.

"Yeah, sure." I start to sidle toward Bran's bedroom.

Her eyes glitter and her tongue darts out to touch her top lip. "Bran hasn't stooped to fucking Americans before. Guess he's scraping the bottom of the barrel."

My jaw drops. What the hell? Who does this chick think she is? I am trying to process. Why does she look so familiar?

"He drooled all over you at the shop."

The shop? Pieces slot together. The Bean Counter. This was the barista who scowled at us behind the counter earlier today. I'm not sure why the redhead has it in for me. Anxiety attaches to my body like a giant squid grappling a whale, threatening to sink me to the murky depths.

"Enjoy being this month's flavor." Her sneer is venomous.

"I've got to—excuse me." I break for Bran's room. When I get inside, I'm in early-stage hyperventilation. Even though it's stuffy in here, I drape Bran's sheets around my shoulders and inhale his musky soap scent in slow breaths until the action steadies me.

Whoa. Bran's got a serious crappy roommate problem.

I sit up on the edge of his bed and look around. The room's surprisingly neat for a guy. I mean, not over the top. There's no color-coordinated pen jars or erasers set in a neat line on the desk—just a general impression of tidiness and order. It's a little lonesome, like he lives here, but doesn't really live here.

There's a creak of footsteps in the hall outside. I don't really want to stick around. Maybe I'll go home. I pull out my phone to message him an invite to come over later. The battery is dead. Crap.

I glance at his desk. Surely he's got some scratch paper in there. I open the top drawer and pull out a piece of card stock.

Dagmar and Christina Lind
are pleased to announce
the marriage of their daughter
Adie Lind

to

Brandon Lockhart
Son of Bryce and Mariana Lockhart

The paper falls from my fingers.

What. The. Hell.

I bend and grab the invitation, shove it back in the drawer, slam it shut. The bottom falls from my stomach.

Married. Bran was getting married last year? He told me he didn't have a recent girlfriend. That was a right fine bit of hairsplitting to leave out the fiancée. Or did he actually get married? Bran's wife? The words sound outrageous. These thoughts don't add up to anything approaching sense.

Married? It seems so old-fashioned for our age.

I hurry around the room, grabbing my things, find my shoes under the futon. Crap, I didn't mean to snoop, but my eyes can't unsee. Double crap, despite my best intentions, here we go—I'm someone else's stupid rebound. My hands grapple the doorknob. I step into the hallway, primed to flee, when a raspy voice bursts in my ear.

"Bella?" Miles hunches in his doorway, scratching his hairy gut. "You seen my lighter? Oh, wait, you're not Bella."

"Haven't seen it." The red-haired girl emerges from the kitchen, eating cereal from a mixing bowl.

Waaaaait a sec. My mind, already ringing from wedding bells, holds up a cautionary finger. This girl is Bella? The "I miss our good-night kisses" texting Bella?

She lives with Bran?

Too much, too much, too much, my brain screams in alarm, threatening to short-circuit.

"Um, I gotta go," I mumble, stumbling toward the front door.

"Who's that?" I hear Miles ask.

I slam the front door but it doesn't mask Bella's response.

"A no one. Just the chick Bran's sticking his dick in this week."

13

BRAN

*T*oday the wind blisters from the north and carries record high outback temperatures over Melbourne. The city is a concrete lung, holding the hot air until we all start to go a bit mad. Take what I did, hooking up with Talia. Stupid. So stupid. And bloody awesome.

I duck into a high-end contemporary gallery for a blast of air-con and freeze beneath an Aboriginal dot painting detailing an abstracted aerial view of a desert landscape. Art's becoming a significant source of livelihood in some indigenous communities. I eye the hefty price tag. Good, they deserve it and more. Whites have screwed the First Nations over since they decided to settle this country and declared it *terra nullius*—land belonging to no one. As if the people who inhabited this continent since forever didn't matter.

The only constant with humans is their innate need to screw someone over.

Fucking Bella.

Hooking up with her was an act of willful idiocy. I'd made

it clear from the start that I wasn't looking for anything and she claimed she wasn't either. But all of a sudden she was. And the more I tried to clue her in that she and I weren't a thing, the more she acted like I was a challenge to win. I'm not a prize, just a dick. But not a big enough jerk to pretend I'm keen on a girl if I'm not.

I don't want to feel anything. Not since Adie and all the shit that went down in Denmark. And I'd been doing better at handling, keeping safe distances, until I met Talia. I tried to give that girl space, knowing she was dangerous. The perfect mix of bright, undeniably American confidence coupled with a vulnerability that sets roots through the shadowed cracks in my heart.

Finally, I did it. Grew a pair and made a play, and Bella screws things up before they barely start. When I got home to a Talia-less house, Miles filled me in on what Bella had said about Talia earlier today as she flew out the door.

I'd like to send my fist straight through the gallery's stark, perfect white wall. It's a bitch to admit but deep down I know Bella didn't mess up the situation. I did. Why couldn't I be straight—tell Talia about Adie, those crap months in Copenhagen last year, the plane, and all the girls like Bella since my return?

Oh wait, because she'd run screaming in the opposite direction.

"Can I help you?" A gallery attendant purses her lips. The polite person's way of saying piss off, dirtbag.

I don't bother mentioning that my dad has purchased at least half a dozen pieces in this place. Or that the gallery owner is a regular at my parents' Melbourne Cup breakfast. The Cup's the one event that brings them home to Australia each year. During the big November horse race, my folks put on a catered breakfast and arrange drivers to shuffle their fancy friends to their private box at the track. The women try to outdo themselves with who has the ugliest hat and the men drone about their portfolios and the price of copper in China or some shit.

I'd rather die than have that life.

"Sir? Can I help you?"

"No," I say, shoving open the door and returning to the anonymous streets. "No, you can't."

Aimless city wanders are stupid in this hot weather, so I catch a tram back to Carlton. Why aren't I at the beach? It's the perfect day to take the Kingswood to the Great Ocean Road. Drive, windows down, past the You Yangs rising above the Werribee plain, the granite ridges where my friends and I go climbing. Cruise past my old boarding school and give it the finger. I could turn toward Barwon Heads, find the place where I kissed my first girl, inside one of the abandoned bunkers that dot Australia's south coast from World War Two. All facing the sea for an enemy that never came.

I think about those empty bunkers sometimes, especially after I got to Europe and everything unraveled. I wonder if waiting for the worst to hit was harder than when the shit went down.

Turns out both activities suck.

I unlock the front door. Bella's bike is gone and Miles is at work. My house is empty for once. All I want to do is sit in a cold bath with a beer and not think about my screwed up life. I head to my room, peel off my shirt, flick on the fan, and fall onto my bed. On the wall, above my head, is a poster of a work by my favorite painter, Sidney Nolan. It's of Ned Kelly, the famous bushranger, Australia's answer to Robin Hood in the nineteenth century. He and his gang made suits of armor from tin and robbed from the rich to give to the poor. He was betrayed and captured not far from the city, and the last words he offered before they hanged him in the Old Melbourne Gaol were "*Such is life.*"

In the painting, the visor to Ned's helmet is open, revealing nothing but blue sky and white clouds. I used to think the artist tried to depict a man with nothing—show a person free from life's bullshit grind.

But now as I stare at the poster, I realize how wrong I've been.

Maybe the heat's made me a little mental, because I'm feeling this . . . this *mateship* with a mythology—an art house poster. It's just me and Ned in here and he's got my back. If someone peered into my mind, what would they see? The sky, sun, life, hope? No, probably stagnant, bitter pond scum.

I knead my temples. So what if living is a bitch sometimes? Things don't have to get screwed with Talia. I don't know how to put things right with her, or even why it matters, but it does. She matters like no one I've ever met before.

Why not dig deep, muster the courage to grab this short time we've got with both hands? Be willing—really willing—to give it a go? At least be friends. I can do that, right?

Because such is life.

And maybe the part that makes everything beautiful, worthwhile, *bearable* is the trying.

14

TALIA

I trail Marti and her girlfriend, Lucy, down a dodgy back-street searching for Skin Tight, a local piercing parlor. No simple tongue barbell for Marti; she wants the big daddy, a clitoral hood ring. The idea makes my toes curl.

She and Lucy dragged me from my room where I holed up from the heat, listening to dark '80s emo and biting my fingernails into jagged edges. The residential hall is under attack from a mice infestation. Tiny shadows skirt the halls, dart out on the stairs, and elicit shrieks in the shower. I'd planned to stay in and Google rodent-related diseases. You know, just in case.

And because I'd rather think about bubonic plague—turns out it still exists in the twenty-first century, who knew—than a certain boy who can't stop infecting my thoughts.

That's when Marti came to the door, ordering me out, despite the fact the temperature hovers in the high nineties.

"Bella, oh yeah, that chick's a trip." Lucy plays with one of her thick rainbow-hued dreadlocks. "Always rabbiting drama. Never shuts up." Lucy works alongside Bella making coffee at the Bean Counter.

Marti's shamelessly pumping her girlfriend for information on my behalf.

I could have contacted Bran myself, but that would mean talking to him. Being mature is not high on my present must-do list. Not after he ditched me alone this morning in the house he apparently shares with an ex.

Not to mention that he was engaged this time a year ago.

Despite my best intentions, I'm falling for a guy who is like a wormhole of rebounds.

"Bran." Lucy's tone is knowing. "Everyone knows that bloke."

I tune back into the girls' conversation with a quickness. "Really, why?"

"You wouldn't think it, but the dude's a total man tramp."

My heart pays a quick visit to my stomach, confirming my suspicions.

Marti notes my stricken expression and grabs Lucy's hand. "Baby, maybe you should tone it—"

Lucy snorts, oblivious to any attempt to silence her. "He drops trou all over town."

I adjust my shirt—the thin cotton feels more like heavy wool. This information settles into my bones, and the hurt ebbs, like I'm in an empty room watching dust motes float in the half-light.

"Why do you want to know about Bran?" Lucy pins me with a penetrating look. "You fancy him?"

"No." My response is automatic. "Well, yes. Kind of. I didn't know he was together with Bella."

"Together? Nah—Bella's all drama. But when it comes to Bran, I can't blame the girl's reaction. He so used her."

Marti rolled her eyes. "Pfffft. He used her." She air-quotes Lucy's words. "Who says she didn't use him right back? Girls are always either sluts or weaklings in these stories. So boring."

"All I'm saying is that Bella was into him way more than vice versa. At work we all saw that. She would have, too, if she ever stopped to pull her head out. Anyway, he's an ass but not bad-looking...for a dude." Lucy slips her arm around Marti's waist, tugs her close. They exchange cute secret smiles.

I want to crack their smug skulls together. I mean not really, but kind of.

A dull ache spreads through my abdominal cavity. Ovarian cancer? The idea twinges a place deep in my hollow chest even though it's almost statistically impossible in my early twenties. I've already been reassured by my doctor that my chance of being struck by lightning is statistically far greater. My chest starts to throb. What if I have a heart murmur? Or a defective rib? Or rib cancer? Or rib cancer *and* ovarian cancer? Or—

"Hey, there it is." Lucy flings out her hand toward the squat gray brick building across the street.

Inside Skin Tight, a sullen guy lounges behind a glass case stocked with gauges and silver earrings. Marti approaches him with Lucy while I zone in on tattoo mock-ups on the wall. Swallowing feels harder than normal at the moment.

I need to calm down. I'm freaking because I've had confirmation that Bran doesn't really care about me. I'm another conquest who fooled herself into believing I was special, that I alone had crawled under his thorns and prickles, glimpsed something deeper.

I'm a huge idiot. All I was to him was a casual hookup. Thank God we didn't have sex.

Eventually I'll probably run into him. Will he call me out, make me explain why I ran?

What would I say? That I didn't travel all the way to Australia to be a notch on his man-whore belt?

Yes, I'm seeking adventure—life experience—not commitment, but that doesn't mean I want to be used. Or snarked at by former conquests while trying to exit his bathroom.

Why can't I have a simpler study-abroad hookup? Like Jazza?

Except Jazza doesn't make me throb all over. Jazza doesn't treat me like a secret waiting to be unlocked. Jazza doesn't push me, pull me, prod me. Jazza didn't tell me I was perfect only for him, make me believe this truth in the deepest part of my heart.

"Talia, come over here." Marti climbs into the wide black chair, wiggles from her panties, and bends down to wad them in one hand.

The piercer, who goes by the name Dice, pops his neck. I try to focus on his impressive tri-colored Mohawk rather than the instruments gleaming on the stainless steel tray.

"You wax, that's good." Dice grunts as he stares between Marti's splayed legs with a clinical expression. "Less pinching."

Ew.

I watch Dice lift a needle. My stomach curls into a tight ball. Jesus. I don't even pluck my eyebrows.

A wayward staph infection probably lurks in the pleather piercing chair. There's zero chance I'd ever get my clit pierced. What if it all goes bad? Who wants to risk a Barbie doll crotch? I close one eye but can't bring myself to look away when Dice leans forward, head nodding in time to the death metal piping in through the crappy speaker system. The rage sounds tinny and I almost snicker except that Marti's eyes form perfect blue spheres.

"Um, is he supposed to stretch it that far?" I whisper to Lucy as

Dice tugs Marti's lady bits out like a rosy pink nub of Play-Doh. I don't think the clit was meant to be pulled like saltwater taffy.

The needle moves into position. Stabs.

"Oh *maman, maman, maman*." Even my rudimentary grasp of French understands Marti is calling out for her mom.

I tear toward the front of the shop, either that or hurl on Dice's combat boots. There's a bowl of peppermints by the cash register and I grab a fistful, unwrap one, and thrust it into my mouth. My tongue feels different. It's not like I normally think about my tongue but I stick it in one corner of my mouth and then to the other. Does it really feel strange or is it me being nuts again?

I need to stop thinking like this. Not healthy. Not helping anyone. I'll probably give myself a gnarly disease from anxiety. Stress kills. Isn't that what everyone says?

I need to control my thoughts.

But my tongue feels so weird and the ache in my stomach is back. I can't control shit. Struggling to think different is like playing a game of mental Whac-A-Mole one-handed.

"What are you doing, love?"

I spin around. Marti and Lucy watch me, hand in hand.

"Are you *bon*?" Marti's brow crinkles.

"Yeah. Sure." I clear my throat, my windpipe thick and claggy. I'm more light-headed by the second. "I should be asking you. Feel good?"

"It pinches." Marti winks. "But Dice says that I'll have orgasms walking up stairs within a few days."

"You outsourcing me, bitch?" Lucy jokingly elbows Marti's rib cage.

My head aches and I dig a B vitamin from my pocket. I pop supplements like candy when I get nervous.

Need to calm down.

My poisonous thoughts cement into place. I shove harder, but they strengthen their grip, little nails dragging across a chalkboard.

How long will it take Bran to move on to another girl? With his track record? Probably not long. Maybe he'll seek out a Canadian the next time.

He drops trou all over town.

I don't even have a right to get upset. We merely hooked up a little. People do it all the time.

It's just…what we shared felt different.

Clarification. I felt.

I felt something that wasn't gray misty sadness shot through with the occasional bolts of terror.

For whatever reason, surly, argumentative Bran made my broken pieces feel…not put back together, exactly, but less brittle, like there could be a chance I could refashion into something different. Stronger.

Well, that hope's gone. No one saves you in real life. It's a dirty lie perpetuated to sell blockbuster Hollycrap movies. There are no shiny armored knights.

Dragons kick ass.

They always win.

I need to get out of here. Away from Dice's thick fingers and bad attitude. And far away from Marti and Lucy's puppy-eyed lusta-love. Why can't I live in the future? A time when unacceptable cognitive functions can simply be deleted? In the twenty-first century we have artificial hearts, electric cars, YouTube, for fuck's sake. Are cyborg brain implants too much to hope for in my lifetime?

My mumbled excuses and hasty retreat garner a skeptical look from Marti, but Lucy is pushing hard for a drink at a pub and it's time I stop being the downer third wheel.

When I get back to the residential hall, there's a Post-it stuck to my room's door.

Stopped by, will come back later

—B

A Post-it? For serious? Does he keep that shit in his pocket for girl emergencies?

I can't deal with this, not right now, not when I'm peaking. The stairwell door props open at the end of the hall. I normally avoid the stairs because they reek of urine and Band-Aids, but right now I need to move. I race down two flights when a small motion catches my eye.

My gorge rises.

A mouse, no bigger than my little finger, lies on its side, rib cage shuddering. The poison bait the facilities crew scattered around the building must have tricked the poor creature. The little guy thought he'd found something good and now he's dying—alone—in one of the world's top ten grungiest stairwells. Its nose twitches, turns in my direction, and I swear the black eyes ask me a single question.

"What have I done that you wouldn't have?"

———

I hunker in the back of a used bookstore. No matter what I do, I can't stop thinking about Bran, the responses he coaxed from me yesterday. He slit the threads I'd spun around my protective cocoon and I slipped out without any butterfly wings, falling to the ground with a sickening smack.

Getting up from my tiny table, I pad to the closest shelf and pull out a random book. It's poetry by E. E. Cummings. I part the pages midway and read.

who are you,little i

(five or six years old)
peering from some high

window;at the gold

of november sunset

(and feeling:that if day
has to become night

this is a beautiful way)

My lower lip trembles involuntarily. Pippa and I shared a room ever since we were born even though we lived in a three-bedroom house. On summer nights when our mom used to put us to bed while the sun nestled high in the sky, we'd pile blankets on the floor and build nests. Curled, side by side, we'd watch the sky change colors out the window while whispering secrets and concocting stories.

Who was my little i?

A girl who didn't worry. Woke up each morning like it was my birthday. Was the kid sister to the coolest, sweetest, kindest person ever.

I want my Pippa alive.

I want my innocence back.

I want to feel normal.

I don't even remember what normal feels like anymore.

There's a lecture on campus I can get bonus credit for attending. Not that I really need it. My grades are kicking all kinds of ass. But that won't fix the fact that I'm not graduating, that I screwed my transcript last year, and that I still need to come up with a senior thesis.

After the lecture, I'll e-mail Bran. Ask him to leave me alone—in a civil way. While it sucks he left me in a house inhabited by a bitter ex–fuck buddy, he didn't do anything really wrong. We have a magnetic attraction, both mental and physical, but are barely acquaintances. He makes me want to feel too much.

And feeling is dangerous. I can barely withstand the sensations in my own body on the day to day. Bran opened something inside me and I need to get that shit recorked before I go crazy. I'm already opting for medication and the pills are barely getting me through. My superpowers are waning and Bran is my Kryptonite. I need to opt for avoidance. Cowardly, yes. But also effective.

Stressing about him has sent my OCD symptoms creeping back. Any second my brain is going to start flashing a red light with a blaring alarm droning, *Danger! Danger!*

A guy is up ahead of me on campus as I walk to my lecture. His height, the fall of the unruly hair, the familiar way his hands are shoved deep in his pockets sends me ducking behind the Law building. I tap my fingers in a special order. It doesn't feel right, so I have to do it again and again. And I miss the lecture.

Fucking damn it.

I had a crush on Tanner, Pippa's boyfriend, for my entire adolescence. When the chance came, the awful, drunken, grief-stricken chance, I let him use me. I offered up my body for a taste of beauty and instead never felt more hideous, like a mutant hobgoblin devouring the crumbs of my dead sister's life.

Bran made me come alive briefly. And look what happened. He burst on me like a wicked storm and when he put his hands on my body, the sensation thundered deep into my bones. Better I stay far away from him. I'm like a trailer in Kansas that narrowly dodged a tornado, lucky to have escaped more or less unharmed.

I head home and fall straight asleep, but my dreams are turbulent. Tangled memories of Tanner's hoarse sob, the sharp burn the moment he buried himself inside me. The first soft brush of Bran's lips across my own. My head bouncing against Tanner's chest while he took me hard, way too hard for my first time. Rubbing on Bran like a sexed-up cat in his shower. Waking up alone under the Santa Cruz Wharf when the high tide reached my bare feet, a homeless guy snoring a few feet away.

I lurch up in my bed, slick with sweat, gulping for air like a dying fish. A bunch of Pippa's pals had gathered at the beach park to commemorate the first anniversary of her death. Tanner and I had both hung in at the BBQ as long as we could, faking smiles, faking we weren't gutted zombies. Dad skipped out, hiding in our backyard to wax his surfboards. Mom had already long bailed, escaping us for a rainbow-colored promise of alohatastic healing.

"Wanna get out of here?" Tanner had unzipped his black backpack, revealing a nearly full whisky bottle.

"Yeah."

I'd followed him down West Cliff Drive on my cruiser. His effortless, graceful skating style turned heads the whole way. He probably didn't even notice. Pippa was the same way. That's what made them such a great couple. They both wore their perfection so casually, like they were fully comfortable in their skin.

We reached the wharf as darkness settled over the bay. For a long time we leaned against a piling, wordlessly passing the bottle back and forth. We drank silently, grimly. The sea air was cold, but my belly grew hot with alcohol and something else.

I'd never spent a lot of alone time with Tanner even though he'd been a regular fixture in our house. He hadn't come by much the year after Pippa died. His pro skateboarding career skyrocketed and he toured with the X Games, and recently he signed a shoe sponsorship, paying off his single and perpetually struggling mom's mortgage.

My mouth stung and the heavy amount I drank wasn't making me feel better. Time didn't heal shit. Another lie people tell you to get through an uncomfortable moment where they don't want to be stuck gawking at your grief. If anything, the year after Pippa's death had turned from a wound into an angry, throbbing infection.

"I miss her all the time."

Tanner's voice had been thick. His hand slid up my knee and when I looked up and saw his tear-wet cheeks, I gave him the only thing I had.

Me.

And it wasn't enough. It wasn't nearly enough.

I'm not perfect. I'm not Pippa.

The air in my dorm room is harder to find. I close my eyes, concentrate on the next breath. That's it. All I need to worry about is the next breath. My heart rate slows.

What I wouldn't give for a goldfish memory.

There's a knock at the door.

Shitabrick.

It's him. Bran. I know it. His presence zings through the cheap particleboard and churns my stomach until I feel like a metham-phetamine hamster unleashed on a wheel.

"Bonjour? Talia?" It's only Marti.

Great. I'm a freak, not a telepath. I brush my arms but my skin remains stubbornly goose bumped, my breath hitching like I'm poised at the top of a roller-coaster drop.

I climb out of bed, open the door, and my senses dip like the roller coaster is flying down the track. My brain screams while my heart throws up its hands in sheer abandon.

Bran stands there, green cat eyes trained on mine. No trace of the dimples. He's deadly serious.

"Oh, hey." I actually stretch my arms like the d-bag I am. "Just waking up."

"He said you wouldn't talk to him." Marti backs away when my gaze cuts her like a lightsaber. Right now I so wish the Force was with me. I'd totally do that Darth Vader choke on her.

"You're avoiding me." Bran's voice is flat.

I force a laugh that sounds worse than the canned soundtracks on sitcoms. "That's ridiculous."

Marti watches us by her door. A few other girls chat farther down the hall. Better to let him come in than stand and bicker in the hall. I can't deal with scenes.

I open the door wide and sweep my hand into the room with a grand gesture. "Come on in."

He ignores my sarcasm and takes a sure-footed step inside my room. "We have to talk."

15

TALIA

*T*alia." Bran's fingers fan my cheek. He must feel how hard my teeth are clenched, for he pulls back, allowing me some much-needed breathing room. "What happened yesterday—Miles told me Bella got to you."

"I nearly stepped on her exiting the bathroom. You live with your ex, Bran. A little heads-up would have been appreciated."

His lips draw a fraction inward, enough to let me know my words make an impact. "Bella called herself my ex?"

"Not exactly, but whatever, the implication was clear."

"I moved into that place a few months ago. Bella and I had the occasional hookup. That's the sum total. Nothing serious."

"I heard..." The words threaten to choke me. "I heard word you get around, like a lot."

He snorts and turns away. His expression is hidden while he runs a hand over my vitamins cluttering the top of my dresser.

I've no idea what to say, but right now babbling's better than this stony silence. "Bran—"

He spins on his heel. "Did you like it?"

"What?" I take an involuntary step backward.

"Being with me?"

"Yes." The truth flies out before I can consider concealing it.

His face loses some of that hard edge. "I did too." He folds his arms behind his head and takes a deep breath. "I...I...Listen, I..."

I sit on my bed, hook my elbows around my knees, and wait.

He shoves his hands into his pockets. "Have you ever been in love?"

My eyes widen. Whatever I thought he'd say, that was definitely not on the list. "Um, yes. I think so. Well, kind of."

I mean, I don't know what exactly I felt for Tanner. I believed my emotions were love, but now I'm not so sure. Sometimes, with hindsight, I wonder if maybe I simply wanted someone to love *me* the same hard-core way he loved Pippa.

Someone who believed, despite all evidence to the contrary, that I was a lock they wanted to open.

Bran rocks on his heels. "I don't believe in love."

Those words shouldn't hurt the way they do. It's not like he and I have time for anything serious. I force myself to roll my eyes.

"What?"

"Figures you'd be the kind of guy who reduces love to something fictitious, like Santa Claus."

"Not following, Captain." There's an edge to his voice.

"Did you wake up one morning and think, love? Mmmm, not really buying that whole spectrum of humanity's experience."

"I did wake up. And realized love's nothing but a word used to excuse a bunch of pretty fucking questionable behavior."

So Bran doesn't believe in love but was practically a child-bride? I bite back the comment, just.

"So you've never been in love. Never felt strongly about anyone, ever?" Oh, I'm baiting now, all right. Put the words on the hook and cast it into the conversation. Fishing for details about Adie Lind and his engagement.

"There was someone serious a while ago. We didn't work out." He shrugs like that's more than enough explanation.

Damn, he got away. He's lying by omission and I can't even get him to own it because of the dodgy way I uncovered the information. But come on, what was he thinking, wanting to get married at our age? He certainly wasn't the religious type. Something doesn't fit.

What if I tell him I accidently snooped, found his wedding invitation? That I know he's been engaged?

"I started sleeping around after my last relationship ended. I needed distance from her, from the memory of us together."

"How's that working out for you?" Better if I keep my mouth shut. He clearly doesn't want me to know, still keeps me at arm's length, hides behind his secrets. Frustration sears my chest. "So why are you here?" I jerk my head toward my bed; apparently my vocal cords haven't gotten the message to shut the fuck up. "You want to get a little more distance?"

"You aren't going to make this easy, are you?"

"I don't even know what *this* is. What do you want, Bran? From me?"

"I...like you." He sounds surprised.

"Wow, is that supposed to be flattery?" The shitty thing is the admission secretly pleases me. And makes me angry. Like am I supposed to drop my panties and cheer for my likeability?

"Who was the guy?" Bran hooks his hand behind his neck. "The one you were kind of, maybe, sort of in love with."

I don't want to talk about Tanner. That time in my life was

chaotic, like the aftermath of a train wreck. "He was my sister's boyfriend. They were together since middle school. He was like my brother, except not, I don't know. In a moment of poor judgment and epic fuck-uppery, I slept with him."

"Your sister's boyfriend?"

"A year after she died." I swallow, hard. "He hasn't spoken to me since."

"Idiot."

Tears blur my vision. I know my actions that awful night below the wharf were slapdick, a terrible mistake. Hearing Bran react so badly makes the remembrance even worse. I clamp my jaw and throw myself over my internal memory chest, the place where I stuff my worst emotions. If I start to feel one thing, I'm going to feel all the things and no way is that happening—I can't lose control.

"Wait a second, hey, look at me, Talia." He crosses the room in two steps, crushes me against him. "Not you. Bloody hell, you thought I meant you?"

I nod, face in his ribs, unable to speak.

"You didn't tie this guy down to do the deed." He squats beside the bed, his hands cradling my face. "Or did you, naughty girl?"

"No." I crack a small smile even as I sniffle. "No ropes were involved. Only Jack and Daniels."

"You got him drunk first, huh?"

I frown at the memory. "Actually, the other way around."

"So you drink with this guy and have consensual sex. But somehow you're the bad guy? Not connecting the dots here."

"You don't understand. Tanner was my sister's epic love."

He tilts my chin. "I get that you feel bad. All I'm saying is it's not your fault. She was *your* sister and you suffered too. Any questionable choices you made—it sounds like you more than paid for them."

I close my eyes.

He strokes my hair in a slow, hypnotic rhythm. "This year, I did things. Lots of things I'm not proud of."

"By things...you mean girls."

"Yeah." His answer is quiet.

"Lots and lots?"

"Yes." Quieter still. "But you're different."

"Oh, come on."

"I'm a lot of things, Talia. But I'm no liar." His gaze shackles me to him. "I don't know what this is between us but I've a mind to find out. What do you want? The ball's in your court here."

Do I let Bran's shadowy former hookups stand between us? Or do I blow them away like dandelion seeds and make a wish that we can start again?

You're only perfect for me. Those damn words stick with me wherever I go, along with the hope that maybe they're true. Hope is scary, even more dangerous than doubt.

He shifts his weight, quiet for once, and waits for me to decide. Maybe I'm an idiot—but I'm going to go for it. For him. Because here's a guy who doesn't run. Who doesn't want me to be someone else.

"Here's my question." I arch my brow and enjoy his nervous fidgeting. "How did you ever score with all those ladies?"

Questions pile up behind those green eyes.

I hook my fingers in his belt loops. "I mean, look, you're hot—"

"You think so?"

"Yeah, although I doubt you need the ego boost. But you're not exactly Mr. Congeniality. When I first met you, at the pub—"

"We first met on Lygon Street. After the fight. I remember exactly."

"Right." *You do?* "Um, yeah, you were dressed like a koala."

"And you were a cute girl in a white dress who stumbled across me at a personal low point. No, I didn't try to fake nice that night. No point trying to impress the girl who knows you're a dick, who watched you get your ass kicked in a koala suit. A girl who's dating your mate."

I flinch. "Jazza and I never dated."

"He's a wanker." His intense look sends a shock of heat thrumming up my thighs. "I wouldn't have let you go."

"Well he didn't really have a choice. I don't like Jazza, at least not like that."

"Who do you like?" He braces his hands on either side of my hips.

My body wants me to give in. My lips scream for me to shut up and kiss him already.

His mouth hovers dangerously close to mine. "If you'd tossed me out, I'd have tried to get you back again. And again. And again. I wasn't lying when I said I can't stay away."

He's waiting for me to kiss him, and I want to, so badly, but I'm scared. The last few days I've felt more than in the whole of last year. I don't know why Bran has this effect but I'm not stupid enough to ignore the lurking danger. Don't want to sleep with another guy only to get bailed on the minute it's over. I want to move forward, but in the slow lane.

Bran sneaks a curious glance at the orange pill bottle on my dresser.

A jolt shocks my system. No one, outside of Dr. Halloway and the pharmacist, knows about those pills. "I . . . I . . . take meds, okay?" Defensiveness curls around my words to shield me from his reaction.

"They help?" His response is remarkably unfreaked.

"I think so, a little, but they're not a perfect solution." Dr. Halloway hadn't been a fan of me going to Australia. He stressed I should take medication in combination with therapy, one without the other might only let me hobble along.

I'm hobbling all right. Stress seems to heighten my symptoms.

"You've always taken them?"

"No. Never. Not until...not until after my sister died. And I started to have problems, dealing, or whatever."

He sits quietly and I feel like I might say more. But how to even start to explain about what happened as I descended into OCD's grip? It's like trying to grab shadows; they keep slipping from my hands. Besides, it's hard enough to get someone to listen about your dreams, let alone nightmares.

"I don't like talking about this stuff," I mumble.

"Why not?"

It's hard to find an easy way to articulate. "Because, if I do..." I take a deep breath, hold it for five counts. "What's happening to me is real, not made up in my head."

He nods, his gaze reflecting only thoughtfulness.

"When my sister was in the hospital, little things began to crop up. Like being afraid to leave my dad without a hug good-bye in case I never saw him again. Or this idea that if I wore red shoes, someone I loved might get hurt."

"No red shoes."

"I threw them away. I threw all my red clothes away. They reminded me of...of Pippa. There was...so much blood. Over time things got worse." I told him about the obsessive thinking, my growing compulsions, and my health anxieties. How I nearly flunked out of school due to my WebMD addiction, because I couldn't find a good reason why I should be alive and healthy and my sister dead.

"You're still here," I said when I'd finished.

He looked down at himself. "Yeah."

"I'd have thought you'd make up a perfectly valid reason to escape my company by now."

"Hell no." He moves beside me and wraps an arm around my waist. "You are one of the bravest people I've ever met."

I draw a shaky breath. "I don't think I can handle sarcasm right now."

"I'm dead serious. What you've dealt with—I can't imagine." He lifts one of my hands and kisses the center of my palm. "Please know this, what happened with your sister, it wasn't your fault."

My chest contracts in a vise, my next breath left to fight its way out.

"It wasn't your fault," he repeats, pushing himself up, brushing his lips over my forehead.

My breath hitches.

"It wasn't your fault," he breathes into my ear.

My sob is short, a single note I quickly swallow. He wants to make me feel better and I'm grateful. But he can't.

He doesn't know his sweet words are a lie.

Because he doesn't know that what happened to Pippa really is all my fault.

16

TALIA

*B*ran stops by my room on the first night of Easter break. We've been seeing each other, tentatively on and off over the last month. Poster children for the notion of "taking it slow." As if we have all the time in the world, which we don't, as I'm heading home mid-June. I've been back to his place a handful of times, mostly so he can grab a jacket or credit card, once to watch a movie. Bella was there and she pointedly snubbed us, and we ignored her. Bran says she barely speaks to him, which I apologized for, even though I wasn't 100 percent sorry. He rolled his eyes and said he was grateful, and added a new guy had been sniffing around, so she clearly wasn't too broken up.

I've never asked about Adie Lind or the mysterious engagement. Bran's never offered. Never even breathed the word *Denmark*. I'd know, I listen. Hiding a secret of this magnitude makes me uncomfortable, but I don't know how to tell him the truth. He'll think I was snooping. I wish we could have everything out on the table, all our cards, but I don't know how to get us there.

"Any plans for the break?" he asks, handing me a paper cup stamped from the Bean Counter.

I take a sip; heavenly Belgian hot cocoa, my complete and utter favorite, made from melted Lindt chocolate. "Oh, wow, that's good." I lick a dollop of whipped cream from my top lip.

Bran stares at my mouth.

We haven't kissed, barely touched except for the odd shoulder grazes and knee bumps, not since he held me crying in my room. It's like we're just friends. Except friends don't gaze at each other's lips for thirty seconds.

"I've finished a couple big papers and midterms went well. Better than well, actually," I say.

"I've meant to ask for a while, why history?"

"What do you mean?"

"Why do you want to study it? I never asked."

"Um, you know, no one's ever posed that question. I mean, it's not the most practical or sexy degree. I think that everyone probably assumes that I'll want to go on to law school or get a teaching degree."

"But you don't want to do either of those?"

"No."

"Hmmm."

"What? Do you think I should have studied something practical?"

He throws his hands up. "I'm only curious, Captain. No need to bite off my head."

"Sorry, you're right. I don't have a planned linear career path and that kind of freaks me out. I picked history to study for a few reasons. I like secret stories. I'm not content with being fed the easy version. There's always more to a situation, you know? I'm curious about the voices during war or large social change movements that don't get heard quite as easily. Maybe I could work at some scholarly press as an editor or researcher. I'm also interested in historic preservation societies, with a focus on alternate history. One of the things that makes Australia so interesting is the convict past, the story of the oppressed tied with the oppressor, plus you had the Aboriginal element of loss of country and—"

"It turns into a mess."

"Terrible things happen. But I love to read cheering letters from women to suffragette prisoners during hunger strikes to get out the female vote or subversive lesbian identities in the nineteenth century, or the way native people turned their struggles into hymns of struggle that slipped under the radar from the masters in the plantation houses." I realize that I'm talking so fast I'm barely breathing.

"Sorry." I raise my cup in a rueful toast. "I get carried away. Dorktastic, I know."

"Shut the fuck up, Talia."

"Excuse me?" I recoil.

"Never apologize for having passion." Bran shakes his head. "Especially not to me. It's rare to love what you do."

"I don't *do* anything, at least not yet."

"Talia, promise me something." He stares at me like I'm to make a solemn vow.

"That's tricky. I don't like to make promises without knowing the terms and conditions."

"Of course you don't." Bran's mouth curves into a private smile that's gone before my next blink. "Don't break your heart trying to batter against the world, okay?"

I gesture ineffectually. It's either that or burst into tears. How can I explain—without sounding like I'm playing the world's saddest violin—that that was the nicest thing anyone has ever said to me?

"I don't have any real concrete plan for Easter break," I say when I trust myself enough to speak. I self-consciously rub one teary eye with the back of my hand. These things Bran says sometimes, they are like little gifts I want to hide in a treasure box. "There's an international student club field trip to the Penguin Parade on Phillip Island that I might check out."

"The Penguin Parade?" Bran blinks, his face clearing. "You don't want to go to that."

"Why not? I've never seen a penguin. They look so cute."

"Yeah, sure, they're cute…or whatever. But here's the thing, you visit the Penguin Parade and it's you and hundreds of other people watching the birds exit the water after sunset. By my parents' place, there's a penguin colony. Sure it's a lot smaller, but if you head there, I guarantee no one else will be around."

I wait after he stops talking, but he doesn't add anything else, like an invitation to take me. "Okay, cool, I'll keep that in mind."

"I'm heading downtown tonight."

I perk up. "Anything fun in the cards?"

"Nah, just going out for a guys' night."

I fall back against the bed. "Guessing that's code for I'm not invited."

"Jazza will be there, if that's of interest to you."

I fall silent. Two can play at this game.

"So I'm out." He walks to the door and pauses. "I'll come by at eleven o' clock tomorrow morning to pick you up."

"Where are we going?"

He looks at me like my brains are broken. "To Portsea, to stay at my parents' house? They aren't around. We'll have it to ourselves. We just talked about this."

"Um, I think that conversation mostly took place in your head."

He gives a half wave. "So see you at eleven."

"Hold up. *If* I go, and note I've never said I will, I want an actual invitation."

His lips quirk in the corners. "Written or verbal?"

"Verbal will suffice."

"Dear Natalia, would you please come to Portsea with me for a few days? I'll introduce you to penguins and a weedy sea dragon or two."

"Now you're making fun of me."

"Sea dragons are real. I'll find you one."

"Let me see." I tap my fingers on my lip, pretending to decide. A few days alone in a beach house with Bran? I can think of a million worse options and none better. "What the heck, maybe it'll even be fun."

"Yeah, I think I can promise some fun." His smile is so naughty that I'm blushing in seconds. Maybe we're ready to change lanes, speed things up a bit. Easter break just got interesting.

———

After a car ride thick with flirty innuendos, the last thing I expect upon entering Bran's childhood room in his family's ultra-modern beach house is for him to crawl under his bed.

He removes a beat-up Vans shoebox while I study the décor, stylish yet soulless, designed for a generic boy, not a real kid. The room feels like an interior design catalog, not a real, practical space.

He flicks through a stack of photographs and selects a few. "If you're visiting Lockhart Penitentiary, you might as well get familiar with the inmates."

"That's a funny thing to call your house."

"Hilarious as a life sentence." He hands me the pictures with a humorless smile. "Here, check these out."

I cross my legs on the comforter, oddly touched he wants to share his family with me, and begin to flick through the pile.

"That's my sister, Gaby." He points at a petite knockout with his same wide mouth. "She's a pain in my ass, but cool, practically raised me."

"You once mentioned your parents traveled a lot."

"Yeah, they were never around. Why bother when they had Gaby and boarding schools to fall back on?" With evident pride, he hands me another picture of two girls clowning around. "These are Gaby's daughters, the troublemakers, Winnie and Claire."

"Which one's the Bieber fanatic?"

He grimaces. "You'll never let me live that down, will you?"

"Nope, it's a gift that keeps on giving."

"Winnie is the wannabe pop star. Claire prefers books and horses. They live in the city's west in one of those McMansion suburbs. Her husband, Joe, is a wanker, raced back in the day."

"Cars?"

"Nah, former jockey."

"Joe the Jockey." I peer closer at the shot of the short guy with the toothy smile. "Was he any good?"

"Yeah. Now he's retired, drinks too much, and talks shit about stallions and share prices."

"Sounds a little boring."

"Like I said, he's a wanker. We don't... get along."

I wait for him to say more, but his shuttered face indicates that conversation is a dead end. I glance back to the dark-haired woman, arms looped over her two identical miniatures. "Your sister really is stunning. She looks like a supermodel or something."

"She did model, a little. But she's vertically challenged. Wait, you'll love seeing this." He shuffles through a few more pictures and selects one, yellowed by age, of a sultry young woman in a clingy red evening gown. "That's Mariana," he says.

"Wow, who's she?"

"My mother. She hates being called Mom. I've had to address her as Mariana since I was five years old."

"Ouch."

"Whatever," he says with a shrug. "She's not the maternal type. Anyway, that picture is from when she was Miss Argentina."

"Whoa—what?"

"Yeah, wild, huh? Dad snagged her a few years later during a business trip to Buenos Aires. How, I'm not sure, because he's a bastard. But I guess money can buy most things. Don't know why they ended up having kids. Still, can't complain, right? Otherwise I wouldn't be here."

There is such a deep sadness behind his sarcasm. A chill creeps through my chest. I mean, don't get me wrong, my family is all kinds of messed up. But even in the darkest times, while Pippa died by slow inches in the hospital, Mom screamed about everything, and Dad never spoke at all, I knew love existed for *me*. Bran speaks about his parents as if they are distant acquaintances and yet keeps their photos stored under his bed. I can't imagine growing up in such a lonely world. No wonder Bran's so prickly and defensive. Does he even know what it's like to receive unconditional love?

"I'm sorry," I say, which is lame. Because I'm so much more

than sorry. I want to take him in my arms and rock him like a lost boy.

"Don't pity me for a single second." His laugh is a poor imitation of the real thing. "Look at all this stuff. Kids grow up way worse."

"We all need love."

"I don't believe in love, remember?"

He acts like his smile is genuine, and I pretend my stomach doesn't flinch.

"Hey, this must be your dad." I switch the subject, no point arguing when he's in a mood. I raise the next picture, which features a smoldering guy in a dark suit, no tie. Except for the crew cut, he's Bran's doppelganger.

"Yeah. That's him. Bigshit Bryce." Bran's voice is tight with a bunch of emotions, none of which sound remotely positive.

"He's total handsomepants." When in doubt, go for humor. Except in this case, I'm serious as a heart attack. I don't have a daddy complex but Bryce Lockhart is *hawt* with a capital *H*.

"Dad?" He snorts. "Really, you think so?"

"Dude, he looks like your twinsie. Super sexy."

Bran's green cat eyes lock on mine. Delicious dimples threaten to put in an appearance beside his parted lips. Maybe I'm shameless, but whatever, a little honesty might improve the suddenly grim situation. Once upon a time, during an afternoon not all that long ago, we hooked up like bonobo monkeys at his place in Carlton. I haven't forgotten the way my body responded when Bran put his hands on me. I want to get us closer.

How would I start, if I want to initiate action? I've never tried to put seductive moves on anyone. What if this all goes spectacularly wrong and I make a total idiot out of myself?

With care, I place the pictures in the shoebox, hoping he can't tell how badly my hands tremble.

"Are you thirsty? Hungry? Want to go on a kitchen raid? Even though my parents barely ever put in an appearance, they hire a housekeeper who keeps the place stocked with dulce de leche and..."

He trails off because I crawl into the middle of his bed. I sit back on my knees and begin to unbutton my shirt, slowly, pretending like I'm someone else. A girl who strips for hot guys like it's the most natural thing in the world. One button, two buttons, three buttons, four, five, six. Every number calms me more.

Here goes nothing.

"Get over here." My shirt falls open. I shrug the thin white cotton from my shoulders.

"Talia." His chest rises and falls; his pupils dilate.

I love when he says my name in that way, like it's something vital to his existence.

"What are you doing?"

"What does it look like?" I unhook my bra, let it slip free from my arms and my breasts tighten from the exposure to the cool air. "I'm going to seduce you."

"Right." He moves across the bed with pantherlike grace. He has on that hunting face, but he's going to learn that I'm the one on the prowl.

I can't believe I'm being so ballsy. I tug down my skirt and panties in one gesture, kick free of my clothes like I'm a total boss. Not a scared little girl afraid he might change his mind at any second.

Bran reaches for my exposed skin and I check him with a single word. "No."

"No?"

"No," I repeat gently, without mercy. "I want to do the touching."

He blinks before his mouth crooks. "You're full of surprises."

"You're overdressed for this party." I peel up his shirt and trace the indents of his stomach muscles. I tug the shirt higher to reveal his pecs and dip forward to take one of his flat nipples into my mouth, worrying the tip with my teeth.

His hands grab the back of my head and I shake him off. "No touching."

He groans. "I don't know if I like this game."

"Remove your shirt and lie down on your back."

"Yes, ma'am." He obeys, and it's pretty hot.

I've reached a part of my mind that I didn't know existed. The place that's confidently sexual, wants to be actively in control, not simply acted upon. Don't get me wrong, I loved when Bran touched me, but right now I want to take the lead. It's the same feeling I had when I rubbed on him in the shower. Except stronger. Dark pleasure curls through me. The tenor in the room shifts. Tension ripples, visible across his flexed stomach when I reach out, undo his jeans' button, and lower the zipper tooth by tooth.

"Please."

I tug down his pants and resist the urge to say, "Whoop, there it is."

Because, serious, wow.

I've never gone down on a guy. The fact had never really bothered me until right this second. I wish I had experience to draw from. There'd been one time, in high school, when I'd discovered a book, *Sex Tips for Straight Women from a Gay Man*, while wandering the basement shelves of Logos Books. I'd lost an hour to flipping through the pages, complete with diagrams and sassy step-by-step "how to" advice, but who'd climb behind the wheel of a Lamborghini after only reading a driver's ed manual?

"Let me touch you," he says, open desire making his eyes more mesmerizing than normal.

I take hold of his shaft at the root and lick my lips, making sure they are wet. He jerks in my hand as I bend down.

"Holy God," he grinds out when I lower my mouth to him. I go easy at first, gentle and tentative, trying not to do anything overly ticklish. There's some time needed to get comfortable and figure out basic mechanics. When I am confident I've found the right rhythm, and my teeth are safely locked down behind my lips, I increase the pressure. Bran cries out, grinds his hips in a silent plea for more.

"Talia." He groans my name and it's more husky, more everything.

My nervousness fades as I begin to enjoy the smooth, firm feel of him on the back of my tongue. I take him in slow, long strokes, all the way to the base. This is good. I got this. My eyes open. Bran stares directly into my face. Something electric passes between us. I keep working, not breaking the contact. There is a heat to his hooded expression that puts my entire body in a fever state. I'm torn. I want to keep going; I want to get him off with nothing more than my mouth and tongue. But I want him inside me so bad, taking us both to the place we want to go.

17

BRAN

*T*alia's mouth is on me. My brain is only capable of producing microbursts of information on a rapid-fire loop. *Want. Her. Want. Her. Want. Her. Want. Her. Want. Her.*

Her hand surrounds my shaft, working me in time to her lips. My mental processing is having a malfunction. I'm brain-dead, but fuck it's a good death. Talia doesn't touch me like she knows what works and wants to show off her skills. Her strokes are a little awkward, some border rough, others softer than how I prefer. But this is Talia, and that makes every touch good—better than good.

I haven't laid a finger on her since that afternoon we got down at my house last month. Of course, I've wanted to. The evidence's right there in the epic blue balls I've endured to spend time in her presence. But sex, the act messes things up. Take Bella—she was cool, almost a friend. We fooled around a few times, then—*bam*— she wants more, wants what I can't give.

I like Talia way more than Bella, or any girl since ... well, in a while. She's sweet beneath the prickly sarcasm, and then there are those glimpses of fragility that practically undo me. I don't want to use her for an easy, forget-my-life hookup, risk messing up what we—*oh . . . oh, Jesus.*

Talia readjusts her speed and pressure based on the way I rock into her mouth. Her whole technique recalibrates, and everything good grows exponentially better. I try not to thrust my hips, almost impossible now that she takes me deeper, sucks harder, works her tongue until my cock can't harden any more. My balls pull tight, start to tingle. I'm close. The intensity builds to jaw-clenching levels.

Not yet, not yet, not yet, not yet, oh, fuck, too late. Thundercats are go.

I yank from her mouth and flip away, coming onto the sheets in a violent burst that nearly levitates me off the bed. I should speak, say something, but my vocal cords forgot how to work.

Talia sits back on her knees; her breasts—smallish but perfectly shaped—rise and fall as she takes a deep breath. Her lips are a little swollen from me. That idea is something I could get used to.

I grab her hand, pull her on top of me.

"Why did you do that?"

She wants to know why I pulled out. Why I hold back. How do I tell her the truth without sounding like a total pussy?

Here's the reason—because if I let her in, I don't know how I'll ever let her go.

———

Talia kicks off her thongs, dangles her feet off the edge of Portsea Pier. She leans over, checking out the shells clinging to the pylons below the surface. Kelp surges with the waves while the world below fades into a murky emerald. I resist the urge to wrap my arm around her waist, steady her, and keep her safe. Not sure where this protective instinct comes from, I'm normally not the kind of guy who frets around like a nervous Nellie.

Between us is an open packet of fish and chips. I select two, dip them in tomato sauce, and raise them to her lips.

She gives me a funny smile. "Two?"

"Stick with me, baby. I know what you like." She bites the chips from my fingers and ducks her head, as if that wall of hair will hide the blush flooding her cheeks, washing down her neck. I don't know why she added the new shiny red streaks. I mean, they look cool, don't get me wrong, but she's perfect the way she is.

And these cheese-dick thoughts make me want to stab myself in the eye.

For some reason, everything Talia does—even the way she eats her food—is fascinating. We've done everything but have sex. For whatever reason, I'm more nervous about that than a virgin. I'm a fucking coward, scared of another girl from a faraway place who holds nothing but the promise of a dead-end future. I'm not strong enough to face that shit storm again.

So I stay away, but not too far, like an abused dog who hovers a few feet back, desperate for a pat but runs off if one looks forthcoming.

Talia's little black shorts ride high on her inner thighs. I love the hint of curve in her legs, and those blue-painted toes threaten to slay me. Even her ankles are nothing short of perfection. I grab my wet suit and sling it across my lap to hide my hard-on.

For fuck's sake, cool it, dude.

———

A half hour later we are suited up, dorked out in snorkels and fins.

I take her hand. "You ready?"

"How cold is the water again?"

"Warmer than the Arctic."

"That's not a glowing recommendation." She squeezes my hand. "Okay, let's do this, before I change my mind."

"One, two, three." She leaps with me and we plunge off the pier. The water is frigid, creating the perfect habitat for the hundreds of marine species surrounding us. The pier's not deep, only five or six meters, ideal conditions to get up close and personal with the trevally, blue devils, zebra fish, rays, and there—I tap Talia on the shoulder and point.

A weedy sea dragon swims toward us, flitting through the kelp to keep camouflaged. The long orange-red body resembles a seahorse except for the leaflike appendages and short spikes lining its back.

We tread together, paddling only when necessary to maintain our position against the current. Here, in this strange world, time slows, life is diluted to the rhythm of tide and waves. I reach out and take Talia's hand, wishing for an irrational second to sprout gills and swim with her down to the ocean's deep, indigo places. Find a mermaid kingdom and hide from the world forever. The sea dragon studies us for a long moment before darting into the shadows.

Talia flicks the snorkel from her mouth. "Oh my God." Her eyes are almost as wide as her smile. "That was incredible. Mystical almost."

"Magic." I stroke closer to her, closing our distance, unable to resist her happy glow. Talia's hair plasters to her cheeks; she's enchanting, a sea witch who's cast a spell on me. Her back hits one of the pilings, and we're beneath the pier, shielded from the tourists promenading overhead, with dragons lurking beneath our fins. I kiss her hard, openmouthed, and don't hold back the groan when her tongue flicks over mine, still a little shy.

I drop my hands below her arms to brace her, keep her well

above the low sets gently rolling by to crash onshore. She wiggles closer and I silently curse our wet suits keeping us from true skin-to-skin contact. Talia's bikini is skimpy and black, exactly how I like a girl's suit. I'd love to pull the string in the back, watch as the top slowly slides off. Since the three-inch neoprene renders that fantasy impossible, I use my mouth to cover every inch of her exposed neck, her high cheekbones, her brow, each of the six freckles dappling the tip of her nose.

"Am I your girlfriend?" Talia sounds offhand, but her eyes tell me she's dead serious.

"Girlfriend?" The word sends a jolt down my spine. "Well…you're a girl and a friend."

"So, no, then?" Her smile vanishes. "I mean, are we seeing each other, seeing other people?"

"Do you want to see other people?"

And if so, who? Tell me so I can beat the shit out of them if they look at you sideways.

"Do you?" Her downturned lips twitch in the corner. She struggles to smile, and to watch that effort makes me feel helpless. I don't want to expose myself, but fuck if I'll hurt her.

"Since I've seen you, Talia"—I pause, clearing my throat—"it's been pretty fucking impossible to see anyone else."

Her fingers thread my hair, bringing my mouth close to hers. "So why do you do this?"

"I love kissing you."

"Me too." She continues to speak through more kisses. "But I mean you keep away, push me back, and then out of the blue act like you want to eat me. It's confusing."

I flinch, force myself to stare right in her dilated pupils. "Not going to lie, Talia. I want you every way you have to give."

"So why the distance, the hot and cold?"

"It's where I'm at right now. I'm trying to figure my shit out, but it's knotted and going to take time. I don't want to use you."

She lowers her lashes. "What if I want to be used?"

Fucking hell.

I do this thing with my mouth on her ear that she loves. "When you talk like that, Captain, you're asking for trouble."

"Your kind of trouble doesn't sound too bad."

How long would it take to strip us from our wet suits, fuck her hard and frantic, the exact way my dick is demanding?

Instead I drop my hand between her legs. With the thick fabric between us, I'm not sure how this will go, but if her ache is anything like mine, we'll do all right. From the way her neck falls back, revealing her tanned throat, and the rapidly pulsing vein, her need is bad.

I rub her, kiss her in the way I don't have words for, and soon her breath is quick, cute, and she's beating me on the chest.

"Stop, stop."

I halt. "What's wrong?"

She takes a gulp of air. "You act like coming is such a big deal. I wanted you to stop. See how it made me feel."

"And…"

Her laugh is shaky. "It sucks. The worst thing ever."

I put my hand back on her and she screws her eyes, grabs my neck, and hangs tight while I take her exactly where she wants to go, where I long to be, if I can gather my courage to take the ride.

18

TALIA

J'm late to meet Bran for coffee at the Sunday market at Abbotsford Convent, a converted nunnery renovated into an arts and cultural space. Since Easter break, we've hung out every day. We've also reached an unspoken agreement to avoid the Bean Counter, although Bella's moved on, now dating a bike messenger. Even with that development, we typically meet here, in my bare little room, mostly because I don't have half-naked bouncers stoned on the sofa at any given hour. We kiss, wander each other's bodies, but always pull back.

Or rather, he pulls back.

I don't know why, but sleeping with me doesn't seem high on his list of priorities. He says he's got stuff to figure out, but what if he doesn't want me as bad? I have no option except to break out Leora night after night. Even my faithful vibrating friend does little to soothe the leg-humping monkey inside. I crave this guy like a drug.

My phone buzzes. It's him. The message is typical and to the point.

?

Sorry, on my way! Looking for my wallet.

My computer dings. Crap. Mom's calling on Skype. Impeccable timing as always.

I toy with the idea of ignoring her, except I've avoided direct contact for a few weeks and that runs the risk of the police showing up at my door to excavate my mummified corpse. Mom can front like she's chillax all she wants, but I know the real truth.

Deep down, we're both anxious disasters.

I click the red answer button. "Hey, Mom."

"Oh, look, you're actually there. Aloha." Her image comes online. Whoa, my stomach drops at her weight loss. Her cheekbones are oversharp, her smile brittle. She must weigh a hundred pounds dripping wet. She's still beautiful, but a wraith. What the hell is going on over there?

She leans in close. "Can you see me?"

"Yes." *More than I want.* I twist my hands on my lap. Exhale. I can only control what I can control. And right now, that's my next breath.

The showy white flower tucked behind her left ear doesn't distract from bruised purple half moons under her eyes. She's visibly exhausted.

"Talia!" Her nose practically touches the screen. "What are you doing with your hair now?"

"You likey?" I rumple my locks. Marti recently added a few auburn streaks.

"It's different." She takes a slow sip from her ever-present teacup. Nope, she doesn't likey.

I pray for patience. "So, how's it going? What are you up to?"

"I'm just back from Logan's. He made lunch after Tai Chi."

Actual food food or a big, tasty bowl of tropical air?

"How's Australia?" she asks.

"Good. Great." Where to start—school? The weather? Marti? Definitely not Bran—that's no-go TMI territory.

"Okay, terrific. Super." She plucks a split end.

"Yeah." Guess I don't have to start anywhere. She doesn't care about my life. What I'm doing here. She probably has "Contact sole surviving offspring" penciled in between Reiki appointments and ecstatic dance class.

Mom deludes herself into believing she can transcend grief. She doesn't want to get her hands dirty rifling through the pain and pointlessness of Pippa's death. Let her ramble about personal journeys and the universal law of attraction until her tongue snaps off. It won't change the fundamental truth.

We're all going to die at some point. The end. It's that terrifyingly simple.

"I'm baking my pineapple upside-down cake this afternoon for Logan. His birthday is tomorrow."

But will you eat it? That's what I want to ask, instead I say, "How old's he turning?"

Does the Wunderchimp know she'll puke up every bite? I used to hear her in the bathroom, making herself vomit, even as she ran the water to mask the retches. She's clearly not given up that crap given that she looks like a rainbow ghost in her flowing Indian cotton and fresh-cut flowers.

I want to tell her it's okay to talk to me, that she can open up, I'll be there. But I've never been her preferred confidante; that was always part of Pippa's job description.

Does Logan notice Mom's weight or does he only see an attractive, wealthy older woman? This relationship is failing to nourish her on so many levels. Shit. I don't want to worry about her. Dad beat his head against that wall for years and look where it got him.

He treated her like a queen and she left him like he was nothing more than a court jester.

She's a taker and I don't have much to offer.

And she still hasn't answered my question.

"Mom? How old is Logan?"

"Oh, yes, sorry." She takes another sip from her cup and coughs into her fist. "Twenty-eight."

If my eyes open any wider, I won't have a face. Mom's forty-seven. "Holy shit, what? I had no idea. You're a cougar." Christ, Logan is closer, much closer, to my age.

"Language, Natalia."

"I had no idea he was a manboy—"

"Don't be cruel. I see you haven't grown or branched out into acceptance as much as I hoped. Careful, you don't want to become stunted." Her frown lines are well grooved. She's turning on that quietly dignified martyred angle. The one that always brought Dad to his knees.

Stunted? I grit my teeth. The bitch. Cruel is leaving Dad and me. We needed her and she tossed us out like end-of-a-winter-cold Kleenex.

Mom loves me. At least, in theory. But there's a disconnect between us, like a stick that's snapped and won't refit no matter how much we maneuver the two broken pieces. As much as she and Pippa looked alike, I inherited her anxious nature. I might not be a borderline anorexic, but I have a hard time losing control and deal badly with uncertainty.

Screw it. This is my mother. I owe it to her to say something, even if it's uncomfortable. I tense my calves, nearly to the point of a charley horse. This is a yellow-light situation, time to enact extreme caution; otherwise she'll blow me off or take offense and shut down.

"Mom—"

"Anyway, I've been thinking about this little adventure of yours. It sounds perfect."

"Isn't that what you're doing in Hawaii?" I regret the words as soon as they leave my mouth. I'm meant to be taking the high road here, but it looks like a landslide of resentment blocks the way.

Her smile fades. "Kauai isn't an adventure, Talia. It's healing."

"Oh, right." Healing. She hides behind that word so that I'm unable to call her out on her bullshit. If she's healing, why does she look like she's disappearing? The thought turns my stomach to bitter sludge. The picture in my head of Pippa diminishing in the hospital is replaced by my mother dying in slow inches, only she's doing it on a tropical island paradise in the company of a man who preaches health and wellness but allows her to wither because at the end of the day he doesn't care.

"Logan and I are coming to Australia."

A stinging burn radiates across my chest. "Come again?"

"There's a spirituality retreat being held in Byron Bay, north of Sydney, in a few weeks, exploring past and future lives."

"You? Will be here? In Australia?" A bolder dislodges from the landslide, rolls in my direction while I yell, *"Noooooooooo!"* in slow motion.

"We both could use a getaway. Logan's been wrestling with a lot of stress regarding his new book, and I know a change of place will be exactly what we need to rekindle the spark."

"Guess the grass isn't always greener in Kauai?"

"Don't you want to see me?"

I honestly don't know the answer to that. "You've surprised me, that's for sure. I mean—I'm kind of doing my own thing here." I want to help Mom, but I am barely getting it together myself. What if she knocks me off this fragile foothold I've gained?

"Byron Bay isn't anywhere near Melbourne. I had thought we'd come for a quick visit, of course, but if you'd rather be Little Miss Independent—"

"For fuck's sake, Mom, come on, I'm not six years old."

"Your behavior is not reflecting that fact."

"I'd like to see you." I speak from behind my hand as if my body wants to catch the lie. Telling the truth isn't an option. And as satisfying as a temper tantrum would be, Mom's paying for me to be here, so I literally owe her.

"Really, I'd love to see you," I repeat, upping the ante a little. Because she doesn't appear convinced. "Send me your trip details and we can make a plan. I'll play tour guide. Melbourne's a cool city, lots to do." I'm already strategizing the best way to keep Bran from Mom's path. He's *mine*. Overwhelming possession charges through me. I don't want to listen to her pass sweeping opinions on his character—which she will—or dare to ever compare him to perfect Tanner, the perfect bookend to perfect Pippa.

Bran's not perfect. Neither am I. And maybe that's fine.

Maybe that's better than fine. We're perfect only for the other.

"I need to get a move on. You've got things to do and I'm late to meet a friend. I'm excited to see you...super stoked." At least I manage to sound more enthusiastic than a water buffalo dying in quicksand.

"All right." Her voice is thick. I wonder if that's actually tea in her fancy cup. "Love you, Ladybug." Confirmation. She only busts out the nickname when she straddles the wobbly line between tipsy and drunk. Once she crosses the threshold, she quickly grows less affectionate, more biting.

"Yeah, Mom. Me too. See ya." *Or what's left of you if you keep this up.* I sign off. Within seconds I'm in my top drawer popping supplements like candy—vitamin B, vitamin C, vitamins D and E. I'm consuming the whole frigging alphabet.

I don't know if they make a difference, but my nerves are red-hot, fried from the cortisol that exploded from my brain during the conversation.

"Let it go, let it go, let it go," I chant under my breath. If Mom can trigger me this hard from the computer, what's going to happen when we're in the same room?

I tap my fingers in my special rhythm until things feel better—barely—but I'll take what I can get. Across the room, my wallet peeks from under my pillow. No idea how it got there. I toss it into my bag along with sunscreen and lip gloss.

I recheck the electrical sockets, nothing plugged in. I'm almost out the door, but my feet won't budge. I need to tap one more time. Then I can go, which I do, fast, like pitchfork-wielding demons give chase.

As I fly down the hall, toward the elevator, I pass Marti's room. A heavy guitar riff slides through the door, along with the lyrics.

"When the world is gone, all you need to do is set yourself alight."

Another girl waits by the elevator. She notes my breathlessness and gives me a strange look. "Going up or down?" she asks, fingers hovering over the button.

"Down," I answer, breathless. Right now I'm definitely going down.

———

"Hey, hey, pretty lady." Bran covers my eyes from behind and my grin is unforced.

"Hey, yourself." He's got a cap squashed low on his head and his hair wings out beneath his ears. I smile and he smiles and for a second that's all that exists.

It's like I'm a regular girl again, not a freak who barely escaped her room.

"What's up?" He links his fingers with mine, pulls me close.

"Nothing."

"Such a pretty liar." His grip tightens as his eyes rove my face, assessing. "Come on, let's walk a bit."

I'm grateful he doesn't push.

"Is this okay?" He swings my arm. "Holding hands?"

"I don't think we're breaking any public indecency violations," I say with a little laugh.

"I'm conducting an experiment."

"With me as a lab rat?"

"A very cute one." Bran leans in, kisses me behind the ear, and whispers, "I'm testing the theory I can be a better person."

"And holding hands will help you get there?"

"Holding hands with you might."

He stabs me in the heart and the pain is addictively sweet. For a second he does it, he lets me in and I'm like a kid balancing a three-scoop ice-cream cone, wanting to savor every drop.

We pass other people, families with kids, old couples shuffling, skinny guys on bikes, pretty girls in spaghetti-strapped sundresses. But they all look like an old-fashioned moving picture. Even though the sun is bright, they are sepia-toned. Only Bran is in color and I float beside him. I'm soaring to the sun.

"I'm leaving town next week."

I am Icarus. I crash to the ground.

"Oh."

He stops and turns me toward him. "Not for good. Jesus, you should see the look on your face."

I clasp my free hand to my cheek.

"I'd be flattered at your reaction, except you look like I drop-kicked your puppy."

"I'm startled, that's all. Where are you headed?" Does that sound casual enough?

"Tassie." He notes my blank look. "Tasmania, remember? Interviewing in person for my program so I can convince my old supervisor for a second chance. Also, I want reassurances I can roll my honors research into a PhD. On the academic food chain I'm somewhere between an amoeba and a protozoa, so I need to be pro-active. Want to come?"

I stand there, speechless. Did I hear him right? No, probably not.

"Hey, don't get too excited." His smile is a little uncertain.

"I'm not sure what you mean."

"Want to come see Tassie? It's an amazing place."

"Go? With you? Like on a road trip?" I slam my mouth shut before this turns into a game of twenty questions.

"I know it's out of the blue and you're in school. I'm not trying to force anything. I need to go down there and thought you might want to tag along. See some things. You've barely gotten out of Melbourne."

"School keeps me busy." I shrug.

"Or is it an excuse to play things safe?" he says after a pause.

He sees too much, this guy.

"Relax, Captain. No need to be a wombat in headlights. Don't overthink."

"That's not really possible." I fold my hands to keep them from shaking.

"We can take my car on the ferry, sail overnight, and drive down the heart of the island. Hobart's good—a pretty city. A history buff like you should be in heaven. It was a penal colony once upon a time and lots of the old buildings are still in good shape."

"Where would we stay?"

"My uncle lives there, in an old whaler's cottage in Battery Point. Chris is a trip. It'd be fun to have some time with you before..." He trails off, tucks a strand of hair behind my ear.

"Before I go home." Not long until my trip's expiry date.

"You'll miss a week of school, but I promise to show you some amazing places. We're talking ten out of ten here."

"Hmmm." My grades are better than good. There are no big assignments due next week, nothing in the pipeline that I don't have a handle on.

"Hmmm, is that a yes or no?"

"I'm considering."

"Okay, I'll give you some time to decide." He steps half a foot away, circles me twice before grabbing my waist from behind. "So?" His excitement is contagious.

"Impatient much?" I laugh.

"When it comes to you, apparently yes."

My stomach flip-flops. Like I'd ever say no. "Yeah. All right. Yes. I'll commit right here, right now. Why not?"

"For real?" He pulls me close and his mouth is warm. Our noses touch and I tilt my head back to deepen the kiss. His hands slot into my jeans' pockets. He draws me closer and my body locks into his like a jigsaw puzzle.

I like this: kissing him, talking with him, seeing him. I like it more than anything I've ever known. But neither of us has mentioned the big issue looming ahead in the not-too-distant future. That I'm leaving Australia soon. I know that's what Bran was trying to say, that Tasmania was a chance for us to have an adventure before I go.

Before I never see him again.

19

BRAN

I steer the Kingswood into the Port Melbourne docklands. A long line of cars wait to board the *Spirit of Tasmania*, the white ferry docked ahead.

"So we sail overnight, and the drive will take three hours in the morning?" Talia likes to keep a handle on things. Earlier, I gave her a Tasmanian road atlas that she hugged like a kid with a shiny new bike.

"Pretty much." A night at sea alone with her. I drum my fingers on the wheel to beat out my nervous energy—hah, like that'll happen. What am I doing here, with her? Is this plan going to blow up in my face?

See, everyone has a number. For one person it might be a hundred. For another it could be zero. Mine hits close to the median of those two points. Talia is a one. She's slept with a single guy, her dead sister's boyfriend and that wanker blew it—left her gun-shy.

She's better off never knowing the specifics of my miserable history. What if she doesn't understand that these weren't chest-beating conquests but acts of fucking cowardice?

She twists her pretty mouth, deep in thought, and my stomach responds in kind. What's she doing here, with me? I haven't earned enough karma to have a girl like her in my life.

"Doesn't it take like an hour to fly to Hobart?" she asks.

"More or less." Should have figured Talia would point out the obvious.

"I mean, don't get me wrong." She speaks fast, like she doesn't want to cause offense. "I'm really excited about the boat."

"I don't do planes." I wait, because here's a girl who won't ignore informational scraps.

"Like...ever?" Her shoulders cave.

"No." I guess her thoughts—she lives an ocean away. Unless I plan on chartering the *Black Pearl*, this presents us with a serious obstacle.

"What happened? A screaming baby break your will to live during a long haul?"

Her nonchalant giggle doesn't fool me. Better give it to her straight. "Engine failure over the Indian Ocean on a flight home from Europe last year."

"What?" Her eyebrows almost reach her hairline. "Are you joking?"

"Made an emergency landing in East Timor." It's like I'm blasted with full-force air-conditioning. I hate talking about this.

"Wait, hang on—you said last year? Holy shit, you were on *that* plane. It was all over the news." She snaps her fingers. "The Miracle Flight, that's what they called it."

I hate the nickname too. "The people who write headlines are hardly poets."

"The engines malfunctioned. You were minutes from crashing, had to coast in for miles."

"Yes, and yes."

"Whoa. Surviving—did it change you?" She stares at me like

I'm some sort of hero. As if anyone besides the captain on that plane actually performed something noteworthy.

"I don't believe in signs, but if I did, I'd say the universe advised me to rein it the fuck in."

"Rein what in?"

"Hope, mainly." The ferry doors open like a hungry mouth. Cars start to creep forward and I give the Kingswood a little gas.

"That's morbid." She frowns.

Why can't I just feed her a fairy tale? How facing death and surviving changes a person, makes everything that matters crisp and focused.

Because that's a bunch of crap. At least in my case. Tension knots my lower back.

"You want to know the truth? Morbid is watching strangers face death. A mom being brave for her two kids. An old woman huddled over a rosary. A couple, probably coming back from their honeymoon, loving on each other. A flight attendant, strapped in the jump seat across from me, staring out the window and crying."

"What about you?"

I flinch. "What about me?"

"There you were, at the moment of imminent death, what thoughts went through your head?" She looks at me like I'm in possession of some big answer. I could lie to her. Maybe I should.

But I don't. She deserves the truth, even if it carries the weight of my darkness.

"I thought about praying, which is something I don't do—ever—but—"

"Seems like an excellent time to start."

"Exactly. But I didn't. Because no god caused our plane to fail or guided us to land. We got lucky. That happens sometimes. And every now and then it's the opposite. All chance, no fate. I sat in my seat. That's it. I just sat and waited to see which way the coin toss would go."

"So no more flying, at all, ever?"

"I prefer control when possible."

"What if the ship sinks? Or you trip on the deck?" She points at the rail high above our heads. "What if you fall overboard? When you think about it—which I try hard not to do—potential disasters lurk everywhere. A minute ago you made control seem like an illusion."

"I can control the decision of whether or not to board a plane."

"But isn't life a game of chance?"

"Look, when it comes to air travel, I prefer not to flip the fucking coin." My words come out sharper than anticipated. Talia doesn't appear offended. Instead, she gives me this thoughtful look.

"What?"

She blinks slowly. "Nothing," she says in a tone that can be interpreted any one of a thousand ways.

I let the topic drop. Unlike some of the other media-hungry passengers, I had no interest in profiting from the Miracle Flight limelight. Parading around talk shows and taking part in weepy interviews sounded like water torture. Shit happens, you move on.

We park the car and join the wave of passengers streaming upstairs to fill the vast windowless cave at the ship's front, outfitted with stadium-style seating.

Talia turns to follow them.

"We go this way," she says, resisting my gentle tug in the opposite direction.

"No, we don't." My planned surprise is going to be muted after the conversation about that fucking plane.

"But—"

"I got us a cabin, Captain."

"A…wait…" Her head comes up. "We're sleeping together?"

My heart quickens as we walk down the narrow corridor. I know what she's really asking—*sleeping* together, or sleeping *together*?

Her breath's unsteadiness rolls me like the ferry's rocked by a storm, rather than docked at port.

How does she walk into the world every day, scared as hell, and not only survive, but also succeed, witty and cute as hell? All I do is sulk around with my black thoughts, replaying a life long lost. This cheeky American with the sad brown eyes has a warrior heart. And maybe it's selfish, but I want to get as close to that, to her, as possible.

"Room two-two-six." I tug the paper scrap from my pocket and recheck the details. "This is us, right here." I open the door.

The cabin is tight, two twin beds. I set our bags on the small table beneath the porthole. Talia puts her hand on my shoulder and leans forward, peering at the shipping cranes and cargo vessels spreading along the bank of Port Phillip Bay. Her body carries a faint vanilla sweetness, the scent warm and reassuring.

I check myself against a mounting anticipation. This girl is like Christmas Eve. I want to open her so bad. Except I'm afraid—what if this moment doesn't live up to whatever expectations we've set?

"Talia." My command is quiet. So low, I'm unsure whether I'll have to say it again. Which would lessen the impact. Finally, she turns.

Her gaze starts at my shoes and ends at my face. Her eyes are gentle, yet so sharp they flay my defenses and carve straight to my bones. "Are we going to the ship's bow to reenact the Rose and Jack scene from *Titanic*?"

Sometimes I don't have a clue what she's talking about. But she looks adorable saying it.

"Come on." She notes my blank stare. "*Titanic*? King of the World?"

"No." I trace her jaw. She's not a girl that I want to take from. She's not a girl I ever want to let go.

Her pupils swallow up her irises. "What are we going to do?"

"What I wanted from the moment I saw you in that white dress on the corner of Lygon Street."

The two furrowed lines between her brows make an appearance.

"Talia—stop, just feel, be here with me."

"Why, why now, after all this time, do you want to do this?"

"Have sex with you?"

She jolts at the word.

Yes, I'm dodging, answering her questions with a question.

"Talia, no more thinking. Sometimes it's better to just roll with this sort of thing."

She gives me a half smile, her eyes questioning. "Okay."

Wait—that was enough of an explanation to satisfy her? I'm not sure what I'm spouting off. All I know is that I made up my mind to go for it, for her, to take this all the way. Maybe I should hit the brakes, but I'm careening forward.

"I...God, I'm awkward," she stutters. "I don't know what to do next. How to start."

"What do you want to do?" I'm fiercely curious. I have no idea what she'll say next. With Talia it could be anything.

She watches me in silence, considering.

"Take off your shirt," she says at last.

I don't let myself smile, don't want her to think I'm laughing.

I seize my T-shirt by the back of the neck and tear it off, tossing it over my shoulder.

Her face doesn't change expression. She's serious, all business.

"Shoes."

I kick off my shoes. "Socks, too, I suppose."

She gives a single nod. Her face is a mask, for once revealing no hint to her inner workings.

Fuck. Come on, Talia. I'm not made of stone.

She unhooks my belt with one finger and pops open my button. My flesh prickles. I'm hard before she tugs down my pants and boxers.

I close my eyes, chew the inside of my lower lip, and anticipate the feel of her hand closing over my shaft. Instead, nothing. I'm about to open my eyes when I feel the brush of her lips on my lids. She kisses one, than the other, the tip of my nose, and both my cheeks. She's not touching me at all except with those few inches of her beautiful mouth. Her gentleness undoes me. She's...she's not using me. I'm no conquest, but something to cherish. I've had girls swallow me to the hilt and felt less than I do in this very second.

"Talia." This is verging on too much. Her lips brush mine and I slide my hands to the flare of her hips.

"No," she murmurs. "Don't touch me. Not yet."

I ball my hands into two fists. "A terrible idea, Captain."

"Really?" She nibbles the side of my neck, down across my chest. "This is terrible?" Her clever tongue circles my nipple and when my moan comes, it's pulled straight from my soul.

"I'll so make you pay for this," I rasp.

Her lips crook in the corners. "I'm kinda counting on it."

She does something with her fingers on my stomach. My seduction plan's unraveling; I'm losing control. And so much for my noble holding-back bullshit because I'm about to come quicker than a fourteen-year-old boy with a smuggled swimsuit catalog.

My balls tighten. Urgent pressure spreads from the base of my dick through my lower belly. Want. Her. Want. Her.

No, shit, summon restraint. I'm more turned on than I can

ever remember being in my life. She skims my shaft. Not even with HER—with Adie—did I ever reach this point so fast.

Okay, mate. Cool the fuck down or you're going to blow this moment—right into Talia's hand.

I jerk my hips back and use the awkward second where she's fumbling with empty air to seize her wrists.

She licks her lips. "Did you…was it…should I do something differen—"

I silence her with my mouth, drive through her insecurities with my tongue. I walk us toward one of the beds and my dick bores into her belly, helpfully leading the way. The problem with Talia is that even kissing her borders on too good. She makes these beautiful breathy sounds and when her thighs press mine, they're quaking.

I drop my head to mouth her breast through her shirt and her gasps are replaced by a groan.

She tugs her hands free from my grasp when the back of her knees knock against the berth. I pull back and see her frantically trying to undo her pants. Her fingers tremble. The sight hits me in the dick like a hot wave of lust. I'm about to offer my assistance when she grinds down the zipper.

"Do you have a condom?" A single lock of hair falls across her forehead and she tosses her head.

"Yeah, hang on." I step toward my discarded jeans and use the measure of distance to draw a deep breath. My wanting burns bright and clear, a flame that draws every ounce of oxygen from my lungs. I dig my wallet from my back pocket, pull out the condom, and tear the foil. The ripping sound makes me sad.

The first time. It never gets better.

This is the moment I've chased all year. The point where addictive lust peaks, the time when everything, for a few perfect seconds, gleams with possibility. A person can believe broken hearts can be snapped back together like Lego blocks in such a place. I love every girl in that white-hot flash. It's in the seconds after, when the heat ebbs and reality sets in that I'm reminded love and lust are different.

And I become guilty. And ornery. But I do it again and again because I'm a junkie to those seconds before, the seconds of possibility.

I roll on the condom and squeeze the tip. I'm an asshole. I tried to resist Talia, I did. But it's like trying to ignore a block of chocolate on the counter day after day. Eventually, you need a fucking taste. I drop between her legs. Bloody hell. She's so wet, tangy and responsive. It breaks my heart a little because she's giving me everything. And I'm going to take it like a greedy asshole.

She trembles, close to undone. I'm on the edge. This is about to tumble to a pitifully quick conclusion. I jerk my head free and rise to my knees.

Her gaze levels on my dick. For a second, insecurity flickers... does she want me as bad as I want—

"Come here." Her eyes are veiled.

"Sure?"

"I'm never sure about anything, Bran," she whispers.

My heart plummets.

"But I know I need you inside me, now."

Before she can change her mind, I crawl on top and brace her hips. My dick nudges against her center. This is it. I kiss her so hard our teeth knock. *I'm sorry*, I want to say as I push deeper. *I'm sorry to do this.* The tightness yields more tightness.

"Oh, whoa. Oh God." She's all wide-eyed wonder, her pretty face framed between my braced forearms. She looks all the way to the stalagmites of my ruined soul.

"Bran."

I rock to distract her, but she doesn't break her gaze. I angle my strokes to hit her where it's good. If I'm going to do this, then I'm going to make her feel pleasure. I grind harder. Still, she keeps looking, and who the fuck knows what she sees.

We go on, riding the build, and this feels so fucking right that maybe I should stop, throw out another bullshit excuse to pull back because I'm never going to regain this moment of possibility.

Instead, I drive faster, my greedy body starved for more. She lets out a raw groan, beyond inhibitions. She's going over and I'd be an ass not to take her all the way. Frustration rips a louder growl propelled from deep within my own ribs. The hell if I'll fail her. I thumb her clit and her lips part, but no sound comes.

This instant is exquisite. Don't want it to ever end.

I kiss Talia again, this time full, wet, and openmouthed, and she starts falling. Powerful waves clamp my shaft, dragging me with her.

Fuck.

Oh, fuck.

God.

Talia.

Holy fucking shit.

"Bran?"

I blink. That's my name, right? I blink again. Talia is beneath me, brows knit in concern.

"Bran, I'm serious, are you okay?"

Am I? Am I okay?

"You blacked out for a second or something. You've been staring but not ... you know ... seeing."

Oh, I saw you, Talia.

I start to laugh from relief, from sheer disbelief, and her features wilt.

"You can't laugh when you're still inside me."

Shit, she looks hurt.

I shake my head before kissing her forehead. "I'm not laughing at you. Really. It's just that—"

"You better make this good."

"Such is life," I whisper, rolling onto my hip, careful to keep inside her. I can't bear to sever the connection. Not yet. I clasp her tight against my chest.

"Such is life?" she echoes, her eyes a question.

There's nothing more to say. All I can do is be here, with her, in this place of quiet touch and soft kisses. If someone looked inside my skull, all they'd see would be blue sky, clouds, and courage.

I'd never have believed it. For the first time in a year, I had sex and not only did regret fail to materialize, but I also exploded into an alternate universe populated by unicorns and fucking butterflies. Whatever just happened was good—better than good—a revelation. And I want to do it again. With her. Only her.

After a few more seconds, I slide free with a pang. Roll off the condom. There's a whole box in my backpack—now it doesn't seem like enough.

She crawls under the blanket and hikes the sheet to her chin. "Bran, sorry, but you keep looking at me strangely."

Is sex with Talia always going to be like this? Or was this a one-off fluke, an outlier?

I'm a scientist at heart. The only way to make new discoveries is to test the hypothesis—repeatedly.

20

TALIA

M ust. Stop," Bran mumbles even as he pushes back inside me.

"Just. One. More. Time," I say, not bothering to open my eyes. I wonder if maybe this is the proverbial straw, that this fourth time will break the camel's back, or at least my va-jay-jay. Possibly there is too much of a good thing and this is a twentysomething version of gorging on Halloween candy. Nothing good can come of it.

He rocks against me and I don't care if this is the sexual equivalent of devouring twelve candy bars in a sitting. His hand dips between my legs, his circling fingers matching his rhythm, and I cry out. Maybe I'll regret this in the morning. Go down in a sugar-rush ball of flames.

But maybe, just maybe, it'll be awesome.

Afterward, we lay in stillness. I haven't cuddled much with guys, but whenever I had, I always liked the cozy protective feeling spooning provides. With Bran, we sleep nose to nose, holding hands. Somehow that's even more intimate and makes me feel like we're two children in a fairy tale. Like Hansel and Gretel while the big bad witch, or in our case, world, lurks beyond our cage.

Except we're not brother and sister, so I'll keep that creepy analogy to myself.

The next thing I know, it's morning. Did last night really happen? Things we did, Jesus, how we moved—I'm going to keep my eyes closed a little longer.

The way he breathes, I don't know him well enough to decipher if that's sleep breathing or if he's awake. He says nothing. Finally I can't take the suspense and peek out one eye.

"Hey, you." Bran's grin is as goofy as my answering smile feels.

Maybe I'm not alone in this. Maybe he feels the same way as me. Like a wrecking ball punched a perfect hole in my chest.

Wrecking balls for everyone!

"Hey." We beam at each other until the speaker blares, ordering us to disembark. There's not much to repack, but the trip down to the car takes a while because we keep pausing to kiss.

Bran drives the Kingswood off the ferry. "Hungry?"

"Famished."

"What do you feel like, a coffee?"

"For sure, and a cinnamon roll. Maybe make that two."

He gapes at me.

"Serious. I could murder some baked goods right now."

"Right-o, to the bakery it is." He checks his phone. "There's a place ahead, here on the left." He parks in front of a shop setting up for the morning.

I unbuckle my seat belt and he sets his hand on my thigh. "No. Stay here, let me get breakfast for you."

"But—"

"I want to." He chucks me under the chin. "This is my modern-day chance to hunt you a water buffalo."

"Well, when you put it that way."

He returns a few minutes later, clasping white bags and two cups of coffee.

"That looks so unhealthy," I say, peering at the cream cheese frosting.

"Should I go somewhere else?"

"Nuh-uh." I'm already biting in, closing my eyes with pleasure. "It's like a party in my mouth."

His laughter joins with mine and we finish eating our huge breakfast in easy silence, watching cars outside the dashboard window drive around the roundabout. I can't believe my luck. Because this is luck, plain and dumb. Bran and I...something passed between us last night. It wasn't just sex. Well, it was sex—hot, hot sex—don't get me wrong. But it was more than that. I now get what it means when someone says sex changes everything. What happened between us wasn't insert part A into part B. It was like our bodies held this intense conversation.

It felt instinctive. It felt natural. And above all it felt real. Like the realest I've been in my entire life.

"Let me get that." Bran leans over to take my garbage and I touch his elbow.

He gives me a quizzical look.

"Hey."

"Hey?"

"I'm really glad I came with you." Even now, even after last night, his wicked grin makes me blush. "I meant to Tasmania, sex fiend."

"Oh, I'm the fiend, am I?" His cat eyes trail down my rumpled clothes with deliberate slowness. I could be in one of those X-ray imagers at the airport where the TSA employees can see straight through my clothes. "I seem to remember a certain someone saying, 'More, please.'"

"Hey!" I grab his hand. "You make me sound like a character in a Dickens novel."

"Captain, if there were a character like you in a Dickens novel, I'd be a literature scholar."

I draw his fingertip into my mouth. Bran's eyes intensify as he watches me sucking him. A nervous humming begins in the back of my brain. Why is this happening—this *thing*—between Bran and I? We've hung out with each other for months now, but we still barely know each other, and besides, he's withholding key information. Even now, he's failed to mention he was engaged. That he almost married someone. Married. I mean, I can't even choose my favorite song, let alone a career path, let alone committing myself forever to a person.

Bran.

My mind weighs the word, uncertain whether to file it as a prayer or a pain.

His nose is a tiny bit too big. His eyes are a little widely spaced. His bottom lip is fuller than the top. Each feature on a whole isn't perfect. But combine them together and his hotness is striking in a singular way, that is him and him alone. And when his restless energy stills, when his eyes drop their surly, protective shield, yeah...I can see why a girl would say yes to a forever with this guy.

I instinctively sense that I could delay until I was thirty or whenever it's more socially normal to meet "the one" and still be waiting for a guy like Bran. He's a once-in-a-lifetime person.

Hold up.

I blink, realizing with a stomach jolt that I'm pondering marriage in a parked car while sucking a guy's finger.

Dude, get a grip.

No telling what Bran's thinking, but it's odd he let me zone out for so long. His eyes look a little unfocused, like maybe he'd been lost in his own thoughts. Well, whatever that weird moment was, it's over.

Bran tugs his hand back and I nip his skin before his finger leaves my mouth.

"Cheeky." He smiles, but it's a little off. He doesn't look annoyed, or sad, or bored. Pensive. That's the word I'd choose if I had to decipher. "I'm going to take care of the rubbish and we'll get under way."

Hobart is at the bottom of Tasmania. The ferry docks in Davenport on the top end, so we drive the three hours on two-lane roads. Much of the way cuts through the middle of what Bran calls the Central Highlands. Wide, brown fields stretch out toward cloud-topped tiers in the distance, empty but for the occasional sheep or dead eucalyptus, white and ghostly.

We watch the stark landscape unfold like a movie while we listen to Triple J, the ubiquitous Australian alternative music station. "Are you sure your uncle is cool with me coming?" I ask after a while.

"Chris'll love you." Bran gives a quick reassuring smile, eyes still locked on the road. "I'm curious what you'll think of him."

"Is it strange, taking me to meet someone in your family?"

"Why do you say that?"

"I don't know. I can't imagine you and my mom hanging out." The idea is like mental fingernails on a chalkboard. How will Mom react if she meets Bran?

"Chris is nothing like the rest of my family. He's cool. Comfortable in his skin, so he doesn't feel the need to change you to justify himself."

"Wow, that's a profound observation."

"Heh. My sister, Gaby, she's cool too—a pain in the ass but she has a good heart. And my nieces are great. But their dad, Joe, he's a wanker."

"So you're either cool or a wanker in the Bran worldview."

"Or a fuckwit."

"Wankers and fuckwits aren't interchangeable?"

"Hell no."

"Please, enlighten me."

"A wanker is someone who knows the decisions they make are shitty. That they are going to hurt someone. And still they do it to make sure they get theirs. That's being a wanker. A fuckwit doesn't have the moral compunction. They more or less stumble through life like cattle getting herded by the media or politicians or society in general to have a certain type of life. The permanent government job. The brick house in the suburbs with the white fence. The two-point-five kids. That's a fuckwit."

"So one can be a fuckwit, a wanker, or cool?"

"There's one more."

"Oh?"

"The bastards."

"So who gets that moniker?"

"People like me."

I wait for a further explanation. Just when I think I'm going to have to get out my verbal pickax and hack away, he resumes talking.

"Someone unpleasant to be around."

"You're not unpleasant."

He arches his brow.

"All the time," I amend with a grin.

That earns a tight smile.

"Can people transfer during their life from one category to another...like being a fuckwit to cool?"

"Once a bastard, always a bastard." His sharp words cut the atmosphere.

There's suddenly less oxygen in the car. My chest hurts. "People can change."

"I'm not sure I believe that." His fingers tighten on the wheel for a split second. "But I like it that you do."

————

I didn't have any set mental image of how I imagined Bran's uncle to look, but I never expected him to be dressed as a woman of a certain age.

"Nephew." A six-foot-plus giant with an elegant gray-haired coif steps onto the doorstep to peck Bran's cheek.

"Ah, and the famous Talia," he says, beaming. Or she. I took a gender studies class last year and know identity can be fluid—or fixed. And in Chris's case, I have no idea. And was given no warning.

I shoot Bran a glare. His uncle Chris dresses in drag, fine. But seriously, isn't that something he could have mentioned beforehand, as a courtesy heads-up? Or is this some sort of bullshit test?

"Great to meet you, Chris." I remember my manners in time to shake his uncle's hand. "Bran raves about you."

"Oh, he does go on, that boy. And on and on." Chris casts a doting smile before shooing us inside the cottage. "Come in, come in."

Bran returns my crusty glare with an amused look of his own. Okay—so this is definitely some bullshit test. What the hell?

Bran Lockhart, you're right; you really are a first-order bastard.

I didn't think we had to play games anymore. My stomach hollows with gnawing disappointment.

Guess I was wrong.

21

TALIA

*C*hris wipes invisible crumbs from the granite countertop in the stylish galley kitchen. "Apologies for the mess, loves," he says, rearranging a brilliant arrangement of cut flowers in a crystal vase.

"Your home's lovely," I say in total honesty, "like a museum." He lives in a whaler's cottage built in 1868. The white bricks are covered by pink tea roses that have grown up over the windows, casting the interior rooms in a cozy romantic light.

"How kind of you to say so." Chris fixes his slanting spectacles. "I hosted a high tea for a few queens. Our friend Larry is fresh out of hospital and we wanted to welcome him home."

A few queens? Did they all look like they lived in Buckingham Palace? Chris resembles Queen Elizabeth, right down to the white gloves.

The creamy parlor walls are adorned with classic oil paintings of the Australian bush and ye olde maritime scenes. Hardwood side tables line the walls topped by sexy male nude sculptures. The effect is grandma's house with an eclectic flare.

"Cup of Lady Grey, anyone?" Uncle Chris bustles past, plumping cushions around the lounge room. "Or perhaps you'd prefer something stronger. A glass of Riesling?"

"Tea sounds wonderful," I say, ignoring Bran to take a seat on an overstuffed white couch covered in throw pillows that appear sourced from indigo kimonos.

I don't even know where to start with him. Every time we take a step forward, he shoves me away. I don't understand. Right now I'm sore between my legs, a dull ache that carries the memory of what passed between us last night, more than a few times.

What we did wasn't just sex. I'm no expert, but that can't be the norm. We didn't touch so much as we clawed into the other, getting as close as possible for two people to be, and, for a second, we really got there.

And now he's built back a wall.

Damn it.

"Dear?" Uncle Chris regards me with a concerned expression.

I didn't just say that out loud, did I?

"Your tea, dear." He passes me a delicate china cup. "And a beer for my favorite nephew."

"Your only nephew," Bran mutters.

"Tut tut, take compliments where you find them, boy." Uncle Chris settles onto a divan, demurely crossing his cream-colored heels. "Now, Talia, it's clear Bran is utterly taken by you."

"Oh, really?"

Bran takes a long pull from his beer. I aimed my voice so that Uncle Chris would think I remained cordial and polite, but Bran would never miss the undercurrent of frost.

We chat politely for another half hour. Uncle Chris is a sweetheart. By day he works as a public servant for the Department of

Transportation, but by night he writes cozy mysteries under the pen name Veronica Lane.

"Agatha Christie in drag," Chris says, dabbing his lips with a lace-trimmed handkerchief. He clearly adores Bran and draws him into conversation about his plans for study, revealing information that I'd not previously known.

Like how Bran dreams of traveling to the Antarctic. Or that he coauthored a paper for a major academic journal while still in his undergrad. Or that Chris isn't on speaking terms with Bran's father.

"Water under the bridge." Chris flicks invisible lint from his spotless skirt. "He doesn't approve of the lifestyle."

"Dad's a bastard too," Bran says, lifting his bottle in my direction.

"That's enough, Bran," Chris reprimands. "You didn't grow up in our house. Your grandfather *was* a hard-nosed bastard. He gave up on me pretty quick. Put all the hopes on your father. He was the one who had to take up footy and cricket, who was pushed into business. He had to be the first *and* second son. I left your father to shoulder a load heavier than any boy should bear."

Bran snorted.

Chris heaves a forlorn sigh. "Sometimes the lack of communication between me and my brother causes me a great deal of pain. But you can't choose your family of origin."

"Guess not," Bran mumbles, peeling the corner of his beer bottle's label.

Uncle Chris beams at Bran, then me, ignoring the two empty feet between us. Distance I put there the moment I sat down. Distance that I hope Bran notices and minds.

———

Our room is decorated like the rest of the house—Grandma's house gone wild. A zebra-striped duvet covers the elegant brass bed while a two-foot replica of *David* graces the top of the rosewood dresser. Outside the dormer window, a junior sail class is on the river, the pint-size boats jumbled together as kids try to adjust their course. Sailing away on a boat right now sounds delightful. Bran crashes onto the bed behind me with a protracted sigh. I hate having talks. Like with a passion, I hate talks.

"You should have told me."

"About what?" he mumbles, forearm flung over his eyes.

"About Chris? Might have been helpful to have some warning."

"Didn't I say something about him?"

"I'd have appreciated a little notice that he likes to dress in drag."

"Because that bothers you?"

My temper flares. "No, of course not. What's annoying is that you basically lied by omission."

"That was hardly a lie, Talia."

"What's the deal? You didn't want to give me a chance to put up my guard, so you designed some bullshit mind-fuckery to root out whether or not I'm a closeted bigot? Which I'm not, by the way. A bigot. Closeted or not. Which you would have known if you'd taken the two seconds to talk to me about it."

"It was a joke, a little messing around. I wanted to see your unfiltered reaction. I didn't think you'd get so mad."

"I'm pissed. And hurt. And irritated."

"Isn't that all mad?"

"I guess if you're a Neanderthal who registers only the most basic human emotions. Me happy. Me sad. Me hungry."

He laughs.

"I'm not trying to be funny."

"You're cute."

"I'm really not trying to be that." No way he's going to dismiss this. Or me.

"Come over here."

"Negative." I place my hands on my hips. "I don't see you and me as a game. This is about wanting a guy that I'm working hard to be straight with to give me the same common courtesy."

He loses the smile.

I need air—and a moment alone. I rummage through my bag for a pair of old yoga pants and begin to change. "I'm going out."

"Where?"

"For a jog." I shove on my running shoes and bend to tie the laces. "To clear my head."

"I'm sorry, okay? Come on, Talia."

"I'm there, Bran. Why don't you decide whether you want to be too?"

I flounce out the door, down the stairs, and into the maze of nineteenth-century streets that make up Battery Point. I count each step in batches of one hundred until I feel somewhat more in control. A pub lights up the dim street corner ahead. Perfect; I have a twenty-dollar note shoved in my sports bra. My jog's not strictly for health purposes. I mean to have a drink, of the scowly alone-at-the-bar variety. I duck inside and heads swivel in my direction. There's a group of guys clustered at the bar, all in grass-stained rugby apparel. They perk, like cheetahs catching a whiff of prey. I'm not in the mood to play gazelle, so I duck back out to the street.

I jog past sweet cottages that would be at home in a fairy tale ... until the street ends. *Damn.* But there's a stairway, with the words KELLY STEPS carved on the worn sandstone column. This seems almost too good to be true, like Hogwarts' Room of Requirement— do these stairs appear when someone needs to escape?

I sprint down and end on a narrow cobblestone street. Sail masts rise from the cove across the road, reflecting lights from the various fine dining restaurants and cafés lining the waterfront. There's another pub ahead; it appears old, like it's been here as long as Hobart itself. The wooden sign creaks in the wind. KNOPWOODS. A homey name, like where Frog and Toad might go for a pint—if one of them was annoyed at their boyfriend.

Boyfriend. Is that what Bran is? We haven't exactly had that conversation, plus I'm leaving in less than a month, so I don't even know what to call him. My lover? Ew, I'm not some seventies disco swinger. My friend? No way—he's way more than that. Fuck buddy isn't exactly socially kosher. So what is he?

I push through the front door and head for the bar.

"What'll you have, love?" A brisk, fortysomething woman waits expectantly behind the taps.

I jump at the sound of her voice. "Um, a cider, please, in a pint." Hard cider, a choice that will complete the ye olde nature of this excursion.

She sets the glass in front of me and I grab a stool. It's quiet here, a perfect place to brood and think.

"Hydrating on a run?"

Apparently quiet time isn't tolerated. I glance over, prepared to tell the conversationalist next to me to piss off—in a really polite way, of course—but the dude looks like my grandfather. Or how I wish my grandfather actually looked. My mom's dad was a Reagan

Republican with rugged yet precise haircuts and carefully pressed casual elegance. This guy looks like Jolly Saint Nicholas right down to the unlit pipe beside him. I swear his eyes twinkle in the bar light.

I glance down at my sweaty jogging clothes and shrug.

"I'll drink to that." He raises his own pint in a toast. "This is the only exercise I get up to these days. That and working my fingers to the bone on the bloody keyboard."

"You a writer?"

"Historian."

I perk, happy to find a kindred spirit. "Hey, that's my major."

"Ah, you're a student?" He eyes me with more interest.

"Well, I'm attempting to finish my bachelor's."

"Finding it a challenge?"

"At the moment, yeah, I guess so." I rock my glass between my hands.

"Wandering?"

"Come again?"

He adjusts his suit coat. "Are you a wanderer? From the sound of that accent, I'd wager you're far from home, indeed."

"I'm Californian."

"Land of sunny skies and warm water."

"That's SoCal. In my neck of the woods we've got fog and redwoods."

His smile is gentle. "Well, aren't you the lucky one?"

"I wouldn't go that far." I take a long sip.

"So tell me how a bright young American finds herself drinking alone in Hobart, Tasmania?"

Coming from another man, that might sound creepy. But this guy—I soon discover his name to be Phillip Conway—is nothing but benevolent kindness and a baffled curiosity typical to those who spend too many hours cooped up with dusty books and their own sizeable brains. After another pint, I learn he's Tasmanian to the core. His great-great-grandfather was transported to this island as a convict nearly two hundred years ago, sentenced to life for sheep stealing. I quiz him on colonial history and we're soon knee-deep in conversation about convict life, the plight of the Tasmanian Aboriginals who suffered genocide at the hands of the British settlers, and the transition of the place over time.

I check my watch and realize dinnertime has come and gone. I wonder what Bran said to explain my absence. I'm certainly not doing a great job at ingratiating myself to Chris. Still, it's cozy here in this out-of-the-way seat, listening to Phillip spin yarn after yarn.

"You're an excellent teacher," I say.

"Oh," Phillip chuckles. "I should hope so. That's what pays the bills."

"Really?"

"I'm a professor of history at the University of Tasmania."

"Dr. Conway—"

"Phillip, please. I simply cannot abide titles of any sort."

"Sorry—Phillip. Am I keeping you—do you need to be home?"

"My wife died last year—cancer."

"Oh God, I'm sorry—"

"Yes, well, I learned, sometimes death can be a blessing. I do have a daughter. She teaches in the Northern Territories. Very remote communities, challenging work."

"She must be special."

"She is. You remind me of her."

"If you don't mind, could I pick your brain a little? See, I need to come up with a senior thesis, a research project, nothing as big as a master's dissertation, but still something substantial. I'm having a total block on what to do."

"Very well, let's start by answering the most important question."

"Okay, that is..."

"What interests you? What topics grab you deep, don't let go, make your soul sing?"

After an hour, Phillip Conway has talked me through my scattered interests and helped me catalog them into one vague, but far more focused category—oral history. Specifically, female oral history.

"Well, there's a term guaranteed to send any sixteen-year-old boy into hysterics."

"What's that?" Phillip's eyes are locked on the corner of the bar's ceiling. Crap, maybe I have taken up too much of his time.

"Sorry, nothing."

"No! Not nothing. Not even close." He shakes his head, refocusing on me. "In fact, if you'd indulge me, I've just had the most interesting idea that might be to our mutual benefit."

22

TALIA

I stumble into the house as the hall clock chimes ten o' clock, my brain buzzing so loudly anyone in a five-foot radius could hear a hum emanating from my skull. I try to close the front door as quiet as possible and tiptoe toward the stairway. I'm tired, hungry, and drunker than I'd meant to get. Leave it to me to get wasted with a sixty-year-old history professor. Yeah, I'm really a prototype for *Girls Gone Wild: The Study Abroad* version.

"Evening, love."

I almost jump from my skin at Uncle Chris's soft voice. I turn to discover him illuminated by a laptop's soft light. He's in a pair of red silk pajamas. Sans wig, he resembles an elegant gentleman. The type you'd see walking a small fluffy dog, with a newspaper tucked firmly under his tweed-encased arm.

"Hey," I say, trying to focus, struggling not to appear like the wayward girlfriend who snuck away to get her drink on.

Chris holds up a small china dish heaped with chocolate cookies. "Come, sit. Enjoy a Tim Tam."

I've got no choice. To bow out would be unthinkably rude.

"Thanks." I select a cookie and take a nibble. Holy shit, my stomach cries out. Sustenance. I force myself not to cram the entire thing in my mouth. "So what are you up to?"

"Trying to hit my daily word count, love." He smiles. "The work of a writer with a day job means I only write at night."

"Sounds hard."

"My characters blather away to each other. I simply turn up and listen."

"So you hear voices in your head?"

"And get paid to record them." He selects another cookie with a boyish grin. "Isn't that marvelous?"

"A pretty good gig." Too bad my own personal brand of crazy isn't creative or lucrative. The voice in my head is nothing but my own, droning on and on about "What if this?" or "Careful, because otherwise that may mean…" Or any other variation of the same boring fear.

"I see you went out tonight." Chris's tone reveals nothing; he's a bit like his nephew in that particular mastery.

I shift in my seat, twisting a pillow tassel around my finger. "I wanted to do a little exploring."

"Brandon told me about your tiff." The open laptop casts a glow on Chris's face, his expression nothing but kind concern.

"He did?" I whisper.

"Well, no. But I heard you leave and when you didn't return for supper, questions were asked."

"You must think I'm a brat."

"Not at all." Chris passes me the dish. I nab two cookies. "Brandon's so much like his father at times."

I choke on my bite.

"Oh my, do you need a mug of warm milk, love?"

I manage to shake my head. "No. I've not heard the most flattering things about Bran's parents, that's all."

"My brother, Bryce, can be a right prig when he so chooses. Did Brandon discuss him with you?"

"Only a little. It doesn't sound like they're very close."

"They are the type of people who see the world in absolutes. True, they tend to fall on opposite sides of the coin, but they're two of the most hard-nosed people I've ever encountered. They have a devil of a time admitting wrongdoing, even when they know they are guilty of it."

"Hmmm." I make a noncommittal noise. It's all fine and good for Chris to nephew bash, but I don't want to stumble into a family drama; I've got enough of my own to worry about.

"I'm surprised he brought you here, after that muddle in Denmark."

"Yes." My foggy brain clears as a shiver spirals down my spine. Of course Chris knows about Denmark, and the girl Bran almost married when practically a zygote. "Adie Lind?"

"Such an awful muddle." Chris settles in his chair with a far-away gaze. "And the whole mess with the pregnancy—I can't blame Brandon for his foul mood this last year."

The what?

"And perhaps I shouldn't blame Adie. But Bran is my only nephew, like a son to me, truth be told, the son I never had. So I'm biased. And I do blame. I blame that girl for breaking poor Brandon's heart." He leans forward and pats my knee. "But it pleases me to no end to discover it's not broken any longer."

"The pregnancy, how hard." I grab another cookie, even though my stomach revolts at the idea of food. I don't want to end the conversation.

Talia Stolfi, you are hereby convicted of spying and being a very large hypocrite.

Bran isn't even aware I know Adie Lind's name. The only reason I'm familiar with anything regarding this mysterious story is because of that damn wedding invitation. I didn't mean to intrude, but I did, and I can't undo it. I deserve the icky uncertain guilt that settles into my gut.

But I can't budge from my seat until I hear more.

"When Adie had the abortion, I almost thought the situation would resolve itself. He was so young. They both were. But poor Brandon. He took it so very hard."

My blank face didn't tip off Chris that this story was news to me. Holy crap, Bran got a girl pregnant and proposed marriage? My stomach, already unhappy to have been force-fed alcohol for dinner, begins to knot. Sweat slicks my palms.

I will not vomit in Uncle Chris's parlor.

"I only met her the once, when I came up to watch her perform in Melbourne. She played so beautifully, first chair violinist and all. Still, Brandon gave up so much to follow her back to Denmark. Such a shame. I could see it from a mile away; she was a girl on her own path. There wasn't room for another to walk beside her. She was driven, utterly single-minded, as you have to be in the hope of advancing in a career as a professional musician. Oh, I don't doubt she cared for Bran. But he cared more. I knew that, warned him to execute caution before he quit school and followed her halfway across the world. He wouldn't have a bar of my advice. He was smitten."

He was smitten.

———

Five minutes later, I spit out my toothpaste into the narrow ceramic basin in the guest bathroom. No light seeps from under the closed door where Bran sleeps. Where I was expected to spend the night. I turn on the faucet and bend to drink directly from the tap.

Let's review the facts as I know them for the hundredth time in the last few minutes. Bran had been in love. He'd gotten a girl pregnant. He'd asked her to marry him and she said yes. She had an abortion. They broke up. This must have been when Bran flew home, had the plane malfunction, and almost died.

These are the events he'd spent the last year trying to gain distance from.

I almost don't blame him for not telling me. Almost but not quite.

I enter the room and ease myself into the bed. Bran's breaths are shallow, not the deep, rhythmic inhalations of someone fast asleep. I tug the blankets around my shoulders and he rolls away, his back a fortress wall that I've no hope of breaching.

I've ripped so many shameful secrets from my belly, held them out, covered in toxic grime for his inspection, but there's no reciprocity. I share and he holds back. This isn't how to build a stable foundation.

The brain creates new synapses every time we make a memory, but not all remain. Some dwindle to gauzy shadows where details are less distinct, feelings stronger than actual facts. Others disappear altogether, like a Chinese lantern floating into the sky, magical for a few short-lived seconds before snuffing out.

I want to extinguish my memories from last night. Those feverish hours when I burned under his hands and foolishly trusted the moment was true. I tricked myself into believing Bran did think I was different, despite the evidence built up behind him like a scandalous mountain. Someone he could trust.

Who doesn't want to be different? Be perfect to somebody? To matter?

Tears drench my cheeks, soak my neck to wet the pillow. But I don't make a single sound.

23

TALIA

*I*t's not yet light when I start awake. I know before opening my eyes that the bed is empty. There's a coldness to the
sheets that suggests this wasn't a quick trip to the bathroom or to
fetch a drink of water. Bran hasn't been beside me for a long time.

"I heard you last night." He's in the chair across the room.

"What?" I rub my eyes, gritty with sleep and dried tears.

"I waited up—decided if you weren't home by ten, I'd search for
you. Even if you were still angry, there's no way I'd leave you out there
a second longer. I was getting my shoes on when I heard the front
door open. When you didn't come straight up, I started to go down."

Oh no.

"That's when I heard Chris telling a story that wasn't his to tell.
My story."

I haul onto my elbows. "Were you ever going to share?"

"Hell, yes, I was. Soon—today even."

I want to believe him, but I'm not sure that I should or that I can.

"But you already knew, didn't you?" His voice is soft, dangerously so.

"The day we first…hooked up. At your place? Bella got to me. I wanted to go home and my phone was dead, so I went in your desk to find scratch paper so I could leave you a note to meet me later."

Bran is a statue. My only reward for divulging this story is an unfathomable stare.

"I pulled out the wedding invite from the top drawer." I swallow. Shame surrounds me like tangled sheets. "I honestly didn't set out to snoop. But I inadvertently did."

"The wedding invitation," he echoes, his voice stripped of any emotion. "*My* wedding." There it was—a hint of something approaching human feeling. Even if it is mockery.

"Yes," I whisper.

"A right fucking fairy tale that turned out to be."

"What happened?"

"Well, you already know, Captain." Dawn has arrived and the dim pink light contrasts with his bitter smile.

"I know facts without context."

He watches me like I'm an exotic fish trapped in a bowl. "And you think you deserve a neat framework, a filled-in background so that everything makes sense? Let me tell you something, life isn't a happy bedtime story."

"You don't need to tell me that," I snap, heat rising up the back of my scalp. "What I did was shitty, yes. I didn't mean to spy into your past. And I'm so sorry. I wanted to wait for you to tell yourself. But your uncle Chris started talking to me like I knew everything and—"

"There was once a kid who had everything. Went to a posh school, had loads of friends, parents who didn't hassle him and gave him money to buy whatever shit he fancied. And guess what? None of it mattered. He was a lonely bastard most of the time. Year twelve arrived and with it came a girl. On exchange from Denmark. She was gorgeous, had this sexy laugh and more talent in her little finger than most people have in their entire body. Everything she tried she was amazing at. She played violin, sang, was bloody brilliant at school."

Maybe I didn't want to hear this story after all.

"For some reason she chose me. She could have had any guy at the school. Everyone made a play. We had the year together—a single beautiful year. And I loved her. I loved her more than anyone else in my entire life. She returned home to Copenhagen and I was brokenhearted. A couple of years later she came back. She found a temporary gig with a chamber orchestra. She could have gone anywhere. New York, London, Moscow, but she came to Melbourne. Because of me. Because she couldn't forget either."

His words fall faster. "But soon after she arrived, the facts became obvious—whatever we'd once shared had shifted. She didn't want to talk about it. I didn't either. But we weren't seventeen anymore. We wanted different things. Everything fun and effortless became strained. But I didn't want to let go. This was my first love. My big love, as far as I was concerned. All I needed to do was work harder. Try more. Adie—she was more practical; she seemed to get that what we had was gone. She pulled back.

"I should have let it go. But I kept trying. And finally she told me it wasn't the same, and left. Here's where the story gets predictable and boring. The condom broke our last night together and she found out she was pregnant once home in Denmark. Sure, I could have let it go. She didn't ask anything from me. But I'm an idiot. So I called my honors supervisor two weeks before my project was set to begin and broke it off. I even raided my mom's jewelry box. Found my grandma's engagement ring and flew to Europe. I arrived at her front door and asked her to marry me in front of her entire fucking family. She said yes, but I heard the hesitation in her voice. And ignored it.

"Her dad owns a wind turbine business and he offered me an internship. I told myself it would take time for her to adjust, for me to change. We were young. Most everyone else our age was making plans to travel, or partying. Adie and I were looking at apartments and talking babies. She grew distant, more so each day. But I ignored it. Because all I had to do was try harder. Be better.

"One day I came home... she knew when to expect me. There was a strange bike by the front door. And she was on the floor, another guy's dick in her mouth—the tuba player. I was trapped in a bad movie that refused to be serious. My pregnant fiancée broke off everything for a balding tuba player. After he ran off, she confessed she had an abortion. I was gutted. I'd given everything I had and it wasn't enough. On my flight back to Australia two days later, the plane almost crashed. The universe rejected me.

"I landed a gig at the Wilderness League and found extra work tutoring environmental studies students. Started thinking about school again. But I needed to forget Adie. What her skin felt like. How she smelled. The way she looked while sleeping." He breaks off and scrubs his face. "I figured the best way to do that was to cram as many other girls between me and her memory as possible. The more it didn't work, the harder I fucking tried, and the lonelier I became. I thought she was 'the one' and that I blew my chance. And then there you were, standing above me in that little white dress. And I got it, even though I didn't want to—at least not at first."

"What?" I inch to the edge of the bed. "What did you get?"

He braces his elbows on his knees, rests his chin on clasped hands. His gaze has its own gravitational pull, sucks me into a dark orbit. "What if there are multiple 'the ones'? Who knows, Talia, maybe you're one of them."

"Wow." A string ties around my heart, cuts off circulation. "You're gifted in making a girl feel special."

"I'm not trying to feed you a line. I'm trying to tell you how my head works and where you fit into my heart. Because like it or not, you're in here now. I'm pissed as fuck, but even still all I want to do is kiss you."

I duck my head. "That's lust."

"Nah, I'm an expert in that area by now." His smile's wry. "This is more than wanting to get in your pants, trust me."

"You're not exactly charming me here."

"I'm not that kind of guy." He gets out of the chair and sits next to me. The mattress sinks under his weight, tipping me toward him. "I don't want to waste time saying things that I think you'll like. Because those might be the wrong things. And if you don't want me for me, I'd rather know straight off."

He glares, like he dares me to reject him. Like he wants me to, like maybe if I do it will be a relief. I know what he means. It's easier not to feel. To merely exist. To survive. But eventually it gets harder to breathe. To choke back the desperate longing to matter, to be noticed, to be important to somebody, to be alive.

To be perfect for someone.

Without a conscious thought, my hand rises, rests on the side of his cheek, in the way I know he loves. "You matter, Bran."

He relaxes into my palm and closes his eyes. "Why do you say that?"

"Because it's true. We're two screwed up people and still, for some reason when we are together, we're okay."

"I know, Talia. This I know."

"I should have told you that I found the invitation. I'm sorry to have snooped in your desk, even if it was an accident."

"And I'm sorry I didn't tell you about Adie. What happened. It's just—I didn't want her here, between us."

"She's not." I give him nothing but a light peck, but still he moans, tangling his fingers into my hair and easing me back against the unmade bed.

"Talia, Talia, Talia," he whispers my name between increasingly urgent kisses. "What have I ever done right to deserve you?"

There is a loud click from the clock radio and the alarm goes off, blasting the AC/DC song "You Shook Me All Night Long."

"Bloody hell." Bran throws himself at the radio. "How do you turn this thing off?"

I clap my hand over my mouth and crack up.

"Oh, you're a right help." He yanks the plug from the wall and the song cuts.

I grab a pillow and shove it over my head, convulsing.

"Get over here, troublemaker," Bran growls, seizing my hips and yanking me down. Our clothes are off in record time.

I pull back. "Where are the condoms?"

"There's one in my wallet," he says, closing his eyes tight as if he's in pain.

I move fast and within seconds I'm sliding the latex over his length, which, swear to God, looks like it's hardened even longer.

I straddle him and he curses under his breath. The details are hazy, but there's a rush of incoherent language, mostly my name. I rub myself over his shaft. I'm so wet he enters effortlessly.

I love this. Riding him—being in control. He likes it, too, from the rapid pulse in his bowed throat, thrusting his hips to meet me stroke for stroke. Our rhythm grows in force and it's good, really good, but I don't think I'm going to come. That's okay; I wanted to do this for other reasons, show myself I could take charge. My sexual inexperience doesn't have to be an ongoing liability.

"I'm close," Bran growls.

"Come." It's the only word I can muster.

"Not without you. Grind on me."

"I am."

He grabs my ass. "Use my body."

"Isn't that what I'm doing?" Hesitation and self-consciousness creep in. I am making this up as I go along. Maybe what feels super sexy and experienced to me looks like one lame amateur hour as far as Bran is concerned.

"Go for it."

"I…" I don't know what he's talking about, but I change my movement, make it shallower, lean forward enough that I put pressure on the place where it's best for me.

Oh.

I do it again to confirm the feeling.

Oh. Oh, wow.

Before it was good, hot, sexy to ride him and watch his responses. The thrumming vibrations felt full, nice, but this is Bran. I don't want nice.

I want this.

I press harder and his eyes roll back into his head.

"Fuck, yes," he says gruffly.

I start to lose myself to the grinding rhythm, chasing something elusive, just out of sight. Bran's made me come before, but always by using his hand. Or his mouth. This is the first time the sensations have ever happened from pure contact, and I'm not sure if I…

Bran tilts his hips, raises them an inch, and things go from wow to holy-shit-I-am-hovering-on-insanity quick smart.

He shudders and moans. "Talia." He sounds like he's choking, in a good way, and I know he can't hang on for much longer. And he doesn't have to because I'm there, too, and it's beautiful.

"Jesus," he says when I finally collapse, spent, on top of him.

My belly trembles in the aftershock. "Is that how makeup sex works?" I close my eyes and breathe in his hot soapy scent, our mingled sweat. Lights flash behind my lids.

He holds me against him. I want to stay like this forever. Take root in his body. "Are you still upset?" he asks into the top of my head.

"I'm lots of things."

"Me too." He carefully withdraws and unrolls the condom. "Talia..." He sounds dazed. "I think I...I am..."

I know what he wants to say. And I feel the same way.

But he doesn't say it.

And I don't either.

24

BRAN

*T*hings are coming together for a change. My honors supervisor is willing to welcome me back into her lab without a word of censure. This is despite the fact that I bailed to Europe last year with only a hurried phone call and a subsequent apologetic e-mail by way of quitting. Then, Talia drops a bombshell. The day we arrived, after I pissed her off not telling her about Chris, she'd hit it off with a history professor at Knopwoods. She'd clearly made a great impression because he offered her a project, for her senior thesis, recording the stories of Somali female refugees resettled to Tasmania. She mentioned it offhand, not giving the idea any serious attention. Despite my few efforts to talk to her about it, she brushed me off.

So I've decided to drop the subject. Focus on the present, this week, and our explorations. This is all we have before we return to Melbourne and begin the death march toward her leaving day.

A date I can't think about right now.

Not when we are arriving at the Museum of Old and New Art. The MONA cleaves into bedrock, plunging several stories below-ground where the giant, windowless rooms disorient us to time. Egyptian sarcophaguses are posed beside modern sculptures composed entirely from human hair.

One exhibit is words appearing for a second in falling water: Killing...Disorder...Beautiful...Triumphant...Unsettled.

"The piece picks up key words from the headlines," Talia murmurs. "It's supposed to reflect the transitory nature of the information age."

Is this exhibit mimicking Talia and I? A word falling in water, visible long enough for our brains to register that something amazing, life-changing even, is occurring?

What will happen if we try to catch the moment? Will it puddle into our hands, become nothing?

Maybe this time we share is enough, a fleeting and bittersweet moment.

My heart pounds as we wander to the next exhibit. Lightbulbs, hundreds of them, maybe thousands, spread along the ceiling, turning on and off in odd rhythms. I give them cursory notice and start to walk away when Talia lets out a delighted shriek.

"Wait, come back. Check this out." She wraps her hand around a lever and looks to the ceiling, her face open with pleasure.

I watch her instead.

"Not me." She gives a furtive smile, blushing in the way that spreads to other places. I'm hard in a second. "Bran, up there."

Reluctantly, I divert my gaze and watch the light in the closest bulb pulse.

"The exhibit records heartbeats," she whispers. "That one's mine. Now it's your turn."

I grab the lever and immediately the bulb lights up, her own rhythm moving down the line.

"Amazing, isn't it?" Talia murmurs. Thousands of bulbs flicker on the ceiling. "These are all people's heartbeats. Each time someone holds the lever, another pulse is added."

She turns to go when I stop her.

"Let's do one together." I'm seized with overwhelming determination.

Her wide-eyed gaze twists my guts. We both squeeze the lever and within seconds the closest bulb lights, an odd, slightly frantic pulse.

"This is ours," I say. Hope ignites in my chest, the glimmer of the craziest idea.

She laces her fingers with mine and we watch as another person walks up, grabs the lever, and our shared heartbeats move down the line.

A light that never goes out.

25
TALIA

*T*he rest of our trip passes in a lightning-quick blur. Bran is filled with manic energy. We stay busy, almost frantic, like he suddenly wants to show me everything. We watch street performers at the weekly Salamanca Market. Check out a Gypsy jazz band at a bar in North Hobart. We drive the Kingswood to Tasmania's southern tip, park in a muddy parking lot, cover ourselves in every piece of his Gore-Tex, and brave horizontal rain to gain a vantage point to see the Southern Ocean. The wild, frigid wind blows straight from Antarctica's ice lands hidden beyond the horizon. We eat kangaroo pizza on Sandy Bay beach near the University of Tasmania, and Bran secures two boards from a guy in his new lab for a full-day surf session at Clifton Beach.

Chris never mentions another word about Bran's time in Europe or Adie's pregnancy. Did he know Bran listened that night and wanted to push the issue into the open? That would be a pretty diabolical level of meddling. My feelings toward Bran stream together in a confluence of light and dark. When I'm with him, I can become incandescent, but there is no telling when a shadow might appear.

Phillip Conway e-mailed me last night, told me again how much he enjoyed meeting me and reiterated his offer for a project. Even though coming back to Australia sounds cool in theory, it's totally unrealistic. Australia is a temporary escape, not a permanent adventure. I traveled here because my life flipped upside down and I hoped that, maybe at the bottom of the world, I might discover a way to turn things around.

How stalker would I look moving here, to Hobart, the exact same town as Bran? I get that he likes me, I like him, maybe even more than like . . . but after all the drama he had last year with Adie, I doubt he's looking for a long-term serious girlfriend. If I tell Bran how much of a place he holds in my heart, he might wall me off again, and I can't face that.

We leave Hobart on a drizzling morning. Chris is dressed in a white shirt and khakis, what he calls his "civilian clothes," for his day job at the office. He won't let us leave until he's pressed two more scones into our hands—not a hardship, as these lemon poppy seed revelations practically melt in my mouth. Probably best not to ponder the amount of butter necessary to achieve this delicious feat of physics.

Bran exchanges a tight hug with his uncle and promises again to let him know the exact date he's moving to Hobart. He'll stay with Chris for a couple of weeks while he looks for his own place. I wonder if when he does, he'll lie in that bed upstairs and think about us, hum the song "You Shook Me All Night Long."

I hope so—I would.

"Good-bye, Talia." Chris presses a dry kiss on my cheek, and as I turn to the Kingswood, he mumbles something low to Bran. I glance between the men, registering the blanching on Bran's face and Chris's inscrutable expression.

So it's something about me. Good or bad, I don't know.

I wait until we get into the Kingswood.

"What did Chris say back there?"

"Nothing." Bran throws the car from first into fourth and we jerk as metal grinds on metal. He swears violently.

"It really seemed like he said something."

"This car is a piece of shit."

"You love this car."

Bran doesn't answer and we drive through the old part of the city, the streets busy with commuter traffic and school kids in their uniforms. Whatever was said, it put Bran in a mood, one I refuse to indulge.

"Why so quiet?" he asks after twenty minutes, turning onto the Central Highway.

"It's easier to throw stones at the moon than talk to you when you're like this," I say.

"Like what?"

"Are you for real? You've been a huge grump since we left Chris's place."

"Have not."

Right when I think we've reached some deeper understanding, I collide into his defenses. "Remind me where we're going again, Bullshitville?"

Bran gives me a sideways glance. "Do you want to know?"

He'd intended the last part of the trip to be a surprise. This is clearly an attempt to fly the white flag, so I've two choices here.

One: throw the effort back in his face and tell him "I don't care," or;

Two: Hike up my big-girl panties and act like an adult who wants to be in a mature relationship.

I really want to go with option one. I can taste how bad. "Yes, please. I'd love to know where we're going."

His fingers relax on the wheel. "I'm taking you up a mountain."

"A what—wait, now?"

"No, tomorrow morning. Cradle Mountain. I booked us a cabin tonight in the national park. We'll head out at first light, hike for the day, and have enough time to catch the ferry back to Melbourne tomorrow night."

"We will?"

"Sure." He side-eyes me. "Unless you hike like a snail."

"More like a slug." I'm not worried about physical exercise. I've been jogging almost every day. Not setting any Olympic records, but if I can run three miles in thirty minutes, I'm pretty sure I'll be able to manage keeping up with Bran on a trail, more or less.

That's not what worries me.

The scary part to this plan is heights. I'm not a big fan of exposure. It makes me dizzy, like the sky is burying me.

"I've wanted to go up Cradle Mountain since forever. I'm stoked." He smiles at me. "I want to share this with you."

I choke down my rising fear. "Can't wait."

"About what Chris said, before we left…" His voice trails off.

"I'm listening," I say quietly.

"He told me you fit me."

"I do?" A flush of adrenaline courses through my abdomen.

"I'm making you a promise." He pinches his top lip with his bottom teeth. "From here on out, I'm going to try to be straight with you, on everything."

"Try?" I say, noticing his gaze cloud.

"It's the best I've got to offer, and I honestly don't know if I can."
He doesn't say anything else, but when he puts his hand on my leg,
he only moves it from that point forth to switch the occasional gear.

When we arrive and I see that the place he rented is literally a
little cabin in the woods. A small kangaroo hops past the car window. "Check it out, we even have friendly woodland creatures."

Bran hefts our bags out of the car. "Let me get these inside. We
can walk down and check out the view."

The mountain currently hides from sight behind this enchanted
forest. Driving into the park, I glimpsed the steep peak. Still, not
exactly Everest. The Tasmanian guidebook doesn't give more than
a cursory idea of the trail conditions, and the lack of information
kind of freaks me out. Okay, it totally freaks me out.

———

A hike to the top of Cradle Mountain seems a fun, if scary idea
until we're here, signing our names into the trailhead logbook. The
mountain looms like two stony fangs and I'm tempted to address it
gladiator-style, *We who are about to die salute you.*

I weigh up suggesting an alternative plan, maybe a leisurely
stroll around Dove Lake, where the water ripples in the light morning breeze. Yes, an easy wander to an out-of-the-way corner in the
park where we can make love among the boulders, lichen, and pen-
cil pines. I open my mouth to suggest the idea—

"This is gonna be great." Bran tightens his backpack straps. His
eyes are bright with excitement and there's no choice. In for a penny,
in for a pound, as my dad says.

"Yeah, great. Awesome. Can't wait to get all over that."

Bran tears up the boardwalk, blissfully oblivious to my misgiv-
ings. I'm in. All in. And need to keep my fear of heights to myself.

What if there's exposed rock scrambling? I should have poured over the trail map last night in the cabin. Why oh why didn't I? That's right—because we were too busy mating like Viagra-addicted rabbits.

I bend down to tighten my laces one last time. Bran checks back and gives me a cheerful thumbs-up.

"Be right there," I call with forced enthusiasm. Bran is usually perceptive. He's either ignoring my fear or more likely hyped up with mountain fever.

I trot to his heels and we clamber scree slopes to where a bolted metal cord helps steady my balance. Bran plows on without a hand to any rock. *O-kay, Mr. Mountain Goat.* We reach a plateau; Cradle Mountain's peak is still far ahead. We follow a twisting path through a scrubby forest; pandanus trees grow over our heads in wild green tufts like something from a Dr. Seuss book.

Tussock grass sprouts along the rocky track. Every shadow seems to slant into the wiry black body of a poisonous snake. Australia is famous for deadly creatures and so far I've not glimpsed a single scale—a record that I'm hoping not to break this trip. I stumble and land on my hands and knees, breath gasping both from the sharp pain and the fear that a pointed head might flash from the underbrush, fangs poised at my knuckles.

I glance up the trail. Bran is nowhere to be seen. He's already skipped out of eyesight. *Damn it.* I gouge my eye sockets, irritated that I'm so annoyed. I don't want him to leave me stranded. Run along pursuing his own adventure while I'm bumbling around in the background. But I should be able to do a classic day hike without whining like a baby.

I clamber to my feet in a huff and wipe leaves and dust from my pants. I march double time. Eerie monkey laughter hoots on my left. I jump, turning to face a dead tree snag occupied by a gray-and-white bird—my first kookaburra, just like the old nursery rhyme:

Kookaburra sits in the old gum tree, merry merry king of the bush is he, laugh, kookaburra, laugh, kookaburra.

Great. The kookaburra is laughing at me. "Join the club, bud," I mutter, giving the bird a dirty glare.

The trail dips ahead and I spy a creek, beautiful, fern-lined, dappled in rich buttery light. Beautiful and Bran-less.

My nervousness ratchets into full-blown irritation. Seriously, where the hell is he? At this rate he'll be sitting on the apex of the mountain while I'm not even at the halfway point. "Dude, c'mon," I mutter to myself.

"Hey! This way."

I flick my head in the direction of Bran's callout. He's reclined against a fallen log, a granola bar in one hand. In front of him is spread out a dishtowel topped by apples, bananas, and a small pile of something that looks an awful lot like raisins and nuts.

"You okay?"

I've been cursing his name while the guy's making me a picnic. So I'm a little bit of an ass. "Wow, so this looks pretty awesome."

"I was getting ready to mount a search party to help make sure you'd eat it."

I point at my mud-stained knees. "I fell."

"Oh, Captain. Get over here."

I drop my pack and trudge toward him. "I'm a dysfunctional hiker."

"So I can see." He runs his hand up under my pant leg and I wince when he grazes my knee. "Are you having fun?"

"Yeah, sure. This is great." He's beaming. I don't want to ruin this for him.

His gaze bores into my face. "You want to go back?"

"No!" And I actually am being 100 percent honest. Failure is not an option. If I ask Bran to turn around and scuttle back to flatter land, I'm going to feel like a total d-bag. Besides, I don't want to climb a mountain to impress him. I want this mountain for me. I need to do this.

"Look." I crouch beside him. "So maybe I failed to mention this fun fact before, but I'm a teensy bit afraid of heights."

"Okay, like how big of a deal is this teensy fear?"

"No big deal, pretty much borderline paralyzed by petrifaction. I once blacked out on the Ferris wheel at the boardwalk back in Santa Cruz."

"The—what? Jesus, Talia." He clasps my hand between his.

"I should have probably said something."

"Might have been helpful."

"I'm sorry. I ... I didn't want to give you a reason."

"A reason?" He pulls me closer, settles me into the crook of his arm.

"To start rethinking things." I address my lap. "That's all it takes, one little difference, a flaw, it seems like nothing at first. Like I don't prefer chocolate ice cream or Scrabble or gangster movies, and the next thing you know we're screaming at each other over who last replaced a roll of toilet paper, filing for divorce, and engaging in a messy court battle over the custody of our traumatized two-point-five children who are now on the road to becoming serial killers."

"Does your mind always process like this?" He rubs my lower back in slow circles.

"Pretty much."

"I've got one question. The two-point-five kids?"

"Huh?" I reach for his picnic. Not hungry, but unable to sit still.

"I'm curious about the point five. That poor kid, is he the top half or the bottom?"

I freeze, handful of raisins halfway to my mouth.

"The top half would be preferable, at least at first thought. But the second half... when you really stop and consider... there's a kid who can run all around, play soccer." He points to the trail. "An uncomplaining hiker. Might be the perfect child."

"You are such a weirdo." I give him a glimpse into my freakish mind and he makes a joke. "My crazy. That's a real flaw."

"You're not crazy, Talia."

"It's nice of you to say so, but really, I am. I'm a high-functioning basket case."

"Like the entire rest of the human species." He leans over and grabs another handful of nuts and presses them into my hand. "Eat, nutso girl."

I pop two in my mouth.

"Do you want to go back?"

"Is that a real option?"

He frowns. "As opposed to?"

"Where you offer but don't really mean it. If I say I want to go back, won't you bully me into making the choice you want?"

"Talia." His tone is a warning.

"Yes."

"Did I or did I not make you a promise?"

"You did," I mumble.

"And that was..." He's goading me, pressing on my pressure points.

"I don't have to repeat it."

"Yeah, you do."

"You promised you'd be straight with me." I sound like a sulky schoolgirl.

"So it would be pretty shitty if I broke that promise straight off, right?"

"I guess so."

"What do you mean you guess so?" he asks.

"People make promises all the time." I turn away to avoid those green eyes. "The trick is keeping them."

"I don't make promises all the time." Bran is on his feet before my next blink. "But when I do, I fulfill them."

I look at him nervously. "You're okay to go back if I want to?"

"Yes. I'd be a little disappointed, but I'm not going to have fun if you're getting tortured."

"I want to keep going." My words march out like soldiers off to war.

"But you said—"

"Yes, I'm scared. I should have told you about my fear of heights. But I'm so tired of being scared all the time. If I don't try to fight back, this feeling is going to drag me down and I don't know if I'll ever get back to me again."

Bran puts his hands on my shoulders. "Natalia Stolfi, you're going to climb this fucking mountain."

I cover his hands with mine. "Brandon Lockhart, I'm climbing the shit out of this mountain."

———

"A few meters more, you're almost there."

It's like we're at the end of some old-school adventure tale, one where the heroes are stoic even as the blizzard rages, avalanches fall, and death hovers like a benevolent ghost.

Well, Bran is the hero.

I'm like one of the minor sidekicks who goes down during some important turning point. My death might even inspire the hero on his journey or teach him a valuable lesson. But at this point in the flick, the minor sidekick should be well and truly dead. Not white-knuckling a column of dolerite rock, thighs gripping the stone like it's the world's best lover.

"That's it, Talia," Bran's voice is encouraging. "You're holding tight, that's great. Now, I'm going to need you to release your left hand and reach up a few inches to grab the next hold."

I grit my teeth. The way he talks, you'd think I'm scaling Everest. Or at least Kilimanjaro. Instead—

"'Scuse, us, we'll be by in a tic. That's the way, Andy, right around the lady."

I'm the lady. Andy is a kid who doesn't look a day over seven who scrambles past me in a flurry of Spider-Man shoes and gap-toothed smiles. His parents bring up the rear, smiling up at their wild monkey child with obvious pride.

And they aren't the first group to pass me.

Five Swedish women, a couple, and a guy who looked to be in his mid-seventies have also shot past me during the course of the last quarter hour.

The top is so close I can taste it. Bran is being nothing but encouraging, but below me is a twenty-foot drop. Not enough to kill me, unless I fall with some sort of suicidal intent, but enough to make me feel incredibly uneasy about the boulder field.

Bran eases toward me. "Talia, take my hand."

"Can't let go."

"Talia."

"No." This is it; this is the reason. Bran isn't going to admit it here, while I'm bordering on a panic attack on a trail being conquered by elementary school children and senior citizens, but there's no doubt this is A REASON to lose interest in me. I'm giving him a big capital-lettered reason, but I can't stop. I physically can't let go.

"Talia. Take a deep breath."

"Breath taken."

"Another."

"Okay."

"Give me your hand, no bullshit. I want your fingers in mine. You'll be safe. I'm going to keep you safe. I need you to trust me."

Somehow I do it. I give him my fingers. He assists me up. We're doing this together. My head clears the boulder and I can see the steel marker that identifies the summit ahead. Holy shit, he's right. I'm going to reach the top.

A few more steps, easy now, and we're there. The kid in the Spider-Man shoes munches a Vegemite sandwich. I want to scoop him up in a smooshy squeeze. Except his parents would likely object, so I switch gears to give Bran a long and passionate kiss.

"I knew you'd get here," he says.

"I didn't."

He turns me to see the view, his hands tight around my waist. "Your place is here, Captain, in the sun," he whispers in my ear. "Don't ever forget that."

————

Our walk back down to the parking lot passes quickly and we say very little. I'm not quite sure what happened up there on the mountain, but I feel connected to Bran more so than ever. By connected I don't mean some vague sense of "I really like this guy." I mean that I finally get *Jane Eyre*, required reading in my History of British Literature class. There's a part where Mr. Rochester tells Jane it's as if he had a string under his rib, connected to hers, and he's afraid their parting would snap the connection and they'd both bleed inwardly. Bran's become vital to me, and our time together has almost run its course. Two weeks more.

Two weeks and back to Santa Cruz.

Two weeks before I'll have to admit to my parents that my OCD train wrecked my academic career.

Two weeks before no Bran.

I plow straight into a wall. Which is actually Bran's body. He's stopped on the trail ahead and I'd been too zoned out, wrapped in my own self-torture, to notice.

"You okay?" He's looking at me strangely.

"Yeah," I sniffle, and wipe my nose. "Hiking is good thinking time."

"You look like you're about to cry."

"I do?" My voice wobbles on the *d*.

"I've been thinking too."

"About?"

"Us." He crosses his arms and my heart breaks into a gallop. "I've got this idea. It's wild, but hear me out, all right?"

26

BRAN

*T*alia stares at me, face afire, eyes glowing, as if I announced having the ability to fly.

Talia, Talia, Talia—why do you make yourself so open? Hide nothing. It's dangerous to be this way with another person, to reveal your soft underbelly, those secret weaknesses. She's granted me the ability to hurt her. That's not a superhero power I want. So with great power comes great responsibility—I guess. And fuck it, I can't pretend I'm not relieved she didn't give me a pitying look and pat me on the head.

"Are you serious?" she whispers. She looks at me like she woke up on Christmas Eve to discover Santa Claus stuffing her stocking. My instinct is to draw back. I'm scared as fuck. This isn't only her soft underbelly on the line. My heart's just lurched back to life. I'm no longer a zombie. I'm Frankenstein's monster with enough stupidity to hope that this time I'll be able to have a happy ending.

"I am." I am, I really am. I am an idiot. The kid who stuck his finger into the electrical socket and ended up in the hospital.

And who's back again because, what the hell—it was fun the first time. But this is Talia—not Adie. They are nothing alike, inside or out. Talia couldn't hide from me, even if she tried. Talia doesn't play games. I wish I had more to offer her than my broken heart, awkwardly stitched together.

"You want me to come back to Australia. Come to Hobart. Live with you?" She sounds dazed.

"Yes. We can do this. I'm not too messy and can cook a mean spaghetti Bolognese. You've got the chance for a great project—that professor is eager to work with you. He said so himself. And even followed up with the e-mail afterward. He wasn't blowing smoke—he means it."

"He did seem to, didn't he?"

"You'll have a chance to do something real. Document important stories about actual people's lives."

"A chance to do something real," she repeats softly, staring at me like I've hypnotized her.

Come on, Talia. Say yes, say yes.

"I'm not going to lie; this is coming from a purely selfish place." *Nice one, Bran.* Still, I told her I would never lie to her. So might as well put this out there. "I don't want to say good-bye to you."

"I don't want to say good-bye either."

"But I'd never ask you to give up your future to try and be with me. I did that last year, for Adie, and it sucked. This way, you don't have to. You could do your senior project down here, at UTAS. My honors year will take a little longer, but only by a few months. After that, we'll see."

"See…" she echoes.

"Where things stand between us."

"What if I come back and live in Hobart? Give this"—she waves her arms back and forth in the narrow space separating us—"a chance. What would happen next?"

No lies. "I have no idea, but who knows, maybe we're destined for greatness."

"Do you really think this is a good idea?"

"I do." I didn't realize how much I meant my words until this second while Talia measures my offer of myself. A flicker of regret burns up my spine. I'm just getting back on my feet; is this really wise?

I like Talia. Really, really like Talia. More than like. But is that enough? Should I be so greedy to want to keep hold of this feeling? Couldn't this moment with her be a beautiful memory, something I can look back on later and smile? Is it better to dream about a what-if than end up in the drudgery over petty fights, the inevitable disillusionment? The moment when she stops looking at me like I'm Superman and realizes I'm Clark Kent.

Maybe this is a bad idea.

"Okay," she says. "Okay. This is insane, but yes, okay, I'll do it."

"You will." I shovel my fear aside. She said yes. Yes to me. I'm not alone here—alone in this with her. I'll deserve this yes.

"I don't know what will happen, but I want to make this work." I'd like this moment to be Shakespearean. Tell her that this is it. I'll love her forever. We'll stumble together toward the sun. Everything is hunky-fucking-dory. But that innocence died with Adie in a brilliant fireball. I got way too close to the sun and nearly burned alive.

Talia is not Adie. Adie doesn't belong here in this moment. That painful memory needs to get out.

Let me be worthy of this strange, lovely girl, who thinks I'm something special, worth taking a chance on.

"This is crazy," she repeats.

"I'm crazy for you."

Her watcher eyes snap from whatever deep thought they're mired in and mockingly roll at my bad humor. "Har. Har."

"I am, though." I pull her toward me, needing my mouth on hers, to feel her, know she's real. "Crazy for you."

I really do want to try. "Want to try" isn't deeply romantic. It's not a love sonnet. But it's the best I've got. Look how far I've come these last months. I can be a better guy. Maybe Talia is my own personal blue fairy and if I work my fucking guts out, I'll become a real live boy again.

27

TALIA

$\mathscr{S}$omeone knocks at my door. Before I can even get off my bed to respond, the raps grow insistent. Bran dropped me off from our Tasmania trip about thirty minutes ago—enough time for a fast and furious quickie before he left for tutoring. I'm surprised he's back already.

I lurch across the floor, only half joking when I mutter, "Dude, serious, you'll kill me if we do it again." I fling open the door and flash-freeze, like Han Solo at the end of *The Empire Strikes Back*. Mom's hair is swept into a ponytail. Her dress hangs low, revealing sharp clavicle bones and a clearly delineated sternum.

"Mom?" She's arrived three days ahead of schedule and I can't muster any genuine excitement. Maybe that's shitty, but them's the apples.

"Hooooooooooney." She draws out the *o* so long I'm certain I must be dreaming.

I'm engulfed in her skeletal hug. This is a waking nightmare.

"Hey." I inject the word with false enthusiasm. "Wow. You're here…in Melbourne…early."

"Surprise!" She throws up her hands.

Time to plaster on a phony grin. "Yeah." I punch the empty air. "Woohoo."

Her smile fades. "You're not happy?"

"No, no, no." *I'm emphatically not happy, Mom.* "You surprised me, that's all. What about the plan—to see you next Monday? Is something wrong?" It doesn't take a rocket scientist's brain or Sherlock Holmes's super sleuthing to deduce there must be trouble in the jungle with Logan the Wunderchimp.

"Of course not." Her tinkling laughter coats me like icy rain; soon I'll topple over with all the grace of a fallen power line.

There's only one thing that can make this moment worse. I glance to the empty doorway. "Is Logan here too?"

"No," she replies, mouth pursing. New lines have formed around her lips; beneath the tan skin and brilliant hair-dye job, my mom looks tired. If she's wasted away this much in months, what will be left of her in a year? "Aren't you going to invite me in?"

"Yeah. Of course, for sure." It's like inviting a vampire inside your home—no going back. "Come on in, not many places to sit but *mi casa es su casa*."

For the next three minutes, I avoid any reference to Bran while getting tortured with TMI about Logan. Turns out Mom discovered him engaging in floor sex with one of his celebrity clients—a twentysomething host of a popular cable dance competition show. He claims to love Mom but wants an open relationship, maintains he's excessively potent.

I grab some Kleenex and dab my face. What he probably wants is an all-access pass to Mom's money and her parents' sweet Kauai vacation home.

Mom grabs an orange pill bottle from the top of my dresser. "What's this, Natalia?"

"Jesus, boundaries." I snatch it from her hands. "Ever heard of them? Handy things, especially in a family."

"Natalia." Her voice hushes. "Are you taking drugs? Popping pills? Ecstasy?"

"Are you kidding me?"

"Language," she snaps.

"Mom, it's my medication."

She snorts. "What's the matter with you?"

"I . . . it settles me down, helps me be . . . me. Only better."

"That's giving up your power."

"Right, sorry, guess I should be consulting guardian angels?" Mom's class at Byron Bay was all about past and future lives, communing with spirits. I hope she's not trying to rope in Pippa for that particular duty. Because if my sister is out there somewhere, she doesn't deserve having to hear the ins and outs of Mom's midlife crisis relationship.

Mom scans my dingy room. "We're booked in at the Crown Hotel downtown, fabulous views. Logan's there now, getting a hot stone massage."

"Come again—he's still with you?"

"I'm considering his offer."

I throw up my hands. "The one where he bangs other women on his kitchen floor?"

"When you get to my age—you realize a few things. Monogamy isn't suitable for everyone."

"Funny, for other people, *of your age*, it seems a more than satisfactory arrangement—take Dad, for example."

She stiffens. "I'm not discussing my marriage or your father."

"Strange, considering you want to share up close and personal details about everything else."

"I came by to give you a nice surprise and invite you to dinner." She turns away. "If my presence is not a welcome one, I can—"

"Mom, it's fine. I'd love to catch up. And wow—getting to meet Logan, what a treat." She'll play the martyr card until I capitulate. Better to give her what she wants, which is time to talk about herself. All I need to do is keep my face polite and switch my brain off.

"I'd really appreciate your opinion." She ignores my sarcasm and smiles like I'm her girlfriend.

I don't want to be her pal. And I really don't want a blow-by-blow about her relationship with a man who's not my dad. I want to say no thanks, but she makes me feel guilty for taking the medication, for being the screwed-up, defective daughter who's left behind.

As soon as Mom leaves, I text Bran to cancel our plans for tonight. His reply is almost immediate.

All parents are mental. I'd like to meet her. Okay, I just want to see you.

I don't want to share him with Mom, but I'm too big of a wimp to deal with her *and* Logan on my own for dinner.

———

That's how I end up leading Bran through a crowded Vietnamese restaurant toward a small table in the back. "Hey, I brought a friend, hope that's cool."

Mom's eyes widen infinitesimally at the sight of me with a guy. Logan's settled into a high-back chair. In the flesh he reminds me of Keanu Reeves, except in a turban and a hand-tooled-looking leather vest.

I bare my teeth in something halfway approximating a smile while Logan folds his hands and bows, labels me a divine goddess.

Bran pulls out my seat and takes control of the conversation, uncharacteristically charming.

Mom's going to burst an optic nerve, gaping at me. She must be wondering how by all the stars and moons I've managed to snag this handsome, well-mannered young man.

I'm also curious—who is this guy? Here's a side of Bran I've never glimpsed. It's not until we order our drinks, green tea for Mom and Logan, beers for Bran and me, the truth strikes home.

This is Bran's mask, the slightly urbane, good-humored chap able to converse politely with my mom about her flight, my grand-parents' estate in Hawaii. I mean, he's even touched on the weather. I don't hear the word *fuck* pass his lips once.

Behold, Brandon Lockhart, son of a wealthy investor, educated in one of Australia's most elite private schools. He's dressed in a faded, threadbare T-shirt and his hair needs a trim, but it doesn't tax the imagi-nation to picture him in a crew cut and polo shirt. A casual tanned entre-preneur reading the business section at a beachside café, checking in to see how many millions he made while waiting for his second cappuccino.

Here's the guy who seduced himself into panties all over town. The idea is morbidly fascinating. So is the fact that Mom is giving Bran serious cougar eyes.

"Any idea what you want to order, Mrs. Stolfi?" Bran asks, peering congenially over the top of his menu.

"Oh." Mom blinks. "I'm divorced. And, please, call me Bee. Otherwise I feel so old."

"Nonsense, you couldn't be a day over fifty." Bran smiles benignly while Mom blanches.

His foot nudges mine under the table and suddenly, despite his mask, I don't feel alone. He's baiting her for me. We're a team, he and I. He might be acting like Brandon Lockhart the Charming, but I know he's still the same surly Bran who thrills at getting under other people's skin.

It's kind of fun to watch when it's not my skin.

Logan twists off one of his chunky silver rings and passes it to me. "Rainbow moonstone," he croons. "Mined in the far north of Canada, land of the aurora borealis. These rocks are precious, diffuse energy through the aura, aligned with galactic consciousness. Dig it?"

It's an effort not to stab him in the knuckle with my chopstick.

"In addition to his chef skills, Logan is a budding healer," Mom says, leaning close to him, letting her hands flirt up his hairy forearm. *Ick.*

"I incorporate gems in my healing," Logan says, fingering his soul patch. "The laying of stones is a powerful force."

I spread a napkin across my lap. "So...you are a crystal healer. Like a real one?"

He blinks, puzzled, keeps rubbing his chin fuzz as if it will yield an intelligent answer.

"And, Logan, how about you, my brother?" Bran bursts in, taking control. "Do much surfing in Hawaii?"

My brother? Bran's starting to overdo the act.

While Logan mouth-vomits words like *enlightened*, *waves*, and *water prayer practice*, I nudge Bran under the table. *Enough*, my foot tells him, *back off a bit.*

He knocks back. *No problem.*

Mom eyes the menu skeptically. She faces mealtimes like other people do horror movies, girding themselves for what's to come, anticipating the worst. I know food is nothing more than a situation she can control from start to finish. For a second I feel a sense of kinship. She and I both have a low tolerance for uncertainty. We both want control in a world that spins wildly most of the time. We have different methods, but at the end of the day, our fears, our primal aches, are frighteningly similar. I smile at her, for a moment feeling no resentment, just a sympathetic camaraderie.

She gives me a little frown. "What are you ordering, Talia?"

"The bánh xèo is amazing." Bran and I have come here a few times because the food's killer and prices are cheap.

She scans the menu. "How's that prepared?"

"Like a pan-fried crepe, not deep-fried or anything."

Mom's little laugh is patently false. "Fried is fried, Natalia." She gives me a quick once-over. "Maybe we should split the soup."

Bran glances at me and I shrug, pretending her words don't sting. In truth, they shouldn't. I should be immune at this point. Why do I ever pretend Mom and I have a nice relationship? Does she realize she's hurting my feelings or is she so wrapped in her own issues that she's totally oblivious?

The waiter comes over. Bran greets him casually and orders bowls of pho for Mom and Logan and two bánh xèos. "Talia and I just returned from Tasmania," he says, handing the waiter our menus. "We didn't get a chance to eat breakfast. She's probably starving. I should have looked after her better."

"Tasmania?" Mom glances up sharply, head swiveling between us. "What about school?"

"She's found an interesting research project down in Hobart." Bran deftly proceeds to chat around the edges of the idea Phillip Conway proposed. The one I'd e-mailed him that I'd be interested in further exploring, during the ferry ride back from Tasmania.

This strange, socially adept Bran touches on the idea of my project so as not to give a complete falsehood, but also not revealing that we've discussed me moving back here. A wild idea still tinged with the aura of fantasy.

He skirts the truth, never quite venturing into outright lies, and

Mom eats up every word. Logan is too busy eyeing the Asian twins at the table next to us. Mom has to notice; he doesn't even try to hide it.

Our food comes and I take a bite, bigger than intended, and choke.

"Talia, goodness." Mom's laugh is self-righteous. "It's not going anywhere. Slow down."

I take a sip of water.

A terrible thought occurs to me. Bran is good at telling people things they want to hear. Almost as good as telling people things they want to avoid. My stomach churns, revolting at the idea of food.

Bran lifts his beer. "Here's a toast, to good food, good conversation, and the company of two amazing goddesses. Am I right, Logan, or am I right?" I don't recognize that smile.

"Oh, Bran, you are an absolute sweetheart. To goddesses." Mom clinks her teacup.

"Blessings to the sacred female divinity," Logan pipes in.

I silently join in, ignoring the thought poking into my brain like a cherry pit. Mom and Logan are clearly a ways out there and Bran is politely rolling with it, giving the genuine impression of listening to every word, revealing nothing of his own thoughts.

What if he does the same with me? And my issues? Tolerates it but inwardly cringes. He has so many layers of defenses. Who is the real Bran? Will I ever know for sure?

"This dinner is so lovely. Isn't this lovely, Logan? Talia?"

"Yeah, Mom." *Look at me,* I silently plead with Bran. I need reassurance, to see him, the real him, not this freaky, charming automaton. *Look at me.*

He must sense my pleading eyes because he gives me a small smile, but his eyes remain blank.

Careful what you wish for.

28

TALIA

om and Logan are leaving town the next morning to tour local vineyards. Their absence is a relief. I can't deal with another round of "getting to know you" dinners with Logan. Bran provides confirmation that the Wunderchimp is an A-grade douche bag.

"Did you see the way Logan checked out the ladies at the table beside us?" he asked, wrapping an arm around my waist, spooning me in his bed. "His mouth may say 'women are goddesses,' but his eyes were saying 'I want to motorboat those titties.'"

"Sick." I hit him on the head with the pillow. Now that we are alone, he is back to being my Bran, but I can't shake the foreboding in my heart.

"Seriously, that dude is fucked."

"Ugh, I know. I don't know what Mom sees in him." Bran opens his mouth and I cover it with my hand. I have my own mask, the one where I joke and pretend everything is fine. "If you say a single word about motorboats, I'm going to pluck out your tongue."

"I thought you were a pacifist?"

"Not where Logan is concerned."

"So"—Bran settles a hand on my hip—"when are you going to tell your mom the big news?"

"About?"

"The fact that you're moving back to Australia."

Do you really want me to return? Are you ready for that?

"Oh, well, I—"

"Talia." He watches me and I return his gaze without blinking.

"I'll talk to her once she gets back to the city. Right before we fly home. It'll be easier that way. I'll say, 'Yo, Mom, didn't graduate. Moving back to Australia to finish school and bone down.'" More joking, more pretending.

He nuzzles my neck. "She'll be so proud."

"Yeah." For once his kisses don't override the icy fear sloshing around the pit of my stomach. "She'll be something, all right."

We've stepped to the edge of truth with each other, but it's like we're daring each other to take the plunge. I'm scared to go first, not sure if he's ready to jump.

———

Mom contacts me after she's back from her wine tour. We are both flying from Australia the following morning. I agreed to come over and meet her for an early dinner before heading to Bran's place for the night.

"Where's the Logmeister?" I scan her boutique hotel, relieved not to see him sprawled on the bed or leather couch. I cross fingers—and toes—that he isn't about to stroll from the bathroom with a fluffy towel slung low around his waist. Don't think I can stomach that sight.

"Logan's left, Ladybug. Or rather, I left him." Mom sits on the edge of her king-sized bed and picks a wine bottle off the floor. She tops off her glass with whatever white she is drinking and now the bottle's empty. This is not a great sign. I chew the inside of my cheek and my rib cage grows smaller, overtight.

"What happened?" I don't want to know the particulars but can't ignore the drunk elephant in the room.

"As you know, Logan and I made plans for a wine tour, but instead we recalibrated and ended up in a village west of here, Daylesford, for a weekend retreat. After the past-and-future-lives course in Byron Bay, I'd begun to question our direction, but I wanted to get a second opinion. So we enrolled in a life-shaping class."

"Life shaping, that's kinda, I don't know…ew?" I say. "I picture you squeezing feelings like Play-Doh. Sounds gross, doesn't it?"

She gives me her look. The one that means I'm annoying, but Mom doesn't use words like *annoy*. Instead, I'm just not "getting" her.

"Please, Talia. The weekend was many things, but not gross. Those two days were powerful. I had a profound experience. Logan isn't the one for me. There's another man waiting somewhere in my life."

Yeah. She's right about that. I call him Dad. But I hold my tongue because you know what? Dad deserves better than Mom and her endless chasing for greener pastures.

"So spirits came and informed you that Logan was *no bueno*," I say with open incredulity. "What did they look like, just out of curiosity?"

She tucks her hair behind her ears. "They were but a feeling, a whisper in the back of my consciousness."

"In other words, a thought."

"Excuse me?" She knits her brows.

"You are describing a thought, an idea in your head that can occasionally do things like suggest logical courses of action. Like, for example, you should wake up and shed your phony boyfriend who's more in love with his own self-indulgence than you."

"Logan is a deeply spiritual man."

"Uh-huh." I tap my foot, one, two, three, four. The order, the predictability, stabilizes me. "Question: If he's so in touch, why are you bailing?"

"Because he wants to be free in a way that I'm not ready to embrace."

"Oh, please."

"He's too much man for one woman. Monogamy is a construct that is arbitrary and overbinding. A reality that we limit ourselves to when we should really be focused on forging cosmic connections with like-minded people."

"Let me get this straight. Douche-bag Logan fed you douche-bag lines about how you should screw your way into serendipity?"

"Really, Talia. Your crudeness is a weakness."

"A weakness, Mom?" I take a deep breath and pretend I'm someone willing to face down uncomfortable truths, like Bran. This is so far out of my comfort zone that I'm not even sure where I am. "Look. I'm not Pippa. I know we don't talk the same way, but I'm trying to help. Someone has to tell you like it is. Guess I'm the only one here for the job."

"I'm all ears, Natalia." Her lips twist in a sneer. "I'd love to hear this life lesson."

I throw back my head. Why do I even bother?

"You are the one with issues, Ladybug. I have tried and tried to give you advice. What you can do to improve, remedy the traps you set for yourself. But you don't want to hear it. You mock my suggestions for yoga even though it would relax you. I suggest tulsi tea and you sneer. You are so smug, act like the world owes you something for your struggle. But the truth is that you are suffering because you can't face life."

"Enough with cherry-picking Buddhism, Mom."

"Is this how you cope, with sarcasm? Because look where it's gotten you. When I see you, I see someone who is surrounded by ego, by id."

"We're veering from Buddha to Freud? You are a pseudo expert in everything, aren't you? Let me pull up a chair so I can take notes on your version of life, the universe, and everything."

"Are you still anxious about your health?"

"Sometimes?" I don't trust the strange, unblinking gaze she's fixed on me.

"And your things…do you still do them?" Her words are softly poisonous.

"Rituals, Mom. Say the word."

"I don't know what to call them. They are something you could stop if you concentrated hard enough, opened yourself to things that are positive and healing. Instead you act like that is beneath you. How can I possibly help if you won't even help yourself?"

"Is that what you really think, Mom, that if I buck up and go to a few yoga classes, start meditating in the morning, I'd be better?"

"It would be a start. It's better than the alternative."

"Which is?"

"Becoming a jaded, ill-tempered young woman."

"Mom, I'm twenty-one. If I'm not jaded or ill-tempered, something is seriously wrong. Look at the world we live in. Look at the state of the country, the state of everything. I mean, global warming alone is going to—"

"Were you ever going to tell your father and I about school, your grades?"

My knees lock. "What?"

She stands and walks to the window, looking out over the anonymous city. "Your father called me before I left. A letter came

from the university. He opened it thinking it had to do with gradu-
ation. Instead, it was a notification you were on academic probation.
What is the matter with you?"

Oh shit.

I start to sit, stand, pace the room in jerky movements. "Mom, I
know how this looks. I was going to tell you. And Dad. Things last
semester, in my head, they got bad. I couldn't focus—"

"Your inattention is dangerous. You make fun of me and the
work I'm doing on myself. Maybe if you'd done what I'd suggested—
massage, herbs, tinctures—you'd have never caused such harm."

"What's that supposed to mean?"

"Your sister. She died because you couldn't control yourself."

I hold up a warning hand. "Are we going there? Because if we
are, we can't come back."

Mom forges on. I don't even know if she hears my cautionary
words. "Pippa died driving to get you. Because you—"

"I was afraid I left the hair straightener plugged in."

"You always thought you left the straightener on, but you never
did. So you went home to check, again, even though you were late.
And your sister came to collect you."

"What about the tweaker who ran a stop sign because he was
texting? That seemed to have a pretty dire consequence."

"You couldn't rein in your compulsiveness, Talia. And Pippa is
dead. Dead." She repeats the word like she can't quite believe the truth.

I feel like Mom's stabbed me in the chest with a dull and rusty
fork. Of course, I've told myself this very same story, countless times.
But to hear it come out of someone else's mouth—to have your fears
validated as fact—that cuts through the remaining unlacerated
parts of my heart.

"Who knows who you'll hurt next?"

I don't hear what else she says because I'm slamming out of her hotel room.

————

It was Dad's birthday. Mom made reservations at our family's favorite Chinese joint. I was biking, late as usual, from class when I started worrying about my hair straightener. Did I leave it plugged in? Yes. No. Yes. No. The idea plagued me for blocks. I had to know for sure, so I texted Mom that I'd be another fifteen minutes late and detoured home to reassure myself.

Pippa and our friend Beth were already at the restaurant table, and knowing Mom and her dislike of anything unpunctual, they offered to run out and pick me up.

I'd felt dumb as I left the house. Not only was the straightener unplugged, but I'd also put it away in the hall closet. I jumped on my bike and started peddling furiously when the first ambulance sirens approached.

I rounded the corner and slammed on the brakes. Mom's old Prius, the one she gifted Pippa when she started at UCSC, was crumpled in the intersection. I stared blankly, unable to tear my eyes from the GOING BOLDLY NOWHERE sticker my sister slapped on the rear bumper last semester. Blood pooled on the pavement beside the driver's door.

Someone started screaming. It took a long time before I realized it was me.

So what if Pippa didn't actually die that day? It's the moment her life ended, trying to cover for me while I obsessed about a stupid straightener.

Mom is right. She only voiced what I'd locked in my chest of repressed fear, that my crazy did, in fact, kill Pippa.

29

TALIA

During the tram ride from Mom's hotel back to the Foreign Student Hall, inner-city suburbs pass in a blur. I let my vision drift out of focus, thoughts on lockdown. Instead I count, let the numbers comfort me. Two hundred and forty-two doesn't judge. Three hundred and ten doesn't blame. Five hundred and seventy-nine doesn't resent. The numbers represent a temporary shelter, a lean-to in the dark woods while outside a storm screams through the treetops.

I arrive at my building but decide not to enter at the last second. Alone, there is too much risk my mental hurricane's mounting fury will break through my flimsy defenses. Instead, I put my head down and follow the familiar route to Bran's place, ignoring the quizzical stares from fellow pedestrians. I wear glasses but doubt the frames help camouflage the mascara streaks raccooning my eyes. His front door is cracked, which is weird but a relief. I don't want to knock and risk Bella answering. The idea of facing that girl with all her jealousy and judgment is more than I can handle.

I duck into the dim corridor, shut the door behind me, and

pause. There's a charge in the air—the kind of atmosphere that prickles neck hair and induces goose bumps. The house is quiet, but I can sense it's not empty. I take a hesitant step toward Bran's room. A floorboard creaks and I jump.

Settle down.

Why do I feel so sneaky? We're together now, right? This trepidation is ridiculous. I'm being oversensitive and paranoid. All I need to do is get over myself and find Bran. Everything will be better when we're together.

I push open his bedroom door and my storm upgrades to a category-five hurricane.

There's another girl in here.

I can't see what she looks like because her face is pressed into my boyfriend's shirt while his is buried in her hair. The room snaps with electricity. My belly stings like it's under assault from mutant wasps. What if I scuttle back the way I came, like a total creeper? But then what? There is zero chance I can pretend I don't have a clue that *this* is going on—whatever this is.

What the fuck is this?

Bran raises his head and our eyes deadlock.

My expression must be murderous because he steps in front of the other girl as if to shield her. Whoever she is turns around and, holy crap, she's gorgeous. A living, breathing Disney princess with those slanted eyes and masses of spun-gold hair spilling down the center of her back. Her pert, upturned nose is pink, as if she's been crying, but that only adds to her air of delicate vulnerability. Under her micro wool skirt, her black over-the-knee boots scream *sexy*.

No one can compete with a girl of this caliber. Especially not when you're me in a saggy knit beanie, tear stains, and scuffed-knee jeans.

"Talia…" Bran's voice is tight, like he's controlling something. Fantastic. Time to play Guess that Cryptic Emotion. What are the choices? Annoyance that I interrupted him? Embarrassment for getting busted? His face reveals nothing.

Here we go, yet another fucking mask.

The girl peeks around his shoulder. Her wide eyes assess me with open curiosity. I'd like to grab those impossibly long eyelashes, whip her around my head, and hurl her out the door.

"Talia?" Bran begins to thaw, regards me like I'm human, not an unwelcome insect who scuttled into the room. "Hey, shit, what happened? You look awful."

Because when I cry that's what happens. I look like crap. Normal people don't cry like whoever this Little Miss Perfect is and walk away with two glistening tears on their cheeks. Crying is raw, aching and real.

My nose threatens to run. I sniffle, hating to expose myself as a regular person. For once, can't I be someone perfect? In fact, right now I'd settle for being anyone. Anyone at all. Just so long as they aren't me.

"Talia? That's her?" The girl looks at me with new awareness.

He talked about me with this girl? Who has a vaguely Scandinavian accent? A dawning realization shines into my fractured brain.

No way.

"Yeah, I'm Talia." I want my voice to sound controlled, but instead I seem high-strung, petulant. Cracks start to fang in jagged bolts beneath my skin. I wrap my arms around my waist to hold myself together. *Don't go to pieces, not here, not in front of … her.*

"Brannie told me all about you." The platinum-haired goddess moves around Bran and edges closer. "I'm Adie."

What's she doing here? I can't compete with this girl and win. The memory of Tanner inside me, while his gaze pretended I was Pippa, is branded in my brain. I won't vie against another first love. That's a hell I'm unable to revisit.

Adie keeps coming until she's right up in my personal space.

Kill me now.

Her arms rise. Maybe she's ready for the task. Nope, this is going from bad to worse. She hugs my wooden body. Her hair is soft against my cheek and smells like meadow flowers. I want to vomit.

"It is so nice to meet you." Her false smile could win an award.

I pat her back awkwardly, not daring to look at Bran. Terrified what I'll see if I do. "Okay, well, this is a...something. You guys must have loads of catching up. Look, I just stopped by to say I..." *Stop talking. Shut up and get the hell away.* "Yeah, so I'm gonna go. I can show myself out."

"Oh no. That's fine. I was just leaving," Adie replied, stepping away, plucking a purse from the futon.

"No! Stay. Please, stay." Is Bran talking to me, to Adie, or both of us? I don't know what to do. If it's not me, I'll fall apart in so many pieces no one will ever put me back together. "I have to go," I repeat, backpedaling from the room. "Right now."

I stumble down the corridor and pause on Bran's front step. This is his big chance to chase after me, call my name, something, anything. If there's ever a moment to buck up and show me how he really feels, this is the moment.

Don't look back. Don't you dare look back.

I turn around. The hall is empty.

I hurl myself forward and rip open the front gate. Going to my packed-up room isn't an option; being alone will only allow my crazy time to sink fingers into my brain. There's no way in hell I'm retreating back to Mom's hotel. I've got literally nowhere to go. It's impossible to swallow. I take a hard left down a street that I don't recognize. And take a quick right. Walk at nearly a jog for a few blocks and veer left again. Lost. I want to get well and truly lost. I'd like to outrun my own name if the option is at all possible.

A plop of water splatters on the tip of my nose. I gasp and glance toward the roiling, dark clouds. A rumble menaces overhead and sprinkles start to dot the pavement. If this were a movie, here's the part where the music becomes dramatic and soul-searching.

A flash of lightning, and it's like a faucet turns on from the heavens. Is this a cosmic joke?

I wipe my face with the back of my hand. If my life were cinematic, I'd gasp, my hair attractively framing my face, and Bran would appear at the end of the street—panting—in a tight white T-shirt that's soaked through to reveal taut biceps.

Don't think about Bran's muscles.

He's not coming. I'm alone—in the rain. And it's cold, uncomfortable, and decidedly unromantic.

High-rise buildings grow taller. In my aimless meanderings, I've headed south and entered the city's heart. Along Elizabeth Street, a woman in an elegant suit and frightening stilettos skitters around me. Her umbrella flips inside out as wind buffets the street. A wet newspaper blows from the sidewalk and smothers my face. I rip the paper off and my frantic walk turns into a full-tilt run.

Another thunder bang crashes overhead.

I want to scream—*I'm sorry.* To Bran. To Mom. To Pippa. *I'm sorry for not being enough for anyone.*

But apologies mean nothing. They don't have the power to change a single thing. Flinders Street train station is ahead. There's an idea. I could catch a train and leave the city. I've never visited the

Dandenong Ranges—the low hills rising to the city's east. I read in one of my guidebooks that the Dandenongs were full of eclectic villages and misty fern glades.

That's what I need—a fast train out of this broken-dream city.

I'll roam used bookstores, sip hot chocolate in a quiet café, go for a long walk through the rain forest, and pretend I'm not someone whose life is one roaring clusterfuck.

I hug my saturated jacket. Great. My clothes are soaked. Maybe the train isn't a well-thought out plan. Correction—this is an epically stupid idea. But I'm going for it anyway because I've already made every conceivable mistake. If all else fails, maybe I'll catch pneumonia and die and won't everyone be sorry?

I cross Flinders Street and duck into the station. The yellow-bricked building is massive, hulking over two city blocks. I search my bag for my public transit card. Crap—my wallet's AWOL. I shove through pens, ChapStick, a loose stick of gum, and a few coins. Damn, I must have forgotten it at Mom's hotel.

I cannot face her in this state.

My life is unraveling faster than I can knot it back together— loose filaments slip between my clumsy fingers. I make my eyes smaller than peas and count to ten again and again until I'm able to wrangle the change from my purse bottom into my hand. I've got three gold coins, worth two dollars each, and another seventy cents: $6.70. That's not much, definitely won't whisk me to the mountains.

My head throbs. What if this is it? I'm going to die of a brain hemorrhage here in the city with no identifying documents. My unclaimed body will be donated for medical experiments.

A beautifully restored classic pub is on the corner across the street—Young and Jackson. I fist my $6.70 and feel the weight. There's enough coins for a cheap beer and at this moment that's my only brilliant idea. I jaywalk, ignoring the blaring horns, and burst into the bar.

The main pub floor is packed on account of the weather, so I wander upstairs. Here the room is quieter.

At the bar, a few men in rumpled suits blearily stare into their pints. I order a Victoria Bitter. On the opposite end of the bar is an oil painting of a naked woman, the brass plaque beside it reading CHLOE. I receive my drink and toast her.

This Chloe's a good-looking girl. Did she ever have guy problems? Drop her defenses, open her heart, allow him to enter and run roughshod before returning to his ex?

I sniffle and take a few deep sips. Why did Adie have to come back? She arrives in town and shatters my turn for a fairy tale. Except in my twisted version the handsome prince didn't believe in love. That reason should have been enough to give me pause. But I held on, believed that despite the evidence, Bran and I had a chance.

Now I'm kicked out of the story, the anonymous ugly stepsister.

My beer's almost empty when I set it down. Good thing I'm currently penniless; otherwise this situation might take me on an alcohol-fueled trip to the danger zone.

"No shit, California? Is that really you?"

I turn, dazed, to find Jazza at the top of the stairs.

"I don't believe it. What's going on, girl? Give me some sugar." He saunters over and engulfs me in a bear hug. I squeeze back, suddenly grateful for human contact.

Jazza takes notice of my empty glass and single state. I swear his nostrils twitch. "What're you doing all by yourself?"

"I fly home tomorrow." I can't hold back a sniffle. "Bran and I... well, I don't even really know if there is a Bran and I. Things are all messed up."

There's a strange flash in Jazza's eyes. I don't know what to make of it because in another blink he's back to his friendly yet dopey self. Turns out Jazza missed his train. He didn't say where he was going and I don't really care. All I know is that right now he's content to fetch drinks for my broke ass. He buys me another round before pulling out his phone.

"You are addicted to that device," I say, crunching on two complimentary peanuts.

"Probably." Jazza nods, thumbs flying over the screen. At last, he sets the phone down, drumming his fingers over the case.

"What are you up to these days?"

"Oh, I'm—"

His phone buzzes. He checks the screen and smiles.

"All good?"

"Yeah, never better." He shoots me another odd look, one that's a trifle smug, like a cat who caught a canary, but the bird is still twitching inside his mouth.

Another beer later and we graduate to liquor: rum and Coke for him and vodka tonic for me. He doesn't ask what I'm doing sitting in a bar looking like the world's loneliest raccoon, sodden clothes plastered to my body. Nor does he fire off a single question about Bran.

That's fine by me because right now I don't want to think about any of that. I'm happy to listen to Jazza drone through some random story that involves a bunch of people I never met, a party down the coast, and a blind ferret.

"It was hilarious." Jazza guffaws at the end.

"Sounds like it." I smile weakly and subtly swing my eyes toward the wall clock.

"I'm glad I ran into you, California. What are the chances, huh?"

The knot lodged in the back of my throat since seeing Bran's arms wrapped around Adie pulls tight. *California* sounds an awful lot like *Captain* to my intoxicated mind.

"You okay?"

"Yeah, I'm—" A sob hiccups from me. "No, I'm not okay. Not really. I had such a stupid fight with Bran."

"Oh, yeah? Tell me all about it."

I love his concern right now.

In halting steps, I give a 30,000-foot overview of what happened.

"Aw, sounds rough." Jazza pats me on the head before pulling out his phone to check another text. "What do you say, time for shots?"

I want to go home and pass out among my half-packed belongings. I've drunk enough that my cramped studio apartment won't be my personal torture chamber. I move to stand.

"Hey, what's the rush? Hold on, girlie." Jazza's hand is on my elbow.

For a few seconds I thought he wanted to steady me, but he's not letting go. In fact, he's closer. A little too close. I try to move away.

"I think it's best if I just go pass out."

"Come on, one more drink." He one-thumb texts.

I fight the impulse to grab his phone and throw it to the hardwood floor. Crack the screen under my heel. Whoa. Need to chill out. I'm a bit of a violent drunk.

The rain pours harder outside the window, a gray unbroken sheet. "Oh no."

"C'mon, California, stick around. My company doesn't suck that bad, does it?"

There's weirdness in Jazza's voice again. Or maybe I'm drunkenly hallucinating drama everywhere I look. I cannot believe what a fool I made of myself back at Bran's. Did he know Adie was coming? Doubtful. Still, that didn't stop him from taking her back with open arms. God, I'm such a stupid masochist. One who can't stop falling for guys who are still caught up with other girls. Who'd Bran prefer? Cinderella or the quirky OCD stepsister? There's no contest.

"All right. One more drink." Maybe that will be enough to erase the memory of the protective way Bran shielded Adie, the way his eyes narrowed, the lean set of his shoulders as he turned away.

Jazza presses another drink into my hand and I take a sip, sputtering. "Oh God, what is this?"

"Ouzo," he says. "It's Greek. You like?"

"It tastes like liquid black licorice." *And I hate anise*, I want to add. Instead, I say, "Thank you." Because I need to remember to fake it. Life doesn't hurt so much when you stop being real.

I swear Chloe, the giant naked woman hanging on the opposite wall, gives me a pitying look. "You ever have these kinds of problems?" I mumble, taking a big sip of the revolting drink.

"What's that?" Jazza invades my personal space. His tone is casual, like we're friends, nothing more. But I'm vaguely aware that his body language is starting to say something else. Something that I really don't want to be happening.

His phone buzzes again.

"Dude, you're on that thing more than a teenage girl."

A fast-beat pop song comes on. "Dance with me." He takes my drink and sets it down.

"Negative." I recoil from his wandering hands. "Dancing and I, we're not really a thing."

"But I love this song." If I lit a match to his breath, it would burst into flame.

"I'm serious, Jazza. I do not want to dance." I clench the bar-stool, wishing I could curl under a table in the back of the bar.

Jazza tugs hard, harder than he should, to be honest, and I tip from my seat, landing straight into his chest, where I choke on his heavy cologne. His pectorals are way bigger than Bran's, but they're meaty and exaggerated. He must lift a lot—too much. I don't like when guys work their body for show. His spicy scent dredges up the memories of our few hookups. I remember his wet lips and roving hands.

Ew, ew, ew.

"Serious, Jazza, I don't want to—"

His thick tongue pushes into my mouth and I gag. He tastes sickeningly sweet, like caramel and Coca-Cola.

I try to shove him off, but it's like he mistakes my hands on his body for assent. The way he sucks my face makes breathing difficult. Dimly, I wonder if I should knee him in the junk or bite down. The upstairs bar's not overly crowded and it's not like he can do much. All I have to do is break free of his gobbling mouth and—

"You have got to be fucking kidding me." That familiar voice slices through my alcohol-soaked mind with the precision of a meat cleaver.

Jazza springs back a good three feet and I'm left by myself, turning to slowly face Bran.

30
TALIA

*M*aybe I crawled under one of the tables and passed out. I close my eyes, hoping that when I reopen them Bran will have vanished. Please let this moment go down in the record books as the worst dream ever.

"So what's up, Talia?"

I open my eyes and Bran remains, slightly out of focus because of the tears in my eyes.

"Please, you don't understand."

"No big thing, bro," Jazza pipes up behind me, and my stomach curdles. I jump as he rests a hand low on my waist. "California and I—well, it didn't really mean anything, Bran. You know how that goes. We're cool, right?"

A muscle twitches deep in Bran's jaw. He moves quick and there's a blur, a feeling of wind rushing past my ear. The sound is heavy, wet, like someone beating a side of meat with a mallet.

I turn and cover my mouth, fighting an instant gag. Jazza's nose spurts blood like a geyser of gore. "Oh God. Oh my God, Bran."

Bran growls something, but I can't make out what he says

because Jazza's laughing. Even though this isn't anywhere close to a funny situation.

Jazza's mouth opens and is covered with blood. His teeth look rusty. "I'd say we're even, mate."

Angry is a light, twinkling feeling full of giggling fairies compared to the expression on Bran's face. "Go away, Jazz, before I use your face to clean this mess."

I take a reflexive step back. I don't mean to touch Jazza, but my back collides with his body and he dips, his breath hot in my ear.

"I always thought American girls were sluts. But if Bran wants to make an ass out of himself over a frigid chick, I'm cool with that."

Bran's fist balls.

"All right, fellas, here's your notice to clear out, or I'm calling the coppers," the bartender orders from behind the safety of the long counter.

I halt Bran with a raised hand and spin around. "That's enough. Get the fuck out, Jazza."

"Look at you, California." Jazza's eyes are squinty and mean. "You're a real hotshot prize, huh?" He shoves past Bran and disappears down the stairs.

"I—"

A barstool flies to the ground with a sharp bang. It takes me a second to register that Bran is the one doing the hurling.

"Mate." The warning's implicit in the bartender's voice.

Bran presses both hands to the side of his head as if he's trying to keep his skull from fracturing.

I touch his arm and he jerks back.

"Don't, Talia, just...don't." Bran's breathing is ragged. I swear for two seconds he's about to cry. He passes a hand over his face and when he looks at me again his features are composed.

"What you saw isn't what you think."

He stares at me with a flat expression.

"Come on, Bran. I ran into Jazza as a coincidence. I didn't have money for a train and he missed his. It's raining."

"Romantic."

"Yeah, right. He bought me drinks and I cried."

"You sounded pretty inconsolable in his texts."

"Wait—what?"

Bran pulls out his phone and flicks the screen. "Here." His voice is impassive.

Jazza: Just ran into Talia, sounds like things are over with you two?

Bran: What are you talking about?

Jazza: She leaves tmr, you won't mind if I give her a go, right?

Bran: Where is she?

Bran: For real, where the fuck are you guys?

Jazza: Sitting right beneath the Chloe painting. Talia kind of looks like her don't you think? Stoked to find out

Bran: Don't do this

Jazza: Ho's before bros, mate

I shake my head, gaze unfocused. "I never had any intention of hooking up with Jazza. You know that, right? The idea is ridiculous. It makes no sense."

"You're talking a lot."

"Because I'm freaked about what just happened. You punched Jazz in the face. That was total crazy town."

Bran's posture is rigid. "People ramble when they feel guilty."

I am tempted to shake him hard and furious. "What are you,

some guy from a true crime television show? Do you believe I'd go from you to Jazza in the space of an hour?"

"Talia, I don't know what to think."

"What does that even mean?"

He shrugs and I understand, wow, bloodlust is a real phenomenon. If I wasn't afraid to break my knuckles on his rock-hard skull, I'd sock him right between the eyes.

"If you throw out accusations, be ready to back them up. What about Adie? How convenient that you haven't mentioned a word about her."

Bran looks around the bar. It's mostly empty still, but we are definitely the stars of the show. Every eye here is locked on us.

"Talia." He grips his elbows hard like he can either hang on or hit something. "If you want to have this out, we need to leave."

"Fine." I bound down the stairs, two at a time, not bothering to check if Bran follows. I push open the heavy pub door and duck into the lashing rain. "Seriously, what's your problem?" I spin around and shield my face with one hand.

Bran ignores the downpour. He's drenched to the bone. His dark hair plasters across his high cheekbones. "You, acting like this. Creating drama. I can't deal."

I draw in a breath between my teeth. "You know what I can't handle? Having my mom tell me that I single-handedly caused my sister to die, Bran. Me, because if I wasn't me, if I was someone normal, a person who didn't freak out, Pippa would still be alive."

He takes a step forward and holds out a hand. "Talia, I'm sorry. I didn't—"

"No, you didn't know." I stomp my foot, ignoring his gesture. "Because you were too busy getting on your ex-girlfriend. The girlfriend who just so happens to be your first heartbreaking love."

"She needed to see me." His face is tight. He won't let me in.

"Oh, I bet she did. You know what? Forget it. Sorry I said anything."

"Don't be like that, Talia. You don't know what's going on. Adie found me to confess. She didn't have an abortion."

"What?" My angry blood flash freezes. "You guys have a kid?"

Bran paces back and forth, the words pouring out. "She lied to me, about everything, because she didn't want to get married. She knew our relationship had changed, that we were growing into different people. But she understood me well and figured—rightly—that I wouldn't give up if I believed she needed my help. So she cheated on me and made up the story about the abortion to drive me away. Her plan worked well. She meant to keep the baby." A violent sob tears deep from his chest. "The baby—it was a little boy—the doctors discovered during a routine ultrasound that he had a congenital heart problem. There was nothing anyone could do. He... he died... eight months into the pregnancy. She had to go through with a stillbirth—even give him a name."

"What was it?" Even though I guessed.

"Brandon." He grinds fists into his eyes. "Her dad is here on business. She's working for him now, as an executive assistant. She took the Australia trip so she could tell me the truth, at last, face-to-face."

"My God. I had no idea. I'm so sorry." Sorry—such a pale, weak word when this is his life, knifed through, red, raw, and vulnerable.

"Me too." He mops rainwater from his eyes.

"How awful that she'd keep something that monumental from you." I reach for his hand. "That's borderline evil."

He recoils like a shot. "Don't talk that way about her."

Whoa, he actually growls.

I shake my head in disbelief, my hand still hanging suspended in space. "This girl cheats on you, lies to you, and still you defend her." No matter how much this will hurt, I need the truth. "Look me in the eye and tell me you're not hung up on her."

"It's not like that." Rain glistens on his spiky lashes and runs down his face, but his face remains fixed on his feet.

"Whatever. For the record, I had no idea what Jazza was texting or that he meant for you to find us together."

He blows out a long breath. "I believe you."

"Thank you."

"Jazz and I—we have history. I slept with his ex on New Year's Eve, before I met you. They'd been broken up awhile. When he found out, I told him it didn't mean anything. Because it didn't. Not to me at least, but obviously he's hung up about it."

"Oh."

"That's why I didn't want to make a play for you at first. If you and Jazza were a thing."

"Which we never were."

"No, you weren't. But I think he hoped otherwise."

"I don't want to waste another second talking about stupid Jazza. Or Adie. Our time—*our time*—together is disappearing fast. I feel like we're running down a hill with a giant boulder at our heels, threatening to squash us."

"We're crazy." He gives a slight shrug. "Totally crazy."

We are crazy or does he just mean me?

"But that's okay, right?" I grab for his hand and this time succeed. His skin is cool and hot, all at once. "Not everything in life follows a set path. When I was with you in Tasmania, on that mountaintop, that's an example of what we can be when we try for the best. When we want to, you and I, we are amazing. That's… that's what I love about you."

There, I almost said it. Maybe if I speak the words, how I really feel, he'll lose that cold shuttered face. Time's up; we don't have the luxury of masks anymore. "Bran." He needs to hear how deep my feelings run. I'm doing this, putting it all on the line. "I should have told you this before but I—"

"Natalia."

Here it is, he's going to say he loves me first.

He yanks his hand free and stuffs it into his pocket. "I can't do this. Me and you. I thought I could, but it's too hard."

My whole body convulses. The words don't penetrate my numb shell; instead they slide down my skin like a toxic ooze, leaving behind a slow burn. "Are you serious?"

He steps back like I'm contagious. "You fly out tomorrow."

"Yeah. I do. Yes." My core temperature plummets ten degrees.

"Right. So good-bye."

"Wait? What?" After everything, the wild ups and grand downs of the past few months, he cannot do this; no way will he leave me in the rain. "Are you for real?"

A muscle bunches in his jaw. "This is what people do. We all eventually have to say it to everyone, right? Better now than later."

My mouth opens and shuts like a fish. Maybe I've sprouted gills. Such an oddity wouldn't make the moment more surreal. I'm drowning here in the empty air that separates us. A bitter pain sears my stomach and the toxic ooze works its way inside, eating out my insides. "But I...I thought we were different."

He turns and shields himself from my disbelieving stare. "We *are* different."

"We are?" If I'm not a dying fish, I'm a dazed parrot.

"I live in reality and you...you want to pretend we're in some fantasy land. You made me believe this story for a while but I'm not deluding myself anymore. There are no happy endings, not for people like us."

The low blow punches me in the solar plexus. "You are a bastard, Bran."

"Tell me something I don't know."

My lips flatten into each other. "Fine. You win. Good luck with that happily-miserable-after you want so much." I wish I had access to a door so I could slam it in his stupid face. I know, without a doubt, my issues are too much for him. I can't change on a dime. There's nothing I can do but walk.

I am not perfect only for him. I'm not perfect for anyone.

Bran falls in step beside me. No emotion is revealed on his features, except for a hint of relief. He's going to ride this out in full-blown stoic mode. We stop because we've reached the end of the road. Here's where the sidewalk ends. The idea is kind of funny if you think about it.

But if I laugh, I'll cry.

"Good-bye, Talia." He says it slow as if the saying of a thing makes it more real. The pedestrian light turns green and he crosses the street.

I stand, as if encased in newly poured concrete, and watch Bran walk out of my life.

31

BRAN

*T*hree seconds after shoving through the turnstile at Flinders Street Station, I realize I'm the world's biggest idiot. I turn around and hurdle the gate, narrowly avoiding taking out a pensioner shuffling for her transit card.

"Hey," she cries, dropping her purse.

I press it back into her hands. "Sorry, love. I gotta go see about a girl." And I race from the building, heart pounding. I was furious at Young and Jackson, but more jealous to be honest. Freaked Jazz's poisonous words might have basis in something approaching reality, which shows how loose my brains were knocked by Adie's unexpected arrival.

Can't think about Adie. We reached a tentative reconciliation; that's the most important thing. She's been through her own hell and I do still feel love for her. But it's for the memory of who she and I once were, not the lies and betrayal we became. I can't sabotage a future with Talia because of what happened with Adie. The black days in Denmark are my past.

That's what I need to tell Talia. That she's vital. I hit Flinders

Street and grind to a halt. She's nowhere to be seen. My arms sink
to my sides.

Okay.

Think, think, think.

She can't be far. I saw her less than ninety seconds ago. I do
a quick crowd scan and try not to get frantic. If I lose my head, I
won't keep rational. Melbourne has a population of over 5 million
people, and right now, with the weather clearing up, it seems like
every single one of them has appeared on the streets.

I take a few steps to the left, scrutinize the anonymous faces,
and turn to the river. Would she go down to the Yarra? I check
Flinders Square. Maybe she'd have a coffee? Or would she walk
back into the city? I glance through the window of a trendy bar but
don't see her blond hair anywhere. Come on, I know this girl, right?
Where'd Talia head after our brutal encounter?

She'd avoid the city, the crowds. She wouldn't want to sit for
a coffee. She'd be upset, anxious, walking fast in that head-down,
straight-arm way she carries herself when she gets agitated.

The river. She'd go near the river.

I start to run toward the water but see nothing. She's wearing
her black-framed glasses today and dark colors. Yeah, great, super
helpful in a city that prides itself on dressing like a black hole. The
Yarra is high and muddier than usual, if that's possible. Little waves
lap and curl at the riverbanks, mocking me because I'm not finding
Talia. With every step, I become less convinced I know anything.

After a mile of hard running, I stop, rooted in place. My leg
muscles tighten. I'm not going to find her. I've lost her to the city.
My stomach goes rock hard. Maybe I've lost her for good. I rest my
head in my hands. My pride and temper outweighed my good judgment and now I've fucked everything up.

I run all the way back to Carlton, and when I reach Talia's place, I'm panting and rain-soaked. Not exactly the look that fires up the girls but right now I don't have a choice. I need to explain what happened earlier today with Adie. How it wasn't what it seemed. Any appearance of intimacy came from us sharing a moment to mourn all that happened. Adie and I had crossed over the threshold from childhood together. We had been with each other when we lost our innocent idea that the world owed us anything.

I pound Talia's door until the hinges creak.

She's not here.

She's ignored you before, comes the whisper from the back of my head.

"Talia." I dig my forehead into the frame. "Please, open the door."

I hear smothered giggling and turn down the hall. Three girls ogle me.

Fucking hell. Let them stare.

I face the closed door. "Talia, I've been an ass and I should have never left you like that back there in the city. I was so angry, at Jazz, at myself, and yes, at you. And that was stupid and unfair. You did nothing wrong. Please, I-I'm sorry for what happened earlier. It was all such a shock. When you came in my room so upset, I couldn't hold everyone's stuff inside me. I cracked, and my shit spilled out on you."

It's oddly cathartic talking to an inanimate object. I press my forehead into the wood. "Open the door, Talia. Please, let me see you."

"She's not in there." A voice startles me from behind.

I turn and find myself getting glared down by the French girl with the hot-pink hair. Marti, I think.

"Where is Talia?"

"She left." Marti's shrug could mean any of a thousand different things. "She took her bags and is gone to stay in the hotel with her mama until their flight."

"Gone?"

"Gone."

"What's the name of the hotel?"

Another shrug. "Pfffft, no idea."

"Fuck." I drag my hand through my hair.

"Yes, you fucked it up." Marti's eyes glitter like she wishes me all kinds of hurt. "You broke the poor girl's heart."

32

TALIA

I pedal my cruiser along West Cliff Drive while green, pink, and gold explosions glitter-spray the fog. Fireworks are banned from beaches in Santa Cruz. A fact universally ignored in the weeks leading up to and after July 4th. Crowds clog the sidewalk as I duck and weave whenever I spot familiar faces. I don't want to chat with anyone or answer questions about Australia. I know I'm only expected to smile and chirp, "It was great," but even that small lie feels insurmountable. The sky darkens, loneliness weighs on my spine, and I turn for home.

My last day in Australia passed like an old-timey movie. The memories are jerky and off-kilter. I never saw Bran after our awful good-bye on the sidewalk in front of Young and Jackson. After I fled to the passive-aggressive torture chamber that was my mom's hotel room, I paced a hole in the bathroom tile before catching a cab to his place. Miles answered the door. Told me Bran wasn't home. That he hadn't been around since the morning. It didn't seem like he was lying. Maybe Bran was out with Adie or picking fights in a koala suit. Wherever he was, I couldn't fly 10,000 miles home without telling him the truth.

I trudged across the street. Lucy was working at the Bean Counter and thankfully Bella had the night off. Lucy loaned me a pen and piece of paper. I wrote my heart out, spilled all the feelings. I used the L-word. Yep, I confessed my love to Bran on the Bean Counter stationery. I went back and Miles let me inside. Bran's room looked neat and orderly, like a guy who's got it together. I placed my sad scrawled note on his pillow and resisted the near-overpowering urge to bury my face into the sheets and breathe in his scent.

Even now, more than seventy-two hours later, the memory of my last hour in Melbourne makes me feel like my legs plunge into an electric current. Humiliation curls insidious fingers inside my throat, threatening slow strangulation.

I'd left Bran my flight information in the letter.

I waited and waited.

But Bran never came.

I dawdled in front of the custom area's metal doors, watching them open and shut with grim finality. Mom's flight to Honolulu departed first and our good-byes were curt, cold. I don't know how we'll ever move past that terrible conversation—the one where she basically accused me of killing Pippa.

After Mom departed, I bent to tie my shoes, rechecked my carry-on, and feigned lots of stretching. I hoped beyond hope that Bran would come to say good-bye. Let me know I wasn't alone in this. There are beautiful places inside him, where laughter comes easy, where sweet words appear like surprises. But I also know his bitter valleys. The dark caves where he hides his fears, his hurts, and his disillusionments.

And he knows mine.

I guess he didn't love my geography the same way. Maybe I wasn't a must-see destination. Maybe my crazy was too much to handle.

He'd come, had a look, and left, been there done that.

My flight changed status on the departure screen from "Go to Gate" to "Boarding."

And so I left.

When the wheels departed the earth, I discovered a whole reservoir of unshed tears. By the time I met Dad by the security gate in SFO airport, I had myself almost convinced it was for the best. That I was home and needed.

That illusion lasted exactly twenty-five minutes. As we turned onto I-280, Dad let the bomb drop.

He's leaving Santa Cruz, putting our house—my house—up for sale. He landed an amazing job giving lectures on expedition cruises, not the big, bloated vessels always breaking down in the Caribbean but small boutique ships that visit exotic locations like Greenland, Alaska, or the Galapagos.

Even Dad is moving on. And when he reaches over to tousle my hair and ask me what my next adventure will be, I somehow don't break into a hundred thousand pieces. My roadmap is full of dead ends.

I steer my creaky bike up the road toward my house—at least my house for the next thirty days. Then who the hell knows what I'll do. Maybe scrape together the last of my savings and buy a van, live by the river.

Fireworks continue to pop behind me, down by the ocean, followed by cheers. The sound reverberates through the chambers of my empty heart. I am hollow. The past few days scoured the inside of my body like a Brillo pad, removing the last traces of feeling.

Survival instinct is amazing. A body can't be expected to hold the hurts, and sometimes, if you're lucky, a switch can be flipped. I know it won't last—it didn't after Pippa's accident—but even a few numb minutes are a blessing.

As much as the van and river daydream seems like enjoyable

self-pity wallowing, I know what I really need to do. Suck it up and get back to school in the fall. Spend the summer developing a kick-ass project and execute it, turn in a senior thesis that will make my advisors weep from my brilliance.

There's a bazillion student rentals around UCSC. It's high time I stop sharing a room with my dead sister and tell her ghost that it's okay to move on. Just like Mom has, like Dad is starting to, like I need to.

I sink my kickstand in front of the garage and spy a dead dandelion by the driveway. I impulsively bend down and blow the puff, send seeds spinning in every direction. My family has exploded; there's nothing I can do to get them back. Life will never be like it used to be.

The porch light illuminates the seeds as they drift into shadow. This sight should feel sad, but doesn't. Because there's this sense, like maybe even though my family's scattering, we share memories and wherever we land, those memories will remain, even as we put down roots and start anew.

I wonder when OCD will clamp down again, the powerful need to rein in an illogical control on life, the ultimate uncontrollable. I don't think I'm cured or anything. But I'm also not so afraid.

I remember something Bran said when we were hiking in Tasmania, about how people believe they see the same river but the water is always different.

I am that river. I'm still me, but I'm not the person I was before Pippa died. Or when I left for Australia. Or after I met Bran.

I am not even the same person I was five minutes ago.

A flicker lights inside my heart, faint, as if even the most gentle breeze might snuff it out. But it's there. And it's hope.

Hope for myself.

I unearth my house key from my bike basket when I sense someone behind me. A muffled shriek flies from my throat as I leap forward, back pressed hard against the front door. Dad's probably in bed, but if I ring the bell—

"Talia?"

The familiar deep, accented voice activates every cell in my body. The warm flicker inside me blazes like it's doused with gasoline.

"Bran." What if I manifested this hallucination from sheer longing?

Or what if this moment is more real than anything that's ever happened to me?

The security light flicks on and Dad cracks the door. "Peanut?" He notices Bran on the bottom step, gripping his backpack straps. "You all right out here? Who's this guy?"

"I'm fine. Just a friend...surprising me." Dad sees him too. Bran's really here, in California, on my front stoop. My smile reaches my ears.

Dad gives a disapproving rumble. "I'm reading in the kitchen, going to keep the door open."

"So"—Bran shifts his weight after Dad retreats—"that's your dad?"

"Yeah."

"He's protective."

"Always."

"Good," he says with a short nod. "He cares."

"I waited, at the airport, but you didn't come."

"I searched for you, but when I found out you were gone, I took off to the beach. I thought it would help. But I'm an idiot; nothing would help—except putting this right with you. After I got home and found your letter, your flight had already taken off. So I drove straight to the airport and bought a ticket. Because I wanted to say I'm sorry and ask if you'll still consider Tasmania. Do the project that professor offered you. When I finish up my honors in nine months, you can pick the next place. We can go anywhere. Do anything."

Too much information, my brain slows. I can only process bits and pieces. "You flew," I murmur, trying to find my bearings. Only one point remains on my internal compass and it's Bran's hesitant smile.

"I white-knuckled it through wicked turbulence near Hawaii, but I made it."

"You conquered a dragon for me."

"Hardly. But I didn't want you to never know that I . . . I love you, Talia."

My heart thunders in my chest. "But . . . but . . . you said you didn't believe in—"

"That was me being a coward and an ass. This is real, Talia. This right here. Since you stopped for me on the sidewalk, I knew."

"Say it again."

He drops his bag and reaches for me. "I love you." A tear drops to my cheek and he kisses it away. "I love you and you don't have to say anything, but I . . . I really think you are in love with me too." His declaration is defiant, like he expects me to argue.

"You really *are* an idiot, aren't you?"

An expression like he's half strangling and half about to strangle me crosses his features.

I brace his face between my hands. "I've been falling for you ever since you followed me out of the pub that first night. You see me, Bran, and you didn't run—you came closer."

"So you'll give us a second chance?"

I can't move, paralyzed by the flood of raw emotion. "Nope."

He slumps against the handrail. Deep bruises half ring his

beautiful but bloodshot eyes. He looks exhausted, spent. Terrible, actually.

He's the best thing I've ever seen.

"Screw second chances, Bran. I am going to mess up way more than twice. Before we take this any further, you need to be crystal-clear about that fact. I might have three separate catastrophes before breakfast."

"I want it all. The catastrophes. The mornings. Every day with you." His hands migrate to my hips and the force of his embrace lifts me off my feet.

"We fit." I kiss his scruffy cheek. "You're my perfectly imperfect key."

"You're the key to everything." He looks directly at me and lets me in, and I see all his fear, and love, and know what this admission costs him.

"I'll move to Australia," I say softly, and he shivers against me. "To finish school and find out if we can live together without going berserk."

"You mean it? Despite the fact that I'm a fucking idiot, you'll really come back?"

"Yes. See, I kinda, sorta love you too."

He dips me and his mouth is a whole lot of hot, like he's branding himself to my lips.

Pop! Pop! Pop! More pyrotechnics shoot from the beach. Fireworks detonate overhead.

I wrap my arms around Bran's neck and return his kiss with everything I've got. Maybe I'm turned upside down, but at last I've landed right side up.

Talia Stolfi has seen more
than her share of loss in her
twenty-one years. Then fate brought
her Bran Lockhart, and her dark
world was suddenly illuminated. But
as much as Talia longs to give herself
over completely to a new beginning,
the fears of her past still lurk in the
shadows…

Please see the next page for a preview of

Sideswiped.

I

TALIA

September

Our California bungalow sits empty, a headstone for a ghost family. The rooms are tomb quiet, devoid of any comforting, familiar clutter. All our stuff, tangible proof the Stolfi family once existed, rots in a long-term storage unit. When the movers hauled off the last cardboard boxes, they took more than precious memories. They snatched my breadcrumb trail. The last stupid, irrational hope that Mom, Dad, and I could somehow find a way back together.

These bare walls reflect the stark truth. We're over. My family's done. A cashed-up Silicon Valley couple craving a beach town escape will snag the house by the weekend.

I pause near the front window and chew the inside of my cheek. Dad's Realtor drives a FOR SALE sign into the front yard. The invisible dumbbell lodged in my sternum increases in weight with every hammer strike. Seriously? Do I need to witness this final nail in the coffin?

If fate exists, she's one evil bitch.

I turn and trace my finger over the hip-high door leading to the under-the-stairs closet. Inside is the crawl space where my older sister, Pippa, and I once played castle. Now I'm the only one left, a princess with a broken crown, my home a shattered kingdom.

Pippa is gone. The result of a stupid, preventable car accident followed by a grueling year where she lay suspended in a vegetative half-life while Dad, Mom, and I clung to a single, destructive lie: She will get better.

I learned my lesson. Things don't always work out for the best. False hope destroys quicker than despair.

Mom checked out, filed for divorce, and hides in her parents' Hawaiian compound where she dabbles in New Age quackery while nursing a discreet alcohol addiction. Dad recently crawled from the rubble, brushed clear the cobwebs, and returned to the business of life. He quit his cushy job with the U.S. Geological Survey and hit the road on his own midlife escapade, giving expedition cruise ship lectures.

The day we turned off Pippa's life support, our family died with her.

Breathe.

Terrible things happen if I allow myself to key up.

Come on—in and out. Good girl.

Better to say that Mom, Dad, and I stumbled to the other side, battered like characters at the end of a cheesy post-apocalyptic flick. I wouldn't go so far as to say life is easy but there's less falling shrapnel. These days, when I brave a glance to the horizon, the coast is actually clear—or maybe I'm just kidding myself.

I check my watch—still no sign of Sunny or Beth. I love my girls, hard. They rallied, stepped up, and closed ranks when I crawled home from Australia in June, heartsick and dazed from the fallout with one Brandon Lockhart. Even after Bran flew in unannounced to commence the world's most epic grovel, they remain suspicious.

Bran.

My heart kicks into fifth gear, like it always does, responding to the mere thought of his name. Tingles zing through my spine as I cover my mouth to hide my secret smile. Tonight, at 31,000 feet, I'll cross the International Date Line. Bran waits for me in Tomorrowland. Here's my golden opportunity to rebuild a life nearly torn from the hinges by stupid fucking obsessive-compulsive disorder.

I'm getting better and I'll only grow stronger. The next few months are organized around two major goals: (1) Give Bran every ounce of my giddy, dizzy love and (2) finish my senior thesis and graduate. My UCSC advisor approved my oral history project and a professor at the University of Tasmania agreed to supervise. Once that baby's done and dusted, our future waits, ready to shine.

"Everything's going to be okay," I whisper to Pippa, as if she's listening.

Either way, the words taste sweet.

"Knock, knock. Hey, who's the creeper out front?" Sunny breezes into the hollow void, once upon a time a disorderly foyer brimming with Dad's surfboards. She stops short and stares. "Holy demolition, Batman."

"Your house!" Beth enters half a step behind and slides up her Ray-Bans. "You doing okay?"

"Yeah, I guess so." My throat squeezes, making the next words difficult. "Looks pretty crazy, though, right?" Change, even for the best reasons, is still effing scary. I'm a California girl, born and raised in Santa Cruz, except for last year's roller-coaster study abroad. When I cruise around town, people here know my name.

And all the hoary, gory details of my family's slow disintegration.

In Australia, any personal details I share will be of my choosing. There's a certain freedom in anonymity. How many people are given a blank canvas, the chance to paint a whole new life alongside the guy who rocks their world?

"Earth to Talia." Sunny waves an ink-stained hand in front of my face. "Want your good-bye gift?"

Beth rolls her eyes. "You're not really giving that to her, are you?"

"Shut your face." Sunny thrusts me a small wrapped package. "It's hilarious. Talia will appreciate it. *She* has a sense of humor."

"Careful," Beth stage whispers, nudging my hip. "Someone's a little edgy this morning. Last night, Bodhi tried to define their relationship."

"Ruh-roh. Not the DTR!" I rip the present's paper along the seam. Bodhi, Sunny's current booty call, works as a diver on an abalone farm north of town. "Isn't that a strictly friends with benefits arrangement?"

"Not even." Sunny readjusts her infinity scarf, brows knit in annoyance. "Friendship implies the capacity for rudimentary conversation. Bodhi sports lickable biceps—no doubt—but that guy's one fry short of a Happy Meal. He's hump buddy material, pure and simple."

"Was he crushed?"

"Like a grape. He cried into his can of Natty Ice."

"Ugh."

"Poor guy, don't mock him." Beth is a whopping whole year older and seems to find life purpose in playing the mature, responsible role. Pippa used to be the exact same way.

When our trio was a foursome.

"He made me hitch home at three a.m. I swear, I'm taking a guy break for a while." Sunny opens her baby blues extra wide as if to prove she really means this oft-repeated phrase.

"Yeah, right, until when? Next Tuesday?" Beth fires back.

These two bicker worse than an old married couple. But Beth has a point. Sunny breaks hearts up and down the coast. You could almost call it a hobby.

I crumple the wrapping paper into my fist. "Seriously?" Sunny's gift swings between my two fingers—a chef's apron with BAREFOOT AND PREGNANT embroidered across the chest. "Um, thanks?"

She giggles wickedly. "That's my prediction for you. By Christmas. Spring at the latest. Except you better add getting married into the equation. I don't want my pseudo-niece or nephew born into sin."

"Riiight, because living with a guy automatically translates into marriage and babies these days. Guys, I'm moving to Australia, not the 1950s."

My friends swap suspicious expressions. After we broke up, Bran flew to California in early July and begged for a second chance. I accepted and the subsequent week devolved into wild beach sex and mad plotting for our future. Beth and Sunny only caught glimpses of the guy who'd wrecking-balled my heart. They remain guarded, like two mother lionesses.

An adorable act if they weren't so annoying.

"Come on, living with a guy is a normal next step."

"Nothing about the Bran Situation is remotely normal," Sunny mutters.

Beth nods in rare agreement.

"I've always wanted to travel, haven't I?" I stuff the stupid apron into my duffel bag.

"This is hardly the Peace Corps." Beth throws my old dream in my face. The one I had before Pippa's accident, before my brains decided to double down on the crazy.

"Forget it." Sunny jumps to my defense and tosses a loose auburn wave over one shoulder. "I just need to get a grip...still can't believe you're leaving."

I force a smile. "You guys have so much going on you won't even notice I'm gone."

Beth's lined up a PR internship over the hill in Silicon Valley, and postgraduation Sunny is...well, the usual Sunny—cashiering at a natural foods store, never finishing her graphic novels, and hunting down her next conquest like a top predator on the African savannah. I hope my smile overrules the fizzy nervousness in my belly. "Don't forget, my visa is only for four months."

"So you keep saying." Beth hasn't dropped the concerned frown. "What comes after? Have you worked out a plan?"

"No, not exactly." I roll my shoulders. If there's one thing I hate in life, it's uncertainty. "Bran says we'll figure things out once I'm there. We have until December thirty-first to wrangle a solution."

The drop-dead date.

"And, what, he's some sort of immigration wizard?" Typical Beth, pushing to ensure every *i* is dotted, *t* crossed.

"Play nice." I sling my arm around her, getting perverse satisfaction from knuckle-mussing her perfectly straightened hair. "He's nervous enough that I might get cold feet and reconsider coming."

"Oh, you'll be coming, friend. Won't she, Bethanny?" Sunny can't resist the opportunity to tickle our girl.

"Get fucked, bitches." Beth squeals, breaking free. She's a gym rat, way stronger than she looks. "What are you guys, five-year-olds?"

"Don't be a poop."

Sunny's pouty descriptor rips startled laughter from my chest.

Beth is almost freakishly beautiful. She rocks her lululemon yoga wear better than a movie starlet. And right now she's not amused. "Sunny Letman, we've known each other since we were, what, zygotes?"

"At least embryos," I toss in my two cents through a giggle. We've been pals since our mothers introduced us in nursery co-op. Sunny and I drew the short straws, mothers who failed their daughters. Mine is lost in a fog of tropical denial while Sunny's mom shacks in a Nevada desert bunker with a wackadoo prepper awaiting Armageddon.

"Maybe it's time to grow up." Beth can front prim all she wants. But underneath that perfect ice-queen exterior, she's a weirdo too.

"Her first." I slap Sunny's butt.

Her response is an awkward twerk that cracks us all up.

I'm going to miss these two.

"Anyhoo." Sunny folds her arms and leans against the banister. "Can I please point out that you're committing a drastic error?"

Seriously?

"Call off the attack dogs, okay?" I say. "You guys really don't know him."

"Whoa, settle down, Miss Defensive. I'm talking about you bailing before October. The best time of year."

"Our time," Beth adds.

"Hmmm. You have a point." October is fantastic in Santa Cruz. The tourists vanish and each morning we wake to perfect bluebird skies, followed by afternoons warm enough for bikinis. The gloomy fog-locked summer retreats into a distant memory as the entire town descends to the beaches, surf breaks, and bike paths, reveling in the coastal goodness. "Still not enough to change my mind."

I love my girls but Bran is the only person with whom I've ever fully been myself. He noticed my OCD symptoms after five minutes and didn't laugh or run away screaming. Sunny and Beth might be my two best friends but even they don't know the real reason I didn't graduate on time. How my rituals and health anxiety spiraled so far out of control that I was placed on academic probation. Even now, I can't bring myself to tell them the truth. The awful facts are beyond embarrassing. Easier that they accepted my simple explanation that I "messed up." I mean, who challenges the dead girl's sister?

Bran's the only one who doesn't tiptoe on eggshells. He treats me like I've got strength, makes me believe I can face life.

Beth checks her phone. "Hey, we need to jet."

"That's all you're bringing?" Sunny points to my backpack and duffel bag.

"Yeah."

"Shut your face. Two bags?" She's a notorious pack rat, hovering on needing a hoarder intervention. Last week, I unearthed third-grade spelling tests from under her bed.

"I decided to pack Zen, practice unattachment."

"Uh-huh." Beth's not having it.

"Do I sound like my mom?"

"A little."

I cave. "Truth? Extra bag charges are a rip."

"Aha, there's the tight-ass girl I know." Sunny grabs my backpack.

"And love." Beth lifts the duffel.

"Oh wait." I grab a small moleskin journal from the stairs and unzip my backpack's top zipper, stowing the journal. The pages chronicle random happenings, unusual incidents, and amusing stories from while Bran and I were apart. Things I forgot to mention during our messenger chats or phone calls. I miss his voice, that surly accent, whispering to me in the dark. My nightly record-keeping allowed me to play make-believe, pretend Bran was nestled on the pillow beside me. The ritual became a precaution against the what-ifs slithering around the edge of my thoughts, ever vigilant, waiting for an opportunity to strike.

What if Bran meets someone else?

What if I say something so stupid he has no choice but to accept I'm an idiot? What if he decides I'm a freak? Okay, fine, he's never given cause for these thoughts, but what-ifs and worst-case scenarios are routine in my world. My brain is hardwired for catastrophic thinking.

Evil thoughts can go suck it.

My friends head out the front door and I need to follow suit.

"Are you okay to lock up?" I call to the Realtor.

"That's my job." Somewhere a tooth-whitening ad wants its smarmy smile back.

"Lucky you," I mutter under my breath while stomping down the front steps.

I shouldn't turn around. Or look at the dormer window where Pippa and I shared a room for nearly two decades. But I do. And I can't hold back the sudden tears.

Sunny pauses to rub my back, saying nothing. If she had her way, I'd cry every morning before breakfast. She thinks it's good for my soul. I find the whole enterprise draining and messy but better than the alternative—becoming an emotionless robot that shuts out the good along with the bad.

I had a great last summer, more or less. Now Bran waits to catch me at the bottom of the world.

"Going anyplace fun?" The Realtor wipes his forehead, perving on Sunny and Beth as they toss my two bags into Sunny's black

Tacoma, the Batmobile. The gnarly old truck is a random vehicle choice for a fresh-faced redhead with a penchant for fairy tales.

Two pelicans crisscross overhead. In the distance, sea lions bark beneath the wharf, the site where I made the worst decision of my life.

Fuck clutching breadcrumbs.

Time to let go.

Embrace the art of getting lost.

What can go wrong, as long as I keep heading in the right direction?

The Realtor shifts his weight.

"Yeah," I say after an overlong pause. "I'm going somewhere great."